THE 17TH STATE

CHUCK DRISKELL

The 17th State

Copyright © 2017 by Chuck Driskell
Published by Autobahn Books
Cover art by Nat Shane

First Edition: January 2017

autobahn
BOOKS

In loving memory of my mother, Betty Gantt Driskell. A beautiful, funny, strong woman who I was blessed with for 26 years. I miss her.

There is no terror in the bang, only in the anticipation of it.
– Alfred Hitchcock

Chapter One

If Roman Littlepage knew what was going to happen tonight, he would have ended this vacation right now. He'd have rushed back to the resort, packed his bags, and taken the next flight to Madrid. But he didn't. He stayed and, by doing so, set off a deadly chain of events that might cost him his life.

Over the past decade, Roman had vacationed in Kauai, Hawaii. He'd been to Roatan, Honduras. He'd enjoyed his honeymoon in Aruba. He'd traveled all over Europe and North America, but never in his life had Roman been to anyplace that compared to Mallorca, Spain. A rocky island in the Mediterranean, Mallorca is the largest of the Balearic Islands and is located east of Valencia and south of Barcelona. With miles of beaches, mountains, cliffs and desert countryside, the island has something for just about everyone. Mallorca is one of Europe's most popular playgrounds, right up there with Ibiza, Cannes and Santorini.

The combination of the climate, of the Spanish locals, of the European vacationers, and the nightlife—oh, the nightlife—created an indulgence Roman wasn't sure he'd ever experience again. Sure, he might come back someday, but Roman was 36 years old. He had a small business that vacuumed up a great deal of his time. He had two children. He had other responsibilities. And, most of all, Roman was no spring chicken—time was running out. He might never get another chance like this one.

Roman—oh, Roman—you should have changed your ticket and gone home with your friends.

Despite all the reasons he had to stay, his strongest motivation was *her*: "The Goddess" he called her. A bronzed 20-something year-old beauty he'd run into no less than six times over the past eight days. He'd not yet spoken to her—he only heard her, speaking German, like half the other vacationers to this island paradise. There were no men in the picture, none that Roman had seen. It was just the Goddess and her friends. On one occasion, she'd even smiled at him. Tachycardia and bliss all at the same time. So, it was her, the Goddess, who was keeping him on this island with all the pull of a Bitter electromagnet.

Unfortunately, the force that pulled him in also paralyzed him. Roman froze every time he saw her. Her appearance always came without warning, too. He'd memorized her friends' faces, hoping they might tip him off to her presence so that he'd be ready to approach her, but thus far there'd never been a warning. It was nothing, nothing, nothing…then, bam!…there she was. Roman's heart would race. He'd sweat. His tongue would even swell, clogging his mouth and rendering him unable to speak.

These were a few of the excuses he made for himself.

Despite the blissful offering of her one-time smile, for all Roman knew, she didn't know he even existed. Regardless, the next time would be different. The next time, by hook or by crook, he was going to walk right up and talk to her. He was going to sweep her off her feet. She wouldn't know what hit her, other than a big fat dose of red-blooded American charm.

"I'm single now," Roman murmured. "What's to stop me?"

"What?" Mitch asked, curling his lip.

Roman averted his eyes. "Just talking to myself."

"You know…that's the second sign of senility."

"What's the first?"

"Asking the question you just asked. Probably why Wendy dumped your pathetic ass."

"It was a *mutual* decision."

"Yeah…right. So says the loser."

They were standing inside the inadequately air-conditioned main terminal of the Palma Mallorca International Airport. It wasn't the Mallorcans' fault that the air conditioning was inadequate. The temperature outside had been in the high nineties all week. Every building was overheated, especially concrete structures such as this one. Despite it being early in the morning, the building was still hot from the day before.

The terminal buzzed with activity. Fresh-faced vacationers arrived, bright with anticipation and a kick in their step, as if each minute spent in the airport was a minute wasted. On the other end of the spectrum, tanned, sunburnt, hung-over vacationers trudged from the taxi stands and bus stops with leaden feet, slogging as if they were headed to their executions. Not a single one of them walked with speed or energy. A few of them sneered at the new arrivals, jealous of the enjoyment that lay ahead for their fellow human beings.

The three old friends, Roman, Mitch and Mike, had gathered near the baggage drop after Mitch and Mike had checked in and received their boarding passes. Mitch, full of his typical energy, was standing. Mike was sprawled in a leather chair, his feet propped up on his carry-on as he silently read from his Kindle.

As always, Mitch used some of that extra energy to give Roman a rash of shit.

"Look at this zoo, dude," Mitch said, motioning to the bevy of people. "You're gonna fold like a cheap suit when we leave. You can't handle being alone, especially around all these strangers."

"Thanks for your concern but I'll be fine."

"My ass. You'll need Mike's teat to suck on. You'll miss spooning with him after those long hot showers you two take together."

Roman chuckled. Mike gave an almost imperceptible shake of the head.

After a week with Mitch, such talk as this was tame.

"I'm serious," Mitch continued. "You're gonna puss out."

Roman shrugged. "You're gonna keep on till you get a rise out of me, aren't you?"

"Yup."

"Well, Mitchell, you underestimate me, as usual."

"Mike, whadya think?" Mitch asked, kicking Mike's foot to get his attention.

Mike didn't even look up from his Kindle as he spoke monotone. "I agree with your prediction. Roman'll puss out. He'll be on a flight tomorrow."

Mitch laughed. "See?"

"I didn't even have to come over here to the airport with you pricks," Roman said, feigning his anger. "It'll be a twenty euro cab ride back. I came over here out of the goodness of my heart."

"Pshh. You did it because you're scared to be alone," Mitch teased. "Right, Mike?"

Still didn't look up. Still spoke monotone. "Definitely scared. Roman's a vagina."

Roman chuckled. "You two should head on through security."

Mitch produced twenty euro, rubbing the bill in front of Roman's eyes. "Here's your cab fare. If you leave tomorrow or on Tuesday, you owe me this, times three. Deal?"

"You're on…and to hell with both of you." Roman shook Mitch's hand and had to slap Mike's Kindle down just to get him to shake hands.

Mitch turned halfway serious, a rarity for him. "You sure you're okay with staying?"

"I am," Roman answered.

"I could probably get you on the next flight and then you could meet us in Madrid." He glanced at his watch and at the departures board. "There's a flight to Madrid every hour. It'd be tight but you could do it." Mitch was a pilot for United Airlines and, as always, was flying as a non-revenue passenger. "I might be able to get them to hold the door open a few extra minutes in Madrid."

Roman shook his head. "My divorce was final twenty-six days ago. I've saved for this trip all year and I've still got plenty of cash. More than anything, this trip's been the best of my life, so I think I can handle staying, *alone*, in Mallorca for a few extra days."

"Okay…I tried," Mitch said, showing his palms, as if Roman's staying would turn out to be a disastrous decision.

Mike nodded. "I bet, tomorrow at three p.m. Eastern time, I'll get a text from you telling me you just cleared customs in Atlanta."

"You two clowns are the ones leaving early," Roman said.

"I gotta get back," Mike replied. "My job sucks. I'm irreplaceable. They need me."

"Yeah, and I picked up a trip on Tuesday," Mitch added. "Need to get back today so I can do some union work and pilot crap in Houston. By the way…they wouldn't let me cancel my room." He pulled a keycard from his pocket. "Here ya go. Paid up until Wednesday."

Mike did the same.

Roman eyed the keycards. "What am I gonna do with three rooms?"

"Throw a bash," Mitch said.

"But they're not all together."

"Go find some hot girls and give them a free place to stay," Mike suggested. "Maybe they'll let you *watch-and-wank* when they bring back some good looking guys each night."

"Yeah, I'll do that," Roman said, his tone flat. "Great idea."

It was time for Roman to leave. The three men half-shook, half-hugged, the way men uncomfortable with another male's touch typically do. Roman nodded one last time at his two best friends. They all chuckled at the awkward moment, filing away another golden moment in their two decades of shared memories. Roman turned and walked away, heading to the taxi stand.

He'd made it approximately one hundred feet when he heard his friend's voice ring out above the din of the main terminal as he obnoxiously relayed one of his personal maxims.

"Do—not—be—a—pussy!" Mitch yelled, his voice echoing and allowing every person in the Palma Mallorca International Airport's ticketing area to hear.

People stared. One woman covered her mouth with her hand. Roman stifled a grin as he walked away. He did not look back.

* * *

This was the tenth vacation to Europe involving some combination of Roman, Mike and Mitch. The three had been in the Army together, stationed in Germany before they'd gone to college and begun their adult lives. All three came from extremely modest upbringings that had bordered on poverty, but all three had been blessed with enough intelligence and occasional good sense to move up a few rungs on life's ladder. They were within a year of each other in age and, inside three months of having been stationed together, the three had become fast friends. Now, even though they typically only saw one another once or twice a year, they stayed in close contact, rarely going a week without talking or texting.

Ten years ago, they'd begun taking an annual European vacation. In the ten years, Mike had missed it only once. Mitch had missed it twice, but now had come six years in a row. Roman was the most recent absentee, having not attended the two previous summers. Things had grown strained between him and his wife and he just couldn't peel himself away. Roman had planned on coming last year, but two weeks before the trip his wife, Wendy, had served him with divorce papers.

After giving Roman a chance to digest the papers in his hand, Wendy had said, "I love you, Roman, but I don't like you anymore."

Roman probably didn't go a waking hour without her words echoing in his mind. The reasons were numerous. More than anything, they'd simply grown apart.

Thankfully, Wendy promised to stay in Franklin, a suburb of Nashville, and she'd been extremely accommodating as they'd negotiated custody. Roman had the kids Thursday through Saturday. He also had them on Father's Day, Christmas and New Year's. He really couldn't have asked for more.

And through it all, not once had he found a shred of credible evidence that Wendy was seeing anyone. Not that he cared all that much, but it hammered home what she'd said to him. She simply didn't like him anymore. In fact, since their divorce, Wendy had grown to be a much better friend to Roman. She'd even suggested that he use a dating website to match him with compatible women.

Who the hell is compatible with me?

"Stop thinking about it," he whispered to himself, stepping from the taxi at the Balearic Resort and Hotel, located right on the water just a few kilometers east of Palma, the main city on the island of Mallorca. It was still early in the day for Mallorca. Most vacationers didn't awaken until early afternoon. Dinner was typically taken around 10 p.m. and the bars didn't even begin to get going until midnight. After fleetingly considering going back to bed, Roman instead grabbed his book, his iPod and a towel and headed out to the beach. The sky was crystalline and the temperature today was supposed to hit 96 degrees Fahrenheit. He'd get four or five hours of sunshine, eat a huge late lunch, grab a long siesta and be ready to go tonight.

When Roman returned from the beach, he ate a sandwich and called the U.S. to say hello to the kids. After speaking with each of them about today's schedule—they were going to a water park with some of their friends—Wendy came on the line.

"How's vacation?" she asked.

"Fine."

"How are your friends?"

"They're okay," Roman said, hoping he didn't have to reveal they left early.

"Are they leaving before you?"

"Why do you ask?"

"Don't they always do that?"

"Wendy, can we talk about all this when I get back?"

"Sure, sure. Meet any girls?"

"No."

"I'm sure you've tried."

"What, are you saying I *can't* meet a girl?"

"No, silly. Listen," she said, her tone changing. "I need to tell you something."

"Okay."

She paused for a moment. "I met someone, Roman, a great guy. I've been seeing him for about two months now."

Roman sat down and dipped his head, staring at the white tile floor of his corner hotel room. He didn't have romantic feelings for Wendy anymore, but it was heavy news to hear from someone he'd spent much of his adult life with.

"Who is he?" Roman asked.

"You don't know him. We met at my hot yoga class and—"

"He does hot yoga?" Roman snorted.

Wendy was silent.

"Go on," he said.

"Anyway, none of this concerns you except for the fact that he wants to meet the children. And, because I respect your wishes, I wanted to ask you first. He's a great guy, Roman."

"You've said that twice."

"Well, he is."

"Is he...you know...spending the night over there? The kids are more perceptive than you think."

"Do you think I'm stupid? No, he's not been staying over here."

Roman, you're on the other side of the world, on vacation, chasing the Goddess all over this Spanish rock. How dare you act like an asshole to your wife who, other than divorcing you (which you deserved for being a distant, self-involved prick) has treated you with nothing but respect.

He shut his eyes, focusing his breathing.

"Roman?"

"Sorry, Wendy, I guess I was just a bit taken aback. You have every right to date. Sure, introduce your friend to the kids. I trust you."

"You sure you're not pissed off? Are you going to get drunk tonight, then call and cuss me out like you did that one time?"

"That was different. I didn't know that big, burly dude was a plumber."

More silence.

"Roman?"

"Yeah?"

"You okay?"

"Fine. Like I said, it just surprised me. I'm...I'm happy for you."

"I'm not talking about what I told you. Before that, you sounded...different."

"I'm on vacation. Lots of good food and drink. And I just came in from the beach, so I'm a little tired and going to try to grab a nap. That's all."

"We'll see you…when?"

"I get back late Wednesday. I'll get the kids on Thursday and have them all weekend, right?"

"Just making sure. Toby and I are actually going to Memphis on Friday."

"Toby? His name is *Toby*? Please tell me you're kidding."

"Roman."

"A guy named Toby…who does hot yoga."

Wendy was silent.

"And you're taking off with him for a whole weekend, are you? Same room, I'm sure. The Peabody, maybe? One of those lovebird room packages with chocolate and champagne on the bed? Good old *quick* Wendy."

"*What* did you say?"

"Just talking out loud."

"Goodbye, Roman." The line went dead.

Roman walked onto his balcony, wishing he had a cigarette. He went back inside, grabbing a cold Beck's beer from the mini-bar. Back outside, he swilled the beer as he stared out over the beach, trying like hell to forget all about Toby the hot yoga man and the weekend sex romp to Memphis.

An hour later, after two beers, Roman lay in a torpor on his bed as sleep evaded him. There were five hours remaining before it would be time to head out. Five very long hours.

But Roman was going out tonight, and tomorrow night…

The Goddess was out there—somewhere. And, after the words of his friends, Roman was determined not to "puss out."

There was no nap.

* * *

During their vacation, Roman and his two friends had spent time—partied, rather—in three districts of Mallorca. Palma, the biggest city on the island, sported a lovely nightlife area down by the water. Truth be told, this was the area Roman felt most comfortable. There were far more revelers who seemed close to his own age and socio-economic level. Additionally, in Palma there was something for everyone. Chic tapas bars. Pulsing clubs. Old pubs. All nestled in the winding cobblestone streets of Mallorca's capital city.

Magaluf, a forty-euro cab ride from Roman's resort, contained ten square blocks of absolute U.K. mayhem. Dominated by Brits, Scots, Welsh and the occasional Irish, Magaluf was a 24-hour party and a study in humanity. Within minutes of their only night there, Roman and his friends had seen two men puking on the streets. Inside the first hour they'd witnessed a dozen hooligans brawling. Later in the evening, when a group of young rugby players found out the trio were "Yanks," Roman and his friends spent the night doing shots and answering questions about the States. One of the ruggers couldn't shake his fascination with "Bigfoot," asking again and again if any of the Americans had ever seen him.

Roman had little desire to ever go back to Magaluf although, oddly enough, he almost always enjoyed people from the U.K. But their area in Mallorca was just too frenetic for his tastes.

Finally, there was the eastern shore district of El Arenal, and its party zone dubbed "Ballermann" by the Germans. This area was predominantly German and Ballermann was the actual reveling style—sort of a cross between Oktoberfest and Mardi Gras. Typical of a German party area, the party music was overshadowed by the group singing of *Ein Prosit* and *Fliegerlied*, and so many other Oktoberfest-type songs Roman had heard over the years. Not unlike Magaluf, with its U.K. essence, El Arenal had a Teutonic flavor all its own.

Roman had seen the Goddess in each of the Mallorcan districts, but he'd seen her in El Arenal three times. So, of course, on his first night alone, he played the odds and made his way back to El Arenal. He deliberately left his cellphone in his room. There was no sense in giving himself the excuse of staring at his phone, texting and surfing the Internet to kill time.

No, tonight he was on a mission and didn't need the distraction.

Today's sun had provided him with a radiant tan, highlighted by his white linen shirt. It was now just after midnight. He'd arrived moments before, sitting at a high wooden keg table at the intersection of the two main El Arenal thoroughfares. If someone were partying in this area, they'd have to walk through this intersection at some point. Roman's vantage point was strategic.

His server was German. Roman ordered a pilsner, speaking his rough bar-German left over from his Army days. A middle-aged lady with a rubicund complexion, the server narrowed her eyes at his accent and grinned. When she returned, she asked if he was British—a standard question on Mallorca, where Americans are rather rare.

"Nope," he said. "American."

"Why would an American come all the way to Mallorca when you've got the Caribbean right there?"

He gestured to the sea of singing, drunken Germans flowing by in both directions. "Where in the Caribbean could I find Ballermann?"

She curled her lip. "You came here for this? I wish I could get away."

"Life's all about perspective." He paid for the large pilsner and told her to bring another one in a few minutes.

Being here alone's not so bad, Roman thought as he sipped his first beer. *Why were Mitch and Mike making such a big deal of it? Sure, it'd be nice if there were someone to talk to; but if I need to talk, I'll just strike up a conversation.*

Because he was alone, Roman drank much faster than normal. The German beers had a much higher alcohol content than American beers. By his fourth beer, his familiar neurosis had kicked in.

Damn, I wish my buddies were here. How the hell do loners do it? It's one thing to be back in Nashville alone, sitting there at my apartment with all my distractions. But it's a completely different prospect sitting here, staring at people like some axe-murdering psycho. I bet girls who see me alone think I'm some sicko creeper…

His server slid his fifth giant beer in front of him and sauntered away.

He looked at his watch. It was nearly 1:30 a.m. That would make it…what?…6:30 p.m. back home. Wonder if Wendy is seeing Toby tonight? Toby…who the hell is this guy, anyway? And what kind of man moves in on a woman with two kids? Yeah…he won't be around long. He probably just wants to add a notch to his bedpost. Or his hot yoga mat.

Screw you, Toby…whoever you are.

Roman had watched the assembled humanity for a total of 92 minutes before he saw *her*. There she was, the Goddess, wearing a simple outfit of stunningly short blue jean shorts and a yellow top. She wore flat sandals, which Roman eventually saw after drinking in her long tan legs. She and her friends were ambling, seeming in no hurry to get wherever it was they were going.

Feeling frozen, once again, Roman's reverie was shattered by a foursome of men who suddenly appeared in front of the German beauty and her friends. After a moment, it was clear the two groups knew one another. Judging by their posture and body language, the men were aggressive and seemed upset by something. The four girls acted disinterested, although to varying degrees. The shortest female, who happened to be the least attractive, seemed to be the only one who was mildly receptive to the male quartet's overtures.

As the center-street rendezvous extended to minutes, the Goddess began to survey the area around her. When her beautiful blue eyes eventually pivoted to the right, she saw Roman. Though her gaze paralyzed him for a moment, he surprised himself when he felt his right hand elevate and manage a wave. He even mustered a smile.

She looked away.

Soon thereafter, the four girls blew off the male suitors, who went the other way in a hail of curses and vulgar gestures. Roman watched the Goddess and her friends until they were set to depart from his line of sight. Just before they did, the Goddess glanced back at him…

And she smiled.

Holy shit! Did I just see that?

I did. I did. I did.

Houston, we have contact.

The Goddess actually moved her facial muscles for him, the movement designed to convey a feeling. It was beautiful and her one tiny, fraction-of-a-second gesture made the entire frustrating evening worthwhile.

Okay, get the hell off this stool and go, Roman. Go now. Follow her. Sweep her off her feet and prove your buddies wrong. Be a man. Take what's yours. Change your life.

And don't be a pussy.

After gunning his beer and wiping the foam mustache away, Roman went.

* * *

He found them.

The four girls had stopped at an open-air bar several blocks north. Roman, Mitch and Mike had visited this bar several nights before, when they'd witnessed a scuffle between several older Russian men. While there were still numerous revelers about, this area was a tad quieter than the Bourbon Street atmosphere at the Ballermann center of El Arenal. Roman approached the bar indirectly, arriving without the Goddess spotting him. The girls were busy viewing a notebook of songs, no doubt preparing to dazzle the small crowd with their karaoke skills.

"Shot of Jack, *por favor,*" Roman said to the bartender. The man didn't even have to move his feet. He grabbed a bottle and a highball glass, giving Roman a generous pour. Then the man slid the glass over, one eyebrow arched as if curious.

Roman gunned the whiskey, making a hissing sound as he dropped ten euro on the counter. Then, after a series of chest-expanding breaths, he walked straight toward the girls.

This was the hard part. Whiskey be damned, approaching a gaggle of girls while flying solo is one of the toughest moves in the business. In the thirteen sticky, tar-like steps Roman took across the small open-air bar, he recalled his days of being single, and just how ballsy one had to be to dare pull off a move like this one.

But I can do it, dammit! Just grab the old stones and say hello. Be confident and just a hair shy of cocky. Keep walking. Don't delay for anything.

Surprising even him, Roman's feet kept right on moving, despite the repellant force of fear and good sense. He reached the foursome but they hadn't yet seen him. They still had the notebook in front of them. Roman leaned as close as he dared to the Goddess and cleared his throat.

"Hello," he said. She turned around, surprised but wearing a poker face.

Was she happy to see him or had he just screwed up?

She'd just opened her mouth to speak when the emcee began speaking German on the microphone. The stage-side speakers that carried his voice were very loud—pain in the inner ear loud. Though Roman's German was that of a toddler's, he knew enough to know that the emcee was pumping up the sparse crowd for the four ladies who were about to take the stage.

Still, Roman waited expectantly.

The Goddess's three friends were already on the stage and one of them grabbed their friend's hand and pulled her up. Roman was left standing there, all alone, like an idiot. As the music started, the Goddess glanced down at him. She made no expression whatsoever.

Oh…what a smooth move this was. Timing is everything, dumbass, and you picked the absolute worst time. Good job, Roman.

He turned and walked back to the bar, feeling all eyes on him. As he approached, he held up his finger for the bartender, who was still standing in the exact same place. By the time Roman arrived, the shot—even more generous this time—was already waiting on him. With a single finger, and again the upturned eyebrow, the bartender slid the drink over.

"Nice work, *mi amigo*," he said, tipping a corner of his mouth up to match his eyebrow. Roman proffered more money but the bartender waved him off, walking to the end of the bar to take another order. Roman gunned the liquid courage, turning back to the stage to ponder his next move.

In a matter of seconds, the girls had drawn a small crowd. And damned if it wasn't the four scummy-looking guys Roman had seen talking to the girls earlier, on the busy street. They were pressed up against the stage, yelling and singing along. It was clear to Roman that the four karaoke singers were happy with their male suitors' presence.

Sonofabitch…cock-blocked by bad timing and euro trash.

Roman watched and listened to the foursome sing, butchering an old Pointer Sisters song. None of them looked Roman's way. The girls' dancing and swaying intensified as their suitors shouted and clapped. One of the Goddess's friends tousled one of the suitors' hair. This was too much…

Well…Mitch and Mike had been correct—Roman now desperately wanted to go home. This mission was over. *Houston, we have a problem.* He checked his watch—2:23 a.m. If he headed back now, he could call the airline and pay the associated fees to fly out around 7 a.m. Maybe he could sleep on the long transatlantic flight.

Roman walked from the open air bar, turning right on the street. The karaoke girls were wrapping up their song with a flourish. Feeling like a defeated six year-old, Roman glanced back to see his Goddess one last time, knowing he'd never see her again as long as he lived. Surprising him, she was staring right at him as she sang the chorus. She smiled, bigger this time. She even waved. Then she shrugged, her body language and expression asking, "You're leaving?"

Whipping his head back around, Roman kept walking, heart racing. His confidence had been destroyed by the earlier brush-off, but now his spirit soared over her three simple gestures. What the hell should he do? Should he buy a pack of cigarettes or chewing gum and then tell her that's why he stepped away? Or should he keep going and forget all about her. Because, despite her smile and wave, Roman couldn't see how he was going to cut through her three friends and the four guys who obviously already had some sort of inside track.

"What do I do?" he muttered to himself, over and over again.

He was reminded of Mitch's final words.

Okay…okay. Roman kept walking, feeling the urgent need to take a leak after the heart-pounding moments he'd just endured. The police here were quite strict about urinating in public—another similarity to Mardi Gras and Bourbon Street.

After I find a place to take a leak, I'll just go back. If I rush back too quickly, I'll look desperate. But a five-minute absence will prove to her that I'm not desperate...in fact, I'm uber-confident.

Yeah, right, Roman.

Unfortunately, there were no bars in sight. He'd exited the El Arenal nightlife area and now walked into a darkened residential area several blocks off the sea. Only a few pedestrians staggered about. Up ahead, he saw a restaurant with a red sign illuminated over the door. The restaurant was called Lemóni. On the side of the building that fronted the main road was a hanging flag—mostly white with some orange. The flag hung limp so Roman couldn't quite tell what it represented. Not that it mattered—he needed to piss, and badly.

As is true with all bathroom emergencies, the closer he got to a toilet, the worse his personal urgency grew. If this restaurant was locked, Roman was heading to the back alley, ticket be damned.

He stepped onto the low wooden porch and pushed on the door. It resisted until he gave it a slight shove, opening with a click. There were plenty of dim lights on in the charming restaurant but nobody was visible. The restaurant seemed to be pricey, displaying fifteen or so tables covered in white linen, sparkling stemware and shiny silver. Though the tables had all been prepared for the following day, Roman noticed a number of drinks on the bar. There was a fresh Heineken, a glass of red wine, a liquor drink of some sort and what appeared to be a glass of ice water.

"Hello?" he called out. He glanced at the deadbolt on the door, seeing that it stuck out a fraction. It seemed that perhaps someone had twisted it, but not fully. Roman's eyes slid to the right as he saw the bathrooms down a short hallway.

"Screw it," he whispered, hurrying down the hallway and depositing what felt like a gallon of used beer and whiskey into the urinal. It went on and on, giving him several shivers. As he squeezed out every little drop, he thought about the Goddess...

"You're damn right, I'm going back," Roman whispered, proud of himself. "I'm gonna walk back in like I own the place. I'm gonna walk right up to her, take her hand, lead her to a quiet table, and then she's going to talk to me and she's going to like me. After that, she's coming home with me." Roman zipped up and washed his hands.

And Toby can kiss my ass.

When finished, he tugged a paper towel from the dispenser. The metal container seemed loose and, when Roman pulled a second towel, the face of the container fell open, resting on the bottom hinge. Sitting on top of the white paper towels was a large coin. The coin was a dull gold color and easily as large as a U.S. silver dollar. Roman removed the coin, eyeing the strange language and markings. It appeared to be Asian in origin and, judging by the nicks and worn edges, very old. He rubbed the coin between his fingers, wondering why someone would have placed it on top of the paper towels.

The last towel that's pulled would cause the coin to drop. Maybe it's some silly little trademark this restaurant had come up with—gold coins for every 100th person who washes their hands?

Chuckling at his silly, giddy line of thinking, Roman rubbed the coin and decided to keep it as his good luck charm. He pocketed his find and smiled at himself in the mirror.

It would be Roman's last smile for some time.

Chapter Two

Feeling like a new man, Roman exited the restroom and walked back into the dining room of the restaurant. He looked to the right—the bar area was still empty with the drinks remaining on the bar. As he grasped the door to leave, he heard a yell. It didn't sound like a pained yell, but more like a protest. Roman turned, still seeing no one. Soon after, he heard several voices, all male. They were indistinct, coming from somewhere in the back of the restaurant. Then came the yell again. This time, rather than a protesting yell, it sounded more like a shout of pleading. One of the other voices grew louder, allowing Roman to understand the heavily accented words, spoken in English.

"Yes, you do. And, so help me, if you don't tell me right now, this is it. No more chances. And why would you hold out for them, anyway? I came here tonight to have a drink with you and get what I paid you for. I didn't come here to kill you."

Roman was transfixed. *Kill you? Did I hear that correctly?*

The voices grew lower, perhaps coming to some sort of an agreement. There were murmurs followed by silence.

More murmurs. Then, a distinct "no." Following the no was a barked command followed by...

"Ayeee!" It was the same voice Roman had heard yell the first two times. The yell transformed into a shriek, followed by growls and grunts. There was a heavy thudding sound followed by several lighter thumps.

Bolstered by a bloodstream coursing with alcohol, Roman walked through the dining room. He passed the bar, turning left through a lightly swinging door that led to the kitchen. There, in the bright white kitchen, Roman still saw no one. He stopped and listened as the smells of a recently-used kitchen filled his nose.

To Roman's left, he heard the voices. They were much clearer and weren't speaking English anymore. In fact, he couldn't place the language. Roman walked down the wide aisle of the kitchen. To his left were stainless steel countertops and sinks. To the right, long prepping tables with a taut cable running down the center above. Numerous alligator clips dangled at one end, ready for tomorrow's orders. Two rows of long knives rested on a white towel. The kitchen was bright, lots of stainless steel and white surfaces, and extremely clean.

The voices were quite clear now. Just ahead, Roman could see a small hallway to the right. It probably led to the restaurant's rear door. This was where the voices were coming from. They were now low and lacking urgency.

Roman continued forward, each step more difficult, as if some powerful glue were attempting to stick his feet to the floor.

These steps were far more difficult than the ones minutes earlier, when he'd approached the Goddess…

As Roman moved forward, the scene slid slowly into view. He couldn't quite reconcile what he was seeing.

One man stood with his back to Roman. He wore what appeared to be a quality suit, blue with a faint chalk pinstripe. The man's shape seemed a bit odd until Roman realized he had no left arm. Oftentimes, when a person is missing a limb, they will simply pin the useless sleeve to their garment. But this man's suit was obviously custom-tailored, appearing smooth and refined where his left arm would typically be. The rest of the suit was tailored traditionally, not in the slim-fit style that seemed so popular these days. It was a power suit and it fitted beautifully. The man was talking and gesturing with his good arm. A lace of smoke rose from his right hand.

Beyond him were two men. They'd not noticed Roman because they had their backs turned. The two men were kneeling and seemed to be struggling with something.

Are they holding someone down?

The man in the fine suit continued to talk in the strange language. It appeared he was giving instruction.

The two kneeling men weren't as nattily dressed as the one-armed man, but their clothing seemed somewhat out of place for blazing hot Mallorca. One wore a heavy gray sweater and the other a fitted leather jacket. Roman took one more step—and that's when he saw the feet.

And the blood.

"Xaná," the man in the suit said. He puffed his cigarette.

The man on the right, the one in the gray sweater, lifted a long kitchen carving knife…

No!

…and plunged it downward. It made a sickening sound, slicing through skin and muscle and skittering across bone. The feet twitched.

The one-armed man puffed his brown cigarette and repeated his phrase again. "Xaná."

The knife-wielding man obeyed. And again. And again.

Roman couldn't breathe. He pressed backward against the stainless steel counter, watching in disbelief. The feet he could see were adorned in sandals. They didn't seem to be the type of sandals worn by most young people. These were large desert sandals, and well worn. At the heels of both sandals—which were no longer moving—streamed a small river of impossibly red blood. It trickled over the tile, seeking the low point at the kitchen floor's drain.

Eventually, the two crouching men stood. The man in the leather jacket spit downward at whoever was still on the floor. The one-armed man murmured something that, in tone, sounded like an admonishment. Leather jacket shrugged and nodded, as if admitting he'd lost his cool.

The three men conferred before the one-armed man began to gesture toward the back door, speaking authoritatively about something.

Roman…get the hell out of here!

Any second now, one of the men was going to turn around and spot him. Then…Roman shuddered to imagine. He turned to go. His back was still against the stainless steel counter. As he began to move, he struck something. It was nothing more than the handle of a large scrub brush, clean and ready for the next day's use. The movement caused a slight scraping sound…

…but, in reality, it caused far more than that.

The three men turned. In that fateful second, Roman drank in their images.

The man in the leather jacket had an angular face, downturned at the mouth and marked by heavy lines. He seemed a cruel sort, almost the caricature of a pirate minus the eye patch. His eyes were ice blue and his head freshly shaved. Roman would later guess him to be a weather-beaten 45 years of age.

Wearing his heavy rag sweater, the second man had a florid face and a head of curly salt-and-pepper hair. His eyes were brown and there seemed to be an air of intelligence about him, though it simply could have been the contrast next to the henchman in the leather jacket.

But it was the one-armed man Roman found most distinctive. Not only was he missing the limb and wearing a fine suit, he was quite distinguished looking. If pressed, Roman wouldn't describe him as traditionally handsome, just…regal. His skin was quite dark and he appeared Middle Eastern. He wore a slim, black moustache tightly above his upper lip. And marking his noble face was a scar on the left side of his forehead. The one-armed man deflated upon seeing Roman, eyeing him with a minute shake of the head. There seemed to be a trace of sadness in his eyes.

"Pity. Now I have to kill you, too," the man's expression said to Roman.

But Roman was already on the run. Drunk or not, he sprinted down the cooking line, grasping the metal table to help him make a hard right turn through the swinging door. He could hear the men giving chase. As he plowed through the dining room, he knocked over chairs to impede his pursuers' progress.

Roman burst through the front door and, rather than run onto the main road, he turned hard to the left and sprinted across the side road into the alleyway. The alleyway was pitch black and partially hidden by a dumpster. Roman halted in the darkest area, peering back at the restaurant. Seconds later, the man in the leather jacket and the man in the sweater emerged. The man in the leather jacket ran straight ahead on the main road, back toward the madness of El Arenal. The man in the sweater turned right, headed to the north, running towards Roman's resort.

Both men had pistols in their hands.

So, after the men went north and south, and with the Bay of Palma occupying the west, Roman was left with only the east. Just as he slid into the shadows of the residential eastern road, Roman heard the back door of the restaurant. After halting behind a dumpster, Roman watched as the one-armed man calmly stepped into the alley. He flicked his cigarette to the ground and lit another, kneeling down and petting what appeared to be an alley cat. Moments later, the man stood and called someone on an old-style flip cellphone. This time the man spoke strangely accented German, but Roman could only make out a few words here and there.

If Roman were to move from his position behind the dumpster, he was afraid the man would see him. Roman continued to check his rear, afraid that the man in the leather jacket might come up behind him.

After his phone call, the one-armed man walked back inside. Without hesitating, Roman sprinted to the east, through the rows and rows of hotels and vacation homes.

And, dammit, if he'd brought his cellphone, he could call the cops right now. But, no, he'd had to leave it behind to force himself to focus on finding the Goddess. Well, it was of no matter. Roman knew exactly where the local police station was. He'd walked right past it earlier. After running five blocks inland, he turned to the north.

He'd speak to the police face-to-face.

* * *

Nearly thirty minutes later, after Roman had made his way several miles to the north via dark side streets, he trudged into the Dirección General de la Policía on the main strand. Roman had been fearful to even walk onto the main strand for more than a few feet, afraid the curly-haired man might still be lurking about. But, as Roman had stood behind the police station, he'd reasoned that he was two miles from the restaurant and more than a half-hour had passed since the murder. It was highly unlikely that the curly-haired man would know to wait in this very spot. After coaxing his hands to stop shaking, Roman hurried around the building and walked in through the front door. The building was gloriously cool, making Roman suddenly realize that he was covered in a film of sweat.

Just being in the presence of the police, and other people, injected Roman with a massive measure of relief. He rubbed his face, thankful to be alive.

The waiting area in the police station was full and reeked of alcohol and vomit and another bodily smell that Roman couldn't quite place—other than being comfortably cool, it reminded him of a New York subway train in the summer. Many people slept in the blue plastic waiting chairs. One post-teen held a bag of ice on his forehead. Small bloodstains marked the left side of his shirt. An older woman with leather tan skin stared at Roman, her blonde wig barely clinging to the side of her head. At the counter, three disheveled but attractive young German women were pooling their money to pay the policeman. Roman listened to their German, realizing they were posting a fine for their friend who was currently in the "drunk tank."

Roman moved beside the women and leaned forward to interrupt. "Excuse me, officer, I have an emergency."

The policeman seemed mildly surprised that Roman spoke English. The officer responded, saying, "You will take a number from the wheel and have a seat. Kindly listen for your number. We will call it only once." The officer smiled, as if he hadn't spoken these rote words in English in quite some time.

Roman turned in disbelief and viewed the number wheel. It was the same one he often saw at a popular butcher shop back home. Was this guy kidding? Roman leaned over again, resting his weight on both hands.

"Sir, apologies, but I'm not here to bail out a drunken friend. I have a true emergency."

"A *true* emergency?"

"Yes."

"As opposed to a false one?"

Roman glanced at the girls and lowered his voice. "Listen, I realize you get a bunch of bar traffic in here. I get it. But I'm doing my best not to cause a panic."

"A panic?" The officer massaged the bridge of his nose and shut his eyes, asking, "Are you drunk, señor?"

"Am I drunk? Are you serious?" Roman licked his lips, dispensing with the formalities, as well as the whispering. "Sir, I just witnessed a *murder.*"

Using "murder" would surely get the policeman's attention.

But it didn't.

The officer exhaled loudly and rolled his eyes. He held up a finger as if to tell Roman to wait. Then he slowly counted the money the women had pooled, eventually nodding. He paper-clipped their money to a yellow form and stamped it. Then, from a drawer to his right, he removed two coins, sliding them back to the women. He stamped another slip of paper and told the women to hand it to the officer in the window to the right. The women walked to the window.

The desk officer then turned to his computer and began to type.

Feeling himself losing control, Roman spoke through clenched teeth. "Officer, I drank tonight, yes. But I just watched two men stab a man to death." He pantomimed the action. "They stabbed him again and again and again while he screamed. Then they came after me. Do you understand?"

The policeman seemed unaffected, but he did turn from his computer screen. "Where was this?"

"El Arenal."

"Stabbed him?"

"Blood everywhere."

"If this is true, why didn't you use a telephone to report it? Why come here in person?" the officer asked, frowning in the manner a parent does to their constantly fibbing child.

"They chased me. I'm here on vacation from the U.S. and I don't have my cellphone with me. Do you not believe me?" Roman asked, realizing he was nearly yelling.

"If they stabbed him and blood was everywhere, why has no one else reported it?" The officer lifted a handheld radio and wagged it. "There's been no mention of a murder tonight."

"I'm the only one who saw it. You can't be serious, questioning me like this. A man was killed and I'm trying to do my duty as a citizen by reporting it."

The officer measured Roman for a moment before nodding. "One moment, sir. Please, take a seat." He lifted his phone and dialed three digits.

Roman found a seat near the window where the women were awaiting their drunken friend. The young woman they'd bailed out finally emerged, bursting into tears as she hugged her friends. Then, oddly enough, they all began laughing. Roman was able to discern enough of their Bavarian German to realize they were already talking about how much they'd have to drink tomorrow to kill their hangovers.

As the girls departed, Roman watched while the officer murmured to someone on the phone. He talked for at least three minutes, glancing at Roman at one point and sharing a laugh with whomever was on the other end of the line. The desk officer noticed Roman watching him so he looked away and continued to speak.

Roman shut his eyes, his emotions in a tangle. He was still quite disturbed over the raw image of the man on the floor—the knife plunging in and out of him, robbing him of his life. That man had been a baby once. His mother had loved him and fed him, tended to him when he was sick. He'd probably gone to school, fallen in love. Maybe he had children.

Sonofabitch, how could someone do that so coldly to another human being?

Roman was tired, his buzz gone. He was sad. He was angry. And now he was humiliated and insulted, not taken seriously by this asshole desk cop.

Back home, Roman always supported pro-police efforts and charities. It was dickheads like this cop who turned people off. Roman glared at him.

The officer hung up the phone and beckoned Roman. *Finally!* Roman hurried back to the desk.

"Señor, the captain on duty will speak to you."

"Excellent. Do I go through that door?" Roman asked, pointing.

"No. He will come to you. Please, be seated."

"Okay," Roman said, mollified. "Right over here?"

"That's fine."

"The captain?"

"His rank is sotinspector."

"Sotinspector…got it. Thanks."

Now Roman was getting somewhere. He checked his watch. Surely the good sotinspector wouldn't be long—not after the report of a nearby homicide.

Five minutes passed.

Ten.

Roman began to fidget.

Fifteen.

Twenty.

Boiling, Roman bolted to his feet and stormed back to the counter. "Where is he?" he snapped.

The desk officer wasn't helping anyone at the moment. Roman could see he was on his mobile device, reading what appeared to be a sports page judging by the soccer image. Probably taking a self-imposed break. The officer rotated irritated eyes to Roman.

"Sir, the sotinspector will come out when he is free. And if you speak to me in that tone again, I will detain *you*."

"Are you kidding me? There are killers on the loose, which you don't seem to care about, but you'll go out of your way to detain me?"

"Alcohol does strange things to a percentage of the population, especially our visitors."

"So, you're again saying you don't believe me?"

"During the summer, I get at least five death reports each day. It is extremely rare that any of them are accurate. The so-called victim is usually just someone passed out drunk."

"I didn't report a death, okay?" Roman answered, using his hands to emphasize his point. "I reported a *murder*. Get it? I watched, and *heard*, the knife plunge in and out of the man. I saw the blood. I heard him scream."

"Yes, you told me," the officer said, his tone and expression patronizing. "Did the alcohol make you forget?"

Roman knotted his lips together and stared at the white ceiling tiles for a moment, summoning patience. When he'd composed himself, he eyed the officer and calmly said, "I'm not exaggerating nor am I hallucinating. I saw two men kill another man. They did so under the direction of a third man."

The officer arched his eyebrows. "Oh? Now there was a third man?"

"There was always a third man. I just didn't say so earlier."

"I see. And now that you've had time to think about it, you're remembering more details."

"I remember all of it…unfortunately."

"Who was the third man?"

"I don't know. Middle Eastern, I think, and he only had one arm."

"Ohhhh…a one-armed man, from the Middle East?" the officer asked, clearly amused. "Did he have a pincher?" he asked, making a lobster-snapping motion with his hand.

Roman knew he was being mocked. "How long will the sotinspector be?"

Just then, the door to the left opened. Through the door came a young man in uniform. His dark hair was slicked severely back. He had a narrow, intelligent face and a serious demeanor. He eyed the desk officer who pointed to Roman while making a "he's your problem now" face. The officer approached Roman and extended his hand.

"Good evening, señor," the man said, shaking Roman's hand. "I'm Sotinspector Reyes. Come with me, please."

Feeling a huge relief wash over him, Roman followed the officer through the door to his office.

As he passed through the threshold, it took all of Roman's willpower not to flip the desk officer the bird.

* * *

There were two other civilians in the lieutenant's office. One was snoozing in a chair in the corner, his wrist handcuffed to an eye bolt that emerged from the wall. He looked to be no more than 16. The other, a tall and stunningly attractive woman, sat on the chintzy sofa against the wall. She winked at Roman as he pulled a chair closer to the lieutenant's desk.

Reyes opened a drawer and licked his thumb, removing three forms, a clipboard and a chewed Bic pen. He handed them to Roman, saying, "Please use block letters and press down very hard. I will also need your passport."

Roman eyed the forms incredulously before raising his eyes to the lieutenant. "Forms? Did you talk to the officer out there about what I saw?"

"Yes, and we cannot do anything until you fill out those forms."

"A murder, sir. I witnessed a murder."

Reyes stared back before flicking his eyes down to the forms. "And when you fill those out, we shall discuss. Would you like some coffee?"

"No," Roman replied, disbelievingly going to work on the top form. "And I don't have my passport."

"Where is it?"

"My hotel."

"In a safe, I hope." Reyes departed the room and disappeared down the hall.

Roman kept writing.

"Don't let their bureaucracy bother you," the woman on the sofa said.

Roman turned to her. She spoke English with what sounded like a Russian accent.

"Where was the murder?" she asked.

"El Arenal."

"Not surprised. Everything else goes on down there."

"So, you believe me?"

"Sure. There are seven murders per year in Mallorca. Who says you didn't witness one of them?"

"Thanks." Roman turned his eyes back to the form.

"Are you here for a vacation?"

Continuing to write, Roman nodded.

"You need to be more firm with your requests."

Roman eyed her. "Who are you?"

"I work in Mallorca."

"Work?"

She went into her clutch and handed him a glossy black business card. In several languages, the card described her as Mallorca's most exclusive escort, available for "memorable dates and companionship."

"I'm Lucy," she said, shaking Roman's hand.

"Pleased to meet you," he replied, feeling somewhat odd over his choice of words. "If you don't mind, I'm going to finish these forms."

"Go right ahead. Just remember what I told you."

The forms weren't as bad as Roman thought. Much of the space was reserved for the police. When finished, he checked them over before sliding them back across the desk. He turned to the woman.

"I didn't mean to be rude."

She shrugged. "I'm not offended."

"Are you under arrest?"

She laughed, showing a wide mouth of straight teeth. "Sort of."

"What does that mean?"

"My business is legal, here. But oftentimes, what you'd think men hire me for isn't reality."

Roman narrowed his eyes.

"Along with companionship, I often help my privileged clients in the acquisition of certain products."

"I see. Your English is excellent, by the way."

"Thank you. It pays for me to speak several languages like a native."

"So, you're *sort of* under arrest?"

"Usually, about once a month, the good Sotinspector Reyes follows me and *detains* me. It's our little game."

"So, you *are* under arrest."

"Not really—just detained. When he leaves work in the morning, I'll go with him. And, five or ten minutes after we go somewhere private, I'm no longer detained. Get it?"

Roman nodded. "I get it."

"He likes me," Lucy said. "Just can't help himself."

Sotinspector Reyes appeared at the door, speaking rapid-fire Spanish to someone down the hall.

"Remember what I said," Lucy whispered.

"Forceful?"

"But polite."

Reyes stepped behind the desk and sat. He glanced at each of the forms, his eyes betraying nothing. "These look fine but we must have your passport before—"

Roman leaned forward and spoke in a stern voice. "Sotinspector Reyes, I respectfully insist we stop with the forms and questions. A man was brutally murdered a short while ago, and every minute that we delay could add difficulty to your solving the case. I've given you no reason to doubt the legitimacy of my claims. Please, sir, since you are *such* a professional, I request you take my claims seriously and act right now."

Sotinspector Reyes straightened. He appeared momentarily angry before the flattery portion took full effect and his face softened. "Very well—we shall retrieve your passport later. How far from here did you witness this crime?"

"Maybe three kilometers? It was just north of El Arenal."

Reyes lifted the phone and spoke several words before hanging up. "My officer is bringing a car around. Follow me."

At the door, Roman looked at Lucy. She blew him a kiss and made a phone gesture with her thumb and pinkie, mouthing, "Call me."

Always be closing. Roman mouthed his thanks.

Seconds later, a uniformed officer named Carrenta whisked Roman and Reyes to the south. The police car's lights flashed but the siren was off. Roman leaned forward and viewed the speedometer—100 kilometers per hour and still accelerating.

Now we're getting somewhere.

* * *

The three men stood on the small porch of the restaurant Lemóni. Though it was nearly 4 a.m., the thudding bass of El Arenal's party district could still be felt, even from four blocks away. The front door of the restaurant was locked and had only been tested by Reyes near the knob's base, in order to preserve fingerprints. Reyes made a call on his radio and, in minutes, a junior officer arrived on a scooter with a large key ring. Again, great pains were endured to make sure no one touched the doorknob or the door. Reyes unlocked the door and used the key to push the door open. He then spoke Spanish to the officer with the keys. Though Roman couldn't understand, it seemed Reyes commanded the junior man to stand watch at the door.

When Reyes and Carrenta went inside, Roman stayed back. His palms were sweaty and he suddenly felt nauseous.

"Señor, you are coming?" Reyes asked.

"I'm sorry but I'm…I'm…"

Reyes drew his pistol. "I'm here, señor. There is no danger."

Roman swallowed thickly and followed, directing them to the rear of the restaurant. Because of the large windows, the front of the restaurant was fairly well lit. But the small hallway that led to the kitchen, and the kitchen itself, was pitch black. Carrenta illuminated his path with his flashlight, using the metal of the light to flip on the switches, again preserving prints.

"Back there," Roman said, feeling his chest heaving as he pointed. He dreaded seeing the body.

"Are you all right?" Reyes asked, seeming genuinely concerned.

"Yeah," Roman answered, sucking in a great breath through his nose. He stepped to the white center table and gestured to the small rear hallway. "It happened over there." Roman shut his eyes, unable to bear the sight.

The policemen walked to the rear entryway. "Where, señor?"

Roman still couldn't look. "Right where that back hallway begins."

"You can open your eyes. There's nothing here, señor," Reyes said.

Roman opened his eyes and made his way to the end of the center table. The floor was clean. No body. No blood.

"Señor?" Reyes asked, clearly puzzled.

"Right there," Roman said, stabbing his finger at the floor. "That's where it happened."

Both policemen moved to the area in question. Upon noticing the rear door, Carrenta moved down the small hallway, checking the bolt. He came back, eyeing the spot of the murder with Reyes.

Reyes looked at Roman. "Are you certain this is the spot?"

"Yes."

"And it couldn't have been another restaurant?"

Roman averted his eyes for a moment. "I know how this looks, but this is where he was killed. You see, this is why I wanted to hurry back down here. I guarantee you that one-armed guy orchestrated this whole thing…cleaned it all up."

The two policemen looked at one another.

Realizing he needed to help recreate the scene, Roman walked to the spot and provided a full explanation. "The man who was killed was lying here on the floor, his feet here, his head here. There were two men holding him down. One was in a leather jacket, the other in a heavy sweater."

"In this heat?" Carrenta asked, the first words of English he spoke.

"Exactly what I thought," Roman said. "I came into the restaurant to go to the bathroom. After I exited the bathroom, I heard voices. I heard a man saying 'no' then yelling. I heard another man—the one armed man—speaking English, telling the man he didn't want to kill him. By the time I got back here, they were knifing him."

"Where was the one-armed man?" Reyes asked.

"Here," Roman answered, standing in the spot and facing the rear door. "I was back there," he said, pointing to the rear counter. "And the one-armed man smoked brown cigarettes. They weren't cigars."

The two policemen looked at each other. "You said there was blood?"

"Yeah," Roman answered. "Pretty good amount, too. I guess they hosed it off."

"The floor *is* wet," Reyes admitted, looking around. "And it's only wet in this area." He pointed to the drain and spoke Spanish to his subordinate. The younger officer stepped away and spoke on the radio.

"He's calling Forensics. If they sprayed the blood away, there will be a residue in the drain. And if they removed his body via the back door, there will probably be drops of blood in the alley. Perhaps there are security cameras, too?"

"Okay, good," Roman answered, feeling slightly relieved. Something occurred to him. "Also," he said, pointing, "there were four drinks on the bar. Maybe they're still there. You can get fingerprints...DNA."

The two men walked back to the restaurant's main dining room. Reyes found more lights, again using his flashlight to flip the switch. Both men eyed the bar; it was clean and dry.

"May I?" Roman asked, gesturing behind the bar.

"Just don't touch anything."

He walked behind the bar, checking the sinks and the trash without leaving fingerprints. The sinks and trash were empty. He used his shirt to open the industrial dishwasher, feeling the blast of wet heat from where it had run on an automatic cycle. The dishes were clean.

Roman looked up. "They cleaned up here, too. There has to be blood in that kitchen drain."

Reyes eyed the front door. "Señor, it was around two a.m. when you were here?"

"Yes."

"How did you get in? The hours on the door read that the restaurant was closed."

"I didn't notice that they weren't open. I just walked up and pushed on the door. Someone had barely turned the bolt lock so the door wasn't shut well. Once I was inside, I didn't see anyone and I really had to take a leak, so I went. That's when I heard the voices...afterward."

Reyes spoke loudly in Spanish, yelling to Carrenta. After listening to the junior officer's reply, Reyes said, "Forensics will be here in an hour, maybe less. They are at another crime scene in Palma."

Roman walked back to the kitchen, trying to think of any other details that might help. He eyed the drain and the coiled hose by the door.

"Clever pricks," he breathed.

* * *

By the time Forensics wrapped up, it was fully light outside although the sun wasn't yet up over the adjacent buildings. The owners of the restaurant had arrived and were whispering in worried tones in the main dining room. They looked to be in their sixties, a husband and wife, and appeared to have been asleep, judging by their clothes and hair. Roman was on the other side of the dining room, awaiting word from Sotinspector Reyes. When Reyes finally appeared, he spoke to the owners first. The conversation wasn't all that lengthy. The owners gathered their things to leave and, at the front door, they both glared coldly at Roman.

After they'd left, Reyes came to Roman. "The owners will allow us to lock up."

"Are they angry with *me?*"

Reyes shrugged. "I wouldn't be concerned. They're probably upset at being dragged into this."

"What did Forensics find?"

"Before I get to that, the owners claim they locked up last night—they didn't allow their employees to stay. They weren't busy so they actually cleaned up and closed a bit early. They know of no way that four men could have had drinks here unless they broke in." Reyes tapped his notepad on his hand. "And they said their staff can verify the closing time."

Roman felt acid building in his stomach.

Reyes gestured to the kitchen. "Forensics has taken numerous samples from a number of areas, including the drain. There is an installed grease collection system that could prove to be problematic. It deploys an enzyme that might have spoiled any residual blood."

"What about blood drops? Fingerprints? DNA? And did you check the hose they used to spray off the blood?"

"Our people took dozens of prints. Those will be checked. There were no blood drops and, unfortunately, no cameras in the restaurant, the back alley, the side streets, or out front. There was also nothing useful on the hose. Whoever used it appeared to have worn rubber gloves, but the owners said the staff wear rubber gloves when they clean up at night."

Covering his face with his hands, Roman shook his head. Then he remembered the two men chasing after him. "You should check cameras up and down the main strand. The two men, when they were chasing me, split up in both directions, north and south. They were carrying guns. That should show up on video."

"We will execute an exhaustive follow-up. But, keep in mind, images from a street camera that show two men running, even if we find any, prove nothing."

"It could help you with identities, give you a place to start."

"Why don't you go home and get some rest? Come see me today when I come back on shift, around 1600 hours. We'll update you on our investigation and ask you some follow up questions at that time."

"Do you think I'm safe?"

Reyes' smile was patronizing, as if Roman were a teenager that was a bit too old to be scared at night. "Señor, Mallorca is an extremely safe island. If there was a murder here, then—"

"You just used the word 'if.' There *was* a murder here. See," Roman said, crooking a finger at Reyes, "you don't believe me."

"At this point—"

"At this point I'm being treated suspiciously, as if I made it all up," Roman said, his voice rising. "Why would I lie about a murder? I'm on vacation. I didn't want any of this. But I saw a man killed, dammit, whether you believe me or not."

Sotinspector Reyes appeared on the verge of losing his temper. His nostrils flared and his lips knotted. He took a series of deep breaths before speaking calmly, but it was obvious his rage was just beneath the surface. "Señor, you snapped at me in my office, and I allowed it. We've both had a long night and I realize you absolutely believe what you've testified. But I will not allow another outburst." He smoothed his tie and calmed down a bit more. "We are taking your testimony seriously. Let us do our jobs. Officer Carrenta will drive you home and I will see you at 1600."

Roman allowed the words to sink in. Though angry, he shook Reyes' hand. "Sorry I yelled at you."

"Your tension is understandable. Rest well, señor."

Roman pondered a final jab. He thought about telling Sotinspector Reyes to have fun "interrogating" Lucy, the escort he'd "detained."

But Roman's good sense won out. He needed sleep.

* * *

Twenty minutes later, Roman ascended in the elevator at his Can Pastilla resort. His fears and his anguish had subsided, replaced by extreme exhaustion. As he trudged down the open air corridor on the 6th floor, he was surprised to see two teenagers bounding the opposite direction with floats and chairs, already prepared for a day on the beach.

"Why did I have to take that piss?" Roman muttered, remembering the way the Goddess had looked at him. Instead of walking up the street, he could have turned right around and used the bathroom at the bar. Then he could have met her and who knows where that might have led? Maybe she'd be in his bed right this second. Who knows, she might have even come back to the States with him.

Roman envisioned his first encounter with Wendy: Late Thursday afternoon. Roman rings the doorbell. Wendy opens the door.

"Are the kids ready?" he would ask.

"They're getting their bags," she'd say, leaning against the door of the home he paid for. "Listen, Roman, I really do want you to meet Toby. I honestly think you'll like…" Wendy's eyes would avert to his idling car. "Who's that?"

"Excuse me?"

"Who is waiting in your car?"

"Her? The tall, tan, blonde beauty? The one whose legs reach to heaven? She's just a friend I met in Mallorca. She'll be staying with me for the foreseeable future. Tell the kiddos I'm in the car. And make sure you tell whatshisname…*Toby*…hello for me." Roman would wink and grin and head straight back to the car, back to his prize.

How sweet that would be. It might even ruin Wendy's Memphis sex romp. Roman remembered, all too well, that everything had to be perfect before Wendy would succumb to sex. And her frigidness had gotten worse with age.

Did you ever consider that maybe she'd grown that way because of you? Besides, none of this fantasy is going to happen, Roman—dumbass—because you had to walk away and take that piss.

Roman opened his wallet and slid his keycard into the door lock. It flashed red. He repeated the process several times. When that didn't work, he breathed hot breath on the magnetic strip. Nope. Cleaned it on his shirt. Nothing. Still locked.

"You gotta be freaking kidding me."

Then he remembered Mitch and Mike had given him their keys. Maybe he was using the wrong one, but he thought he'd slid their keys behind his American Express. He stood there for another minute, trying all three. None of them worked. Now he'd have to go back downstairs and wait on someone at the front desk to make him a new one.

He was so damned tired.

Roman tramped back toward the elevator when he came to Mike's room. It was three rooms away from his own. Primarily out of curiosity, Roman produced the three keycards. On his second try, Mike's lock flashed green and, when he pushed the door open, Roman was greeted by a blast of cold air from the room's air conditioner.

Stepping into the room, Roman saw that the maids had given it a thorough cleaning. He walked all the way in and viewed the aquamarine protected bay of Can Pastilla in all its morning brilliance. Roman glanced back at the freshly made bed, so clean and inviting.

"To hell with going back downstairs." He slid the blackout curtains shut, stripped down to his underwear and plopped right onto the plush duvet.

Roman was asleep in seconds.

Chapter Three

The red digital letters of the clock read 2:58. Roman groaned, unable to remember where he was. As he'd slept, he'd managed to pull the duvet cover over his midsection for warmth. He stirred, seeing the brilliant outline of sunshine around the heavy drapes.

Daytime.

Fighting the urge to burrow under the duvet and go back to sleep, Roman sat up. Something in the back of his mind reminded him that he had an obligation, even though he couldn't remember exactly what that obligation was.

He stood and staggered across the room, squeezing his eyes shut as he tugged the drape open. The warmth of the summer sun through the glass felt good against his skin. The air conditioning had been set so low that now he was very cold. He turned, easing his eyes open and remembering that he'd slept in Mike's room.

Then, in a matter of two grim seconds, Roman remembered everything. The worst of his recollections was the vision of the long knife plunging down into the man on the floor. The sounds. The blood. The yells.

The clock now read 3:01. Roman was due at the police station in an hour. Monday was already more than half over. He needed a shower, fresh clothes and some caffeine. He slid on his pants and shoes and stepped into the empty corridor, deciding to try the keycards one last time before journeying downstairs. Check-in here was at 3 p.m., so Roman feared he'd have to wait too long if he went to the front desk.

Carrying his socks, shirt and belt, Roman neared his room. As he drew closer, he cocked his head. The door was cracked open. Would the maid be there this late in the afternoon? But there was no cart outside the door. With the fog of sleep still hanging heavy in his head, Roman pushed through the door and stepped inside.

"Hello?"

Nothing.

Since Roman's room was at the end of the hallway, it was laid out a bit differently from Mike's and Mitch's. Theirs was more of a standard layout. A small hallway, a sleeping area and a sitting corner. Roman's, however, was more like a suite. You walked in and made a right turn into the sitting area, overlooking the bay. To the right, in another room, was the bedroom. Wondering if the maid had accidentally left his door askew, Roman walked in and turned right, into the bedroom.

He knew right then that he'd been burgled.

His clothes were scattered everywhere. His suitcase lay splayed on the floor. Papers from Roman's briefcase—work he'd brought for the plane rides—were strewn all over. Roman stepped back into the sitting area, seeing that his backpack had been rifled. But a quick inventory demonstrated to Roman that nothing of value was missing. Oddly enough, Roman's mobile phone was exactly where he'd left it. In fact, it was the only item that hadn't been moved.

Roman's blood ran cold as he pondered who'd tossed his room. He went into his suitcase, reaching into the concealed pocket as he shut his eyes. For a moment, he thought it wasn't there. But then, his hand touched the thin booklet. Roman removed it, staring at his passport.

Thank God.

He pocketed the identification and also grabbed his phone, confirming that it was still set to airplane mode. Then he took a set of clothes back to Mike's room. After quickly showering, Roman left the hotel via the stairs, exiting in the dark basement and walking out the rear door, located in an alleyway behind the resort restaurants. Roman walked the length of the alleyway, coming out in the heart of Can Pastilla. He still had 20 minutes so he sat in the rear of a small café, drinking a strong coffee and thinking.

Was that just a random burglary? If so, why wasn't anything stolen? Since nothing was stolen, it couldn't have been a random burglary. It wasn't a burglary at all.

Therefore, it had to be the one-armed man and his thugs.

Despite the heat, a chill went through Roman's body.

How the hell did they know who he was?

* * *

Roman burst into Sotinspector Reyes' office. "They just broke into my hotel room."

The officer who'd led Roman to the rear of the police station frowned and objected in Spanish but Reyes waved him off and shut the door. He sat on the corner of his desk and crossed his arms as he considered Roman.

"Did you hear me?" Roman asked, opening his arms and gesticulating. "They broke into my hotel room and tossed everything."

"Who did?"

"Last night, when your guy dropped me at the hotel…this morning, rather…my key wouldn't work…one of those credit card keys, you know?" Roman slid the three card keys from his wallet to demonstrate. "So, my buddies had just left yesterday. They'd prepaid their rooms so they gave me their keys. You with me?"

"I think so. Go on, but please slow down, and *calm down*."

"Well, when my key wouldn't work, I was so exhausted that I didn't want to go back downstairs to the front desk. So I crashed in my buddy's room. I woke up today around three and went to my own room to try my keycard again, just so I didn't have to stand in line downstairs. Anyway, when I got there, the door was open. I went inside, and my entire room had been tossed."

"Tossed?"

"Someone broke into my room and went through everything I own." Roman gestured around the office. "And I mean everything. My stuff is strewn all over."

"What did they steal?"

"Nothing. And that tells me that it was them."

"Who?"

"The killers! Don't you see? The one-armed man knows who I am," Roman said, poking his chest. "I had to sneak down the stairs and out the back door of the hotel in case they'd staked out the lobby."

Reyes frowned and gnawed his bottom lip. After a moment, he motioned to one of the guest chairs at his desk. "Please...sit."

Roman did, pressing his hands back through his hair. "Look, I know I'm a bit keyed-up, but to see what I saw last night, followed by this break in. Well..." Roman cut himself off and shook his head. "These guys are killers and they know who I am. If they find me..."

Reyes walked around his desk and sat. He laced his hands together on the blotter. "Forensics found nothing to indicate a murder, or even violence, occurred at the Lemóni."

"That's impossible. There has to be some sort of evidence."

"Our forensics team is quite good, señor."

"The blood in the drain?"

"They cut meat there. Fish. Poultry. The catch system uses an enzyme to break down naturally occurring substances. We discussed this last night."

"And?"

"And, there was very little in the drain other than water and the enzyme. We've sent it off for testing, but that will take weeks—and we're not optimistic."

"They flushed that drain," Roman lamented. "I bet they dumped fifty gallons of water in there."

"Additionally, after further searching, we found no cameras nearby and no other witnesses have come forward. We've even canvassed the area, asking residents, store owners, anyone. You're the only person claiming anything about what happened last night."

Roman fought the urge to panic. "I saw a murder."

"Furthermore, we have no reports of anyone missing, and nothing else other than your testimony to indicate anything untoward occurred." Reyes arched his eyebrows. "In fact, in the kitchen area of the restaurant, the only fingerprints we found that didn't belong to the staff...belong to you."

"The killers cleaned up their mess."

"I remember your theory, señor."

"What about my room? Shouldn't you come take fingerprints? Maybe they left a stray hair with DNA? Maybe there are cameras in the hallway?"

"If it happened, hotel break-ins aren't that uncommon here."

"If? Did you just say *if*, again?"

Reyes didn't answer.

Roman white-knuckled the spindly arms of the chair. "Sotinspector Reyes, do you believe I witnessed a murder?"

"Señor, I took your testimony seriously. I did everything in my power to determine what happened. And other than your words, I have absolutely nothing to go on. Please, put yourself in my position."

"Dammit, I'm a trustworthy and ethical man. I'm also an Amer—." Roman halted himself. "I'm a stable man with no criminal record. Yes, I drank last night, but I don't do drugs or anything that might impair me. I know what I saw," he said, poking his chest. "And today, my hotel room was turned upside down. If you don't help me, those men are going to find me and kill me. I need your help!"

"Please, calm down."

Roman cocked his head. "Oh, there's one more thing: I want to know how the hell they found my name and hotel."

Reyes paused. "You're insinuating that I told them?"

"No. Not you. But someone on this police force. Who else knows that I reported the murder?"

"Let's not connect the break-in so quickly, señor. Most hotel burglars look for expensive watches, cash, jewelry. They don't waste time with phones, computers or the like. So, please, set that aside for the moment."

Roman took a deep breath and nodded.

"I believe you about the murder, señor…I do…but I have no other evidence to support your claims. It's difficult to investigate a murder with zero evidence and no reports of anyone missing." Reyes leaned back in his chair and considered Roman. "But, if I didn't believe your testimony, I would charge you with, among other things, filing a false report."

"So, that's it? No evidence. No body. Case closed?"

Reyes' response was biting and clinical. "Along with the drain water testing we've ordered, we've alerted every single law enforcement official on this island about these three men. The man with one arm should be quite easy to spot. Okay? We've also sent canvassing teams around the neighborhood of the restaurant, and they're still trying to find anyone who saw something. Also, the man who was killed should turn up missing at some point, so we may have that to go off of, too." Reyes' face softened and he paused for a deep breath. "Now, please, there's nothing more you can do *right now*. Go and enjoy your vacation. If I need you, I will call you."

"I'm not turning my phone back on. And I'm afraid to go back to my hotel."

"I think that's unnecessary."

"Regardless, I'm still afraid."

"When do you leave, señor?"

"Wednesday morning."

"I'll send a team to your hotel. They will check the cameras, search your room for evidence, prints and such…and they will bring all your personal effects here when they're finished. Fair enough?"

Roman nodded and suddenly felt pretty small. "I'm…uh…I'm sorry for doubting you and acting the way I did."

Reyes stood and extended his hand. "At least you didn't insist that you were correct because you're American. But you were very close."

For the first time since before the murder, Roman smiled.

* * *

Three hours later, Roman exited his new hotel in Palma—a solid 7 miles away from his previous hotel. He nodded at the proprietor of the small boutique establishment, a kind older gentleman who'd been lenient enough to rent Roman a room without any identification. Roman claimed he'd lost his wallet and passport and was currently awaiting assistance from the Canadian Embassy in Madrid. Roman had cash, however, and agreed to pay a bit extra for the man's accommodations. All of this was done with a false name, of course.

Knowing there was nothing else he could currently do, Roman vowed to attempt to have a pleasant evening. He'd stay here in Palma, near the hotel, and have dinner and a few beers. He wasn't sleepy, but he also didn't feel like partying. And despite all that had happened, he'd love to reconnect with the Goddess. But Roman didn't dare entertain going back down to El Arenal, where he'd last seen her.

No way in hell was he ever going back there.

The knife plunging in and out of the man…

Roman stopped at a kiosk, where he purchased a 500-minute international calling card. He then took a seat in the rear of a nearby Greek restaurant. The restaurant was quiet, other than a few people at the bar. Roman ordered a beer and, as he was waiting on his server to return, he pondered the break-in at his resort hotel. How had the men known who he was? The only people who knew Roman Littlepage had reported the murder had been the local police, correct?

What about the hooker? Would she somehow know the killers?

The only other thing Roman could think of—and this was a long shot—was the possibility of the killers collecting Roman's fingerprints from the restaurant. But they couldn't have managed that, could they? In the span of a few hours, they killed a man and then sanitized the restaurant of, not only his body and blood, but of all collateral evidence. And what sort of resources would they have had at their disposal to run Roman's fingerprints, then connect them with his identity, then use said identity to find Roman's resort?

Too far-fetched.

Meaning, they somehow found out through the police. Maybe they were members of local organized crime. Roman had worked around local government long enough to know that influential mobsters usually have tentacles in the resident administration. Perhaps, here in Mallorca it was no different. Regardless, despite whatever local influence they might have, they wouldn't find him now because Roman was currently anonymous. In fact, he had enough cash that he wouldn't have to expose himself electronically until he checked in at the airport.

Speaking of that—would Reyes prevent him from leaving? Roman couldn't see why, especially since the murder had been all dead ends.

As sickening as it seems—the murderers getting away with it—I'm just going to have to leave it all behind and find my peace at home.

When the server returned with his beer, Roman asked her if there was a telephone in the restaurant.

"No cellphone?" she asked in English.

"I don't have an international plan," he answered, showing her the calling card.

She showed him into a back office that seemed more of a storeroom, judging by the perilous stacks of boxes. It held the smell of cardboard and, oddly enough, mimeograph ink that reminded him of elementary school.

"Your boss won't mind?" he asked.

"My papa is my boss, and he's not here."

"Thank you."

"Make sure you pay the long distance with your card," she said playfully, wagging her finger. "Or I will get in trouble." She smiled and pulled the door shut.

She's kinda cute...

Tonight certainly was proceeding nicely. In the privacy of the cluttered office, Roman suddenly felt better about things. All he had to do was make a conscious effort to enjoy the vestiges of his vacation in anonymity. Heck, tomorrow he might even rent a jet ski and explore the various beaches around the island.

Roman placed the calling card on the disarranged desk. He used his recently found good luck coin to scratch off the silver residue so he could see the card's PIN. Then, after punching in what felt like 100 digits, Mike's cellphone rang five times. Roman was greeted by Mike's perfunctory voicemail message.

"Mikey," Roman said. "Hope you made it home safe. I'm still here. Some big shit went down and, no, I'm not joking and it's not good. I slept almost all day so I'll try you in a few more hours. You're not going to believe what happened. Talk later."

There was no sense in mentioning a man being stabbed to death on Mike's voicemail.

Roman repeated the process with the digits, dialing Mitch's cellphone. After mis-keying once, Roman started over and eventually heard the American ringtone.

"Yeah?" Mitch asked abruptly.

"It's me."

"Holy shit, dude!" Mitch yelled. "What happened? Where are you?"

Roman stood, taken aback by Mitch's tone. He was normally unflappable. Now, however, he was clearly alarmed—uncharacteristically alarmed.

"What do you mean?" Roman asked. "What have you heard?"

"I got a call this morning from some guy in Mallorca. Said he was a detective, or something like that, and said you'd been a witness of a major crime. He wouldn't say what had happened. He said they were trying to find you and asked me fifty questions about where you might be, where we stayed, if you have a rental car, places we ate and shit like that."

"Are you kidding me?"

"No. I didn't tell him much because something about the whole thing seemed...I dunno...off."

"Was he Spanish?"

"Yeah. He said he was a detective, or whatever their title there is. I tried calling your cell like ten times."

"It's in airplane mode. Gimme a second." Roman put the phone down, rubbing his temples as he thought about this. It wouldn't have been Reyes. Maybe, when the report of the murder flowed through Mallorca's law enforcement divisions, someone hadn't gotten the memo about where Roman was staying. Maybe that's where this came from—bureaucratic confusion. Roman lifted the receiver.

"It was probably someone with the local police who didn't get the full story."

"What full story?"

Roman sat back down and told Mitch about going out in El Arenal last night. He made the story quick, but was clear about where he was because Mitch and Mike had been with him in the same area. "So after I found her at that open air bar a few blocks north of the center of El Arenal...remember, we saw those old Russians taking swings at each other in there?"

"I remember. Go on."

"Well, the Goddess started singing karaoke with her friends. I was thinking of bailing, so I left. When I got a few blocks away, I changed my mind but I had to piss so I went into a restaurant that was already closed for the night. You with me?"

"Yeah."

"Anyway, I took my leak and then I heard voices in the kitchen. I went back there and saw something I'll never forget…" Roman felt his voice cracking.

"You all right?"

"Not really," Roman answered, hardly able to get it out.

"Just say it."

"They killed him, Mitch. Some man was on the floor in the kitchen. Two men were on top of him and one was stabbing him with a huge knife."

"Are you shitting me?"

Roman dipped his head, taking deep breaths. Something about telling this to his friend made it seem far more real. "No…I'm not shitting you. There was some guy watching and giving orders. He had one arm."

"One arm?"

"I know it sounds weird."

"What happened next? You try and stop 'em?"

"No, it was too late. They saw me so I hauled ass. They came after me. I thought I was a dead man. They had guns."

"Are you being a hundred percent serious? This isn't some joke you're playing on us?"

"Hell no, dude!" Roman snapped. "And now I'm lost. I don't know what to do. They're after me."

"Take it easy, brother," Mitch said, clearly uncomfortable with having to comfort Roman. "What about the other people in the restaurant?"

"It had been closed for a few hours. It was just me and the killers and the guy who got murdered."

"How'd you get in if it was closed?"

"The door wasn't shut all the way." Roman spent the next ten minutes explaining about the lack of evidence, the suspicion the police had treated him with and the fact that his room had been broken into.

"Are they gonna let you leave?"

"I don't know. I just want to get home."

"Why aren't the cops giving you protection?"

"Like I said, I don't think they believe anything happened. Besides, I don't want to sit at the police station for two days."

"Okay, well…you've done all you could do, right? If you're scared those psychos are looking for you, then just lay low. Mallorca's a pretty big island. Just don't use I.D. or credit cards."

"Way ahead of you."

"And relax. You're fine, okay? You're a smart guy. You'll get through this."

"Thanks. I appreciate you listening, Mitch."

"Did you change hotels?"

"Yeah. I came to Palma, just up the hill from all the bars in the old city. Like you said, I didn't use my name, credit card…nothing. I even called you on a restaurant phone with a calling card."

"Which restaurant?"

"It's near the Irish pub we went to, Molly's. Northeast of there. I'm getting ready to have dinner and a few beers. Need them badly."

"Good. Drink a bunch and sleep late tomorrow. As long as you keep your phone off and stay anonymous, they have no way of finding you."

"Thanks, Mitch.."

"You got it, dude. If you're bored, call me tonight when you get back to your room. Use the calling card!"

"Will do."

Roman replaced the receiver and sat there taking deep breaths. He felt much better. Just the slight release of emotion when telling his story had a cleansing effect.

Once he was back at his table, Roman took Mitch's advice and deliberately relaxed. He stayed at the rear of the restaurant, able to see a soccer match on the big screen TV. He enjoyed a fine meal, drank several large beers and had a nice flirtation with his server—who grew cuter by the minute.

It was past 11 p.m. when Roman left the restaurant. He now felt quite good—almost back to normal. The beer had removed the rough edges of his last few days. And after sleeping so late today, he wasn't all that tired. He made a right turn and walked to Molly Malone, the nearby Irish pub he'd enjoyed earlier with his friends. He stayed until 2 a.m., chatting with three Brits who lived in Mallorca as English teachers. Roman made no mention of the murder and, for the first time today, he felt back to his old self.

As he was conversing with his new friends, Roman had no idea that a related murder occurred at precisely 12:13 a.m. local time.

But he'd find out soon enough.

Chapter Four

Shortly after 2 a.m., Roman plopped down on the side of his bed. Tonight had indeed been therapeutic. After the long conversation with the British teachers, he'd chatted with the owner of the Irish pub and his three comely servers. Once again, being American in Mallorca made Roman stand out. The owner had poured a final shot of whiskey for everyone, toasting their new American friend. Although he'd staggered home on deserted and dark streets, Roman didn't feel a bit of fear. Tomorrow night would be his last night on Mallorca, and he'd probably repeat exactly what he'd done tonight.

Sitting bedside, listing slightly, Roman produced his calling card and went through the digits to call Mike. Once again, he received Mike's voicemail but this time, at the end of the message, Roman was informed that Mike's mailbox was full. Mike hadn't used his phone in Mallorca so Roman assumed he hadn't yet cleaned out his voice mailbox when he'd returned home.

A quick glance at his watch informed Roman that it was just past 7 p.m. on Monday back in Houston. Mitch had to fly tomorrow so he'd probably be having a tame evening. Roman dialed the numbers and listened to the ringtone.

"Hello?"

Roman frowned. Mitch didn't sound like himself. "Mitch, that you?"

"Who is this, please?"

"I meant to dial Mitch Cardell. Did I reach the wrong number?"

"No, sir, you did not. This is Lieutenant Nathan Fitzsimmons of the Houston Police Department. Who is this?"

Police? "I'm Roman, Mitch's friend. Where's Mitch?"

"You're not his blood relative?"

"No."

"Sir, I cannot go into specifics about Mister Cardell. But, may I ask, what's the nature of your relationship with him?"

"Wait…are you in his apartment?"

A pause. "Yes."

"Is he okay?"

"I cannot divulge any—"

"Holy shit," Roman breathed, the room spinning.

"Sir…"

"Wait a minute…lieutenant…is Mitch dead?"

"Why would you ask that?" the man asked, his tone one of suspicion.

"I was just with him," Roman gasped, unable to go on.

"You were with him today?"

Roman lay back on the bed. "Give me a second."

Is Mitch dead? Is he? He has to be, right? Why would a cop answer his phone?

"Hey," Roman barked. "You there?"

"I am, sir."

"Are you a homicide detective? Tell me that."

There was a pause. "I *am* a lieutenant in our Homicide division, sir. I need to know who you are and what you and Mitch did today."

"Oh, shit!" Roman cried. He let out a long, mournful wail. This all had to be some sick, twisted nightmare. There was no way this was really happening.

Then, the thudding question cut through all the alcohol and anguish.

Is this somehow related to what happened here? Could that one-armed bastard somehow have gotten to Mitch? No way, right? Unless those three men, and the man they killed, were part of something much bigger.

Roman was fuzzy from the booze and the shock of the news he'd not yet confirmed. He struggled to see any connection to what he'd gotten mixed up in—but there was only one way to find out.

"Lieutenant," Roman said, struggling to speak. "I wasn't with him today. I'm in Mallorca, Spain. Mitch was here with me just yesterday. He flew home."

"Thank you. We did find evidence to that effect."

"Listen to me, sir. This is important. Last night, about twenty-four hours ago, I witnessed a murder." Roman told him the entire story.

After hearing the tale, the lieutenant cleared his throat. "Sir, I cannot speak to what's happening in Mallorca. That's in the Med, right?"

"Yeah."

"If what you say is true, I can't envision how anyone related could have possibly traveled to Houston and committed another crime."

"What I say *is* true. Look, I promise I won't call his family." Roman took a steadying breath. "Tell me…is Mitch dead?"

"Yes, he is. I'm sorry."

Roman squeezed his eyes shut.

"Sir?" the detective asked.

"Gimme a minute." When Roman was able to speak, he insisted Mitch's murder was connected with the Mallorca murder.

"Again, sir, it's technically possible, but highly unlikely." The lieutenant replied. "Besides, Mister Cardell lives in an upscale condominium and this appears to have been a burglary."

"No…no…they made it look that way. They're a part of something bigger," Roman said, surprised at his own words. "And somehow, someone from their organization got to Mitch because he and I talked just two hours ago and—"

It suddenly hit Roman—like a bag of hammers—that he'd told Mitch where his new hotel was. Mitch knew where the hotel was; where the Greek restaurant was; and where the Irish pub was.

The detective continued to speak. "Sir? Are you there?"

"They know where I am. Oh shit. Oh shit. Oh shit."

"Sir, I need to get some information from you. Please give me your—"

Roman hung up the phone and stared at the door of his hotel room. If they somehow got to Mitch, they'd have tortured him. He would have talked. As tough and stubborn as Mitch was, he'd have talked. Everyone talks. And now they'd know Roman had eaten at a Greek restaurant, gone to Molly Malone's…

…and taken a hotel room in Palma.

What did I tell him? Think! I think I said I got a room in Palma, just up the hill from the old city, or something like that.

There are, what, six or seven hotels in this block?

Oh no…

Calm down, Roman. Relax. There's no way they could know.

Right?

Heart racing, Roman slipped his shoes back on. He eased the door open and checked the hallway while holding his breath. Empty. Roman relaxed just a bit before tiptoeing to the stairwell that led downstairs. He was on the second floor of three and, when he reached the stairwell, he heard the low hum of male voices in the small lobby. He crept down the stairs, peering over the bannister to the lobby.

What he saw sent a rusty spike of fear through his heart.

There, at the front desk, was one of the killers. It was the man who'd worn the heavy sweater and done the actual knifing. The man with the curly hair and florid face. He was now wearing slacks and a dress shirt, and there was a badge hanging from his belt. He was murmuring to the hotel owner who was standing behind the desk in his bathrobe. The curly-haired man was showing what appeared to be a photo to the hotel owner.

Roman nearly pissed himself with anxiety. The hotelier began speaking and gesturing upstairs, towards Roman's room.

Earlier, when he had come in from the Irish pub, the lobby was dark. The hotelier had no way of knowing Roman was currently in his room—did he?

Fearful the curly-haired man would see him, Roman tiptoed away and hurried back toward his room. They'd be coming if they weren't already on their way.

Roman eyed the hallway, seeing no alternate stairs at the opposite end. The hotel was extremely old so it was probably grandfathered-in when it came to fire codes. He went into his room and shut the door, dead-bolting it and also using the chain lock. After just a moment's thought, he hurried to the window and pulled it open, staring down at the street below.

The fall was no less than 15 feet—the landing area consisted of uneven cobblestones. Broken ankle city.

Roman heard them. He turned, seeing shadows moving in the strip of light under his door. There was a knock before the hotelier called his false name.

"Señor Maison, open your door, please." Another knock. "Señor?"

After sliding his wallet into his pocket, Roman looked down. *Damn, that's a long fall…*

Then came a much louder knock and a phrase Roman didn't understand.

Roman decided it would mitigate the fall if he hung from the ledge jutting out from the windowsill. That would leave only about 9 feet from his toes to the ground. He stepped onto the ledge just as he heard the key in the door. When he was crouching to lower himself, the door opened, halted by the chain lock.

The hotelier grunted when he realized the chain lock was employed. Roman heard the man say something about "*uno momento.*" He saw the shadow move as the man began to walk away. He probably had a special tool to disengage chain locks.

But the killer obviously had no desire to wait. He kicked the door, sending splinters flying.

The curly-haired man who, 24 hours before, had plunged a long kitchen knife in and out of the man on the kitchen floor, joined eyes with Roman for a split second.

Only a split second, because Roman jumped…

Sixteen years before, Roman had been a soldier. He was just a normal soldier, with no special training other than 5 jumps at the U.S. Army Airborne School in Fort Benning, Georgia. His lack of experience made him one of the thousands of soldiers affectionately known as a "five jump chump." Though he only made the required 5 jumps at the school, he made an estimated 1,000 Parachute Landing Falls, or PLFs, during the three-week course. The PLF was designed to dissipate the sudden impact with the ground over the entire body. This was far easier on the body than trying to stand upon landing, whereas the feet, ankles and knees absorb too much force. And because he'd done 1,000 or more PLFs, Roman planned to rely on muscle memory for executing this coming maneuver.

The killer lurched into the room, led by a very large pistol. Because Roman had seen the curly-haired man in action before, he knew the pistol wasn't for show. In fact, Roman would now remember him as the curly-haired killer. And because of the killer's quick entry, there was no time to execute the hanging maneuver. Though Roman knew the fall was going to hurt, it seemed a far better choice than taking a bullet.

Down Roman went. 15 feet. Whoosh. Thud.

Ouch.

The cobblestone road was sloped, leading to a natural downhill PLF. Unfortunately for Roman, he hadn't executed a PLF since the Clinton administration, and he twisted his ankle in the process. Additionally, he didn't tuck his head, as he'd been taught, leaving it exposed to whip down onto the cobblestones at the end of the maneuver.

So much for muscle memory.

Instinct took over, thankfully, and Roman was up and limping away, tucked up against the building to prevent the killer from seeing him. The narrow ledge above him concealed him just enough to prevent the killer from getting a positive shooting angle. It wasn't until moments later that Roman felt throbbing pain on the side of his head. He touched it with his left hand, feeling a large knot that seemed to be growing with each second.

Despite the pain of his ankle, despite the fogginess from hitting his head, Roman knew the curly-haired killer probably wasn't alone. The other men might be on the street or nearby. Thankfully, Roman's room had been at the rear of the small hotel. Now he was headed south into the bar district, where he'd had dinner at the Greek restaurant and too much to drink at Molly Malone's. Most of the bars were now closed, save for the mega clubs several blocks down the hill at the waterside. As Roman continued to move, his head and ankle worsened.

He continued on, every inch of separation precious.

Hurry, Roman. Haul ass.

* * *

Roman reached the bottom of the hill, limping and out of breath. In front of him, the bay twinkled majestically, unaffected by his life or death situation. He turned left, crossing the wide Avenue d'Antoni Maura and moving into the expansive Parc de la Mar. Quite possibly the centerpiece of Mallorca, Parc de la Mar was a sprawling waterfront common below the iconic Palma Cathedral. The cathedral was certainly Mallorca's most recognizable monument, and it would be impressive even in a picturesque city such as Rome or Paris. Situated on a hill overlooking the Bay of Palma, the colossal cathedral was imposing and statuesque. As Roman staggered into the park, hundreds—if not thousands—of people lounged about, waiting for sunrise. Some strummed guitars. Others toked hashish cigarettes. People made out. Dope dealers lurked like jackals. When the bars closed, this was the place to be.

Roman and his buddies had come here several times after their reveling. It was a mellow place to have a few beers, to hang out, and to finish the day. Several people told them that sunrise in the Parc de la Mar was a Mallorcan tradition that dated back hundreds of years.

The sea of people was the perfect place for Roman to blend in.

Wasting no time, he stripped off his t-shirt and rolled his jeans up over his knees. If the killers were to see him from a distance, his change in appearance might do enough to fool them. He hobbled forward, wading into a crowd of 20-somethings. They were on the broad green lawn, sitting in chairs and lounging on blankets, drinking and smoking.

I've got to blend in. I can't keep limping along or they're going to spot me.

Roman viewed the faces. Half of the people here appeared drunk or had the thousand-yard-stare of the extremely stoned. Most were younger than him, although the crowd was dotted with several people who were much older: tattooed, bearded globe-hopping 60 year-olds who always knew where the party was.

Just plop down anywhere, Roman. You've got to blend in right now!

He'd just found a small slice of unoccupied grass when he saw her…

The Goddess.

He couldn't believe his eyes.

Near the middle of the throng, she was lounging on a dijon blanket with one of her friends. She'd spotted Roman and stared at him with a cocked head.

Knowing he had only seconds, Roman limped forward and threw himself down on the blanket between the Goddess and her friend. The friend made a protest sound but the Goddess simply slid a few inches to her right.

Roman rolled over and dug out his wallet, coming out with ten euro. He handed it to the Goddess and pointed to the people on the next blanket. They had a large cooler.

"Will you get me a beer, please?"

The Goddess held the money and stared at Roman quizzically.

"Please," Roman said. "Just a beer. *Habla Ingles?*"

"Yeah, *yo hablo* pretty good."

She leaned over and handed the closest man on the next blanket the money. He was a white, leathery-tanned Rastafarian. His body was covered in psychedelic tattoos and, from six feet away, Roman wondered when the Rasta man had last taken a shower. Several days, at least, based on his scent. Seconds later the Goddess handed Roman a tall can of sweaty Estrella beer. Roman eased back to his elbows and held the beer in his left hand.

Eyeing himself, he felt he'd pass a quick muster. No shirt. Pants rolled up. Beer in hand. He didn't think he'd even earn a second glance—unless he was scrutinized.

"Do you have sunglasses?" Roman asked the Goddess.

"I do."

"May I wear them?"

"They're women's sunglasses."

"I don't care."

She handed Roman a pair of leopard print Wayfarer-style glasses. They were perfect. He pulled his shirt off his head and dumped a bit of the beer in his hair and gave himself a hair-hawk.

"Are you okay?" the Goddess asked with a chuckle.

He leaned back again, still watchful but reclining as far as he could.

The two ladies spoke in their native German over Roman. Finally, the

Goddess eyed him again. "Mister American, if you're going to share our blanket, would you mind telling us your name?"

"Sure," Roman said, his eyes widening as he thought he saw one of his pursuers. "One second."

He lifted all the way up and stared toward the avenue. There he was— *shit!*—the curly-haired killer. He'd jogged into the plaza in the same area Roman had entered. Upon seeing the large crowd, the killer slowed and lifted a phone to his ear, his eyes scanning left and right.

Roman flattened himself on the blanket. He covered a portion of his face with his t-shirt and leaned the beer up against his jeans. "If anyone asks," he whispered, "I'm passed out."

With the jeans rolled up, no shirt, the sunglasses, the hair-hawk and the partially obscured face, Roman felt he could get through this.

He lay there, able to see glimpses of the curly-haired killer out of the corner of his eye. The killer wandered the perimeter of the plaza, patiently eyeballing each group of people. The phone was still pressed to his ear. He walked past the blanket, pausing when he was only ten feet away. Roman could hear him talking. His language was fast and Roman didn't recognize it. The curly-haired killer looked Roman's way. Roman shut his eyes and lay perfectly still. He dared not look, dared not breathe.

Time slowed.

"Hey," the Goddess eventually said, nudging Roman.

"Yeah?" Roman whispered.

"Was that man with the phone looking for you?"

Unsure of what to say, Roman told the truth. "Yes."

"Why?"

"It's a long story," Roman whispered, still afraid to move. "Where is he?"

"He's gone. He ran back up the avenue. He had a bulge under the rear tail of his shirt. Was he carrying a pistol?"

"Hell yeah, he was. A big, long silver one." Roman sat up, seeing the curly-haired killer jogging up the Avenue d'Antoni Maura before he disappeared behind the first building.

"Who was he?" she asked.

"Like I said, it's a long story," Roman breathed, deflating. Almost instantaneously, his head and ankle began to hurt again.

"Are you okay?" she asked.

"I'm fine."

"You sure?"

"Yes. Where are you from?"

"Germany," she replied.

"Lots of Germans here."

"Do you know what the Germans call Mallorca?" she asked.

"No."

"The Seventeenth State."

"Why?"

"There are sixteen states in Germany. But there are so many Germans here, we call it the seventeenth state." She waved her hand around. "I'd bet three-fourths of this crowd is German."

He rubbed the knot on his head. "Sorry…hit my head. I'm a little slow. Where in Germany are you from?"

"All over, really. I've spent most of my life in North Rhine-Westphalia."

"The northwest."

"You know it?"

"I lived in Germany for a while. I'm Roman," he said, extending his hand. He turned and shook the Goddess' friend's hand, too.

Consistent with most Germans under 50, the Goddess spoke excellent English. She pointed to the avenue. "That man who was looking for you, is he a policeman?"

"No," Roman breathed.

"Please tell me he's some sort of law enforcement."

"He's not a cop of any type."

"And he had a gun?" she asked, mildly alarmed.

Roman suddenly felt dizzy and reclined on the blanket, rubbing his head. "Excuse me but now I don't feel too hot. I just jumped out of a hotel window. I twisted my ankle and hit my head."

"You don't look very good," the Goddess agreed.

"That guy had a badge," Roman slurred. "But I'm positive it was bullshit."

"Roman, your eyes are bouncing."

"So that's why everything is jumping ar…"

The Goddess said something. Roman heard it, but it was garbled.

He heard nothing else. It was as if he swirled down the drain into the blackness.

* * *

Roman Littlepage opened his eyes. They were rimmed by pain. The side of his head ached ferociously. His feet were elevated on top of a battered wicker basket. He slowly propped up on his elbows and looked around. It took him a moment to clear his fuzzy vision. There were still a number of people gathered in the park but only half as many as before. The Goddess lay next to him, separated by a foot of space. Her eyes were open and her friend was gone.

"Hey," Roman croaked. "How long was I out?"

"Forty minutes, maybe."

"Where's your friend?"

"She went back to the resort."

"But you stayed?"

"I was worried about your head. I checked your pupils with my phone light. They continued to dilate, which was good."

"You know your stuff," Roman breathed, easing his head back to the blanket. "Really, I'm okay. It just hurts…in several places."

"People have died from hitting their head and then sleeping. After I checked your pupils, I checked your pulse and watched your breathing—both were normal so I decided to stay and keep an eye on you."

Roman massaged the knot on his head. It seemed to have gone down a bit. "You a doctor?"

"I'm a nurse."

"Seriously?"

"Yeah," she smiled. "I have a diploma and I even wear a stethoscope around my neck."

"Sorry. Have you seen the curly-haired guy again?"

"No. It's been quiet."

The gravity of tonight's events came back to him. The chase. The gun. And how on earth could Mitch be dead? It didn't seem real. And if they got to Mitch, who else could they get to?

"You said you have a phone?" he asked.

She nodded.

"May I use it to call the States? I'll pay you for the minutes. I'll pay you whatever you need."

"I have international calling," she said, handing him a large Android in a black and gray case.

"After I make this call, you might want to turn your phone off for a while."

"Turn off my phone?"

"So they can't track your signal," he answered. "I'll understand if you don't want me to use it."

"Here. Make the call." She handed him the phone and sat up, crossing her legs and lighting a cigarette.

Roman dialed the series of numbers, satisfied when he heard the American-style ringing.

"Hello?"

"Hey, it's me."

"Oh," Wendy replied, her voice devoid of humor. "How's the big vacation going?"

"Not good. Wendy, I need you to listen very carefully to what I'm about to say to you, okay?"

"Are you drunk? Is this about Toby? My gosh, what time is it there? It's past nine here. Oh, no, Roman. Let's don't start a pattern of you drunk-dialing me. I knew I shouldn't have told you about him."

"Will you please stop and just listen." Roman paused, glancing at the Goddess. She, too, was listening. He touched his finger to his lips and spoke to his ex-wife. "Last night, I saw a man get murdered here."

"Roman…"

"I'm not kidding, dammit!" Roman bellowed, clutching the knot on his head afterward.

"Okay, I believe you. Calm down," Wendy replied.

"It wasn't just a random killing I saw. The men who did it are…you know…*connected* somehow and now they're after me. They're trying to kill me."

Wendy was silent.

"Are you there?"

"What do you mean connected?" she asked, her voice lacking concern.

"Professional criminals, Wendy. Big time."

"Okay, but I honestly don't know how to react to all this. Before you left, I was worried, Roman…about your mental state."

"My mental state?" he asked, screwing up his face. "When have I ever shown a trace of instability?"

"The kids said you were acting strange."

"And you weren't? A divorce is a big deal, Wendy, but I'm perfectly sane." Roman had growled the last part.

"Well, first you hear about my boyfriend Toby and then you call with something like this. Seems odd."

Roman shut his eyes and composed himself. "This has nothing to do with Toby, okay? I'm not trying to get back at you in any way. I'm calling you because I think you're in danger."

"Danger?"

"Yes, danger."

"Are you serious?"

"Completely."

The following conversation was lengthy and strident, but eventually Roman persuaded his ex-wife to leave the house with the kids. They were to take no phones, iPads or anything of the sort. Roman forbade them from checking email or anything that might leave electronic signatures of their whereabouts. He even insisted that she not drive her own car.

"All this because you witnessed a murder?" she asked, exasperated. "That doesn't make sense."

"Whoever they are, they want me dead. And they'll go to great lengths to find me."

"I don't see how they could get to me in Nashville."

"Just trust me, please," he said, hoping he didn't have to tell her about Mitch.

Wendy was quiet for a moment. "What should I drive?"

"Get your Mom's SUV."

"She's going to be pissed and she'll ask a million questions."

"Don't answer any of them."

"And where do we go?"

"Not to your mom's. Don't go to your sister's, either. You think the Pages will let you use their river house?"

"I guess I can ask." The Pages were mutual friends and owned a comfortable weekend home on the Cumberland River. If Roman's family had to remain in hiding for a few days, the house was perfectly equipped to keep the kids from going crazy.

Roman paused as he thought the plan through. "If you can't get the river house, I need you to go somewhere you won't be found. No family and not Toby's. Be smart. Please. No phones. No credit cards. No email. No Internet. And don't drive your car."

"This is insane, Roman. I realize you must be in a stressful situation, but I don't think you're seeing this clearly. You're on an island and, if it seems like someone is after you, then I can understand that it might make you a little crazy. But to think that they could somehow reach me and the kids here in Nashville is patently absurd."

"They *are* after me—and it's not absurd that they might come after you."

"Is this some crazy, contrived, desperate attempt to keep me away from Toby?" She paused. "You know what? It is. You even mentioned that I shouldn't go to his house. Real cute. Roman, I can't remember you ever being this jealous…except in college, when that beefy football player tried to make out with me at—"

Roman shut his eyes. "They murdered Mitch."

"*What?*"

"That's why I'm pushing you to do this, Wendy. They killed Mitch—in *Houston*. Did you hear me? Houston. All just so they could learn where I am."

"Why was he in Houston?"

"He went home early like he always does."

"Oh my God."

"Think about it, Wendy…they killed him, in Houston, less than a day after I witnessed the murder here in Mallorca."

"But how could they get there that fast?"

"I think they're a part of something bigger. But all that matters is, if they can kill him in Houston, they can kill you in Nashville. So you and the kids need to go, right now, and take everything I said seriously."

"I don't believe this. How would they gain anything from hurting us?"

"I don't know. Maybe they want information. Maybe they want to get back at me. I do *not* know. What I do know is the danger is real. And I can't go on if something happens to you or the kids."

Wendy was quiet for a moment before she said, "The kids love you, Roman."

"I love them, too. I'll call the river house tomorrow. Do not use their phone to call anyone connected to you. Not your parents, Toby, anyone. You just have to go dark until we figure out what's going on."

"Be careful, Roman."

"I will. Please be safe."

He pressed the red button on the phone.

The Goddess eyed him, her face a swirl of emotion. "I'm sorry to listen in, but..."

"I know. Crazy, isn't it?"

"Is everything you said true?"

"Yeah, I'm afraid so," Roman breathed. He touched his throat. "I'm really thirsty. Do you have any water?"

The Rastafarian and his friends were sleeping—or passed out. She went into their cooler and brought Roman another beer. He drank half of it in one gulp.

"I'd take the battery out of that phone," he said.

The Goddess removed the case and slid the battery off the back.

"I can head out if you'd like," Roman said. "No point in dragging you into all this."

"I want to hear all of it," she said. "Tell me everything."

He shook his head. "Listen, as much as I hate to say this, because I've wanted to meet you since I first saw you, you'd be much better off if you leave now."

"I don't want to leave." She held her index finger between them. "But tell me one thing, first..."

"Yeah?"

"Was that your wife?"

"Ex-wife."

She narrowed her eyes.

"She's my ex-wife. Honest. She divorced me."

"I did hear you say something about a divorce, and about someone named Toby?"

"That's her new boyfriend," Roman said, managing to get it out without inflection.

The Goddess nodded and situated herself on the blanket. "I'm not leaving you. We've got plenty of time before sunrise so, please, tell me the full story."

Roman drank two of the beers as he told her the entire story in detail. The Goddess was an excellent listener.

Chapter Five

A prodding stick awoke Roman. The woman touched his bare calf with it, giving him a firm nudge. He opened his eyes, squinting due to the bright sunshine—the intense light felt like a million needles in his eyeballs. When his eyes eventually adjusted, Roman could see the woman behind the stick was a policewoman. She spoke rapid Spanish, pointing to a sign in a nearby tree. It was obvious she was telling Roman to leave.

Far more surprising than where he was, was Roman's blanket-mate. Not only had the Goddess stayed, he awoke to find himself pressed up behind her. In fact, she held his hand to her stomach. When the female officer moved on, the Goddess nuzzled back into him and murmured that the police would give them another hour before they really got serious.

"How do you know?" he mumbled.

"We've slept out here three times this week." She breathed deeply and seemed to resume her slumber.

Roman rubbed his head, feeling the localized pain where he'd smacked the cobblestones. Though the knot was gone, the residual discomfort radiated through his skull in the form of a throbbing headache. He was quite thirsty, too. He wiggled his ankle, feeling the stiffness. Standing was going to be a chore.

Last night, after calling his wife and telling the Goddess everything, Roman phoned Sotinspector Reyes. He told him about the pursuit at the hotel and also told him about Mitch. Reyes sounded dubious but promised to send someone to the hotel. Regarding Mitch, Reyes quickly dismissed it as a tragic coincidence.

"While you were talking, I accessed the crime statistics for Houston, Texas," Reyes had said, academically. "They had 239 murders last year, señor. While I'm sorry about your friend, I fail to see how it could be related to our investigation here."

"Okay, then check the hotel in Palma. The owner actually brought the curly-haired killer up to my room."

"Why would he do that?"

"The killer had credentials of some sort, like he was there on an official investigation. I had to jump out of a window to get away. Surely there's security video, fingerprints, that kind of thing," Roman reasoned. "And now you've got a witness, other than me, who's seen one of the killers. I'm sure the owner wasn't happy about the guy kicking in his door."

"I will send someone, señor. Where are you now?"

"I'm hiding. Look, Sotinspector Reyes, I know you're struggling to believe me. But if you don't find these guys soon, they're going to eventually catch up to me. When they do, some other vacationer will be in your office reporting a murder…mine."

After that call, Roman lay back on the blanket and stared up at the Palma Cathedral. The Goddess had lain next to him. At some point Roman's mind shut down and now here he was, spooning with the woman he'd dreamt about since he'd first seen her.

He rested in silence for 30 more minutes before he sat up. "Hey," he said, giving her a light shake. "Where are you staying?"

"Can Pastilla," she answered, rolling over and shading her eyes against the powerful morning sun.

"Are you serious? That's where my resort was."

"I thought so. I saw you and your friends on the beach more than once."

Roman shook his head. How had he missed her, dammit? Oh well, there was no point in being upset about it now. "Are you and your friends staying in a hotel?"

"Yes. It's a resort that's set off the beach, back behind the row of restaurants."

"You wouldn't happen to have your own room, would you?"

She turned her head and smiled. "The four of us are sharing one room."

"That won't work." He cleared his throat. "Don't take this the wrong way, but if I give you cash, will you book a hotel room for us in your name?"

"Later. Need more sleep."

"But, will you?"

"Sure, I will."

"Last thing…I was kinda drunk last night, and a little woozy. Did I tell you everything that's happened?"

"Yeah, and you used my phone to call your ex-wife and the local police."

"Does being around me scare you?"

She turned. "I hadn't thought about it. I guess, since they already checked here, the people who are after you don't know where you are, right?"

"Hope so."

"Then we're safe."

"What about later, once we leave?"

"I'll help you stay hidden. How hard can it be?"

Despite his exhausted, bewildered, frightened condition; Roman felt his heart flutter at the thought of spending significant time with the Goddess.

"When are you supposed to leave Mallorca?" he asked.

"Five more days. Let's get thirty more minutes of sleep." She pulled his hand close, holding it to her trim stomach.

"Okay," Roman breathed, shutting his eyes.

As he lay there, unable to sleep, he thought about his flight reservations.

Surely, if these murderers were resourceful enough to kill Mitch in Houston, they'd know when Roman's flight was due to leave. They'd be waiting on him.

So, why shouldn't I surprise them and go to the airport today? Don't pay in advance, which will just tip them off if they're truly connected. Just show up a day early with the old Amex and pay the exorbitant fare at the counter.

But what about her, the Goddess? All this time you've dreamt of her. Now, you're willing to just walk away?

Roman pressed into her, feeling her reaffirm his presence with a slight push backward from her derriere.

Get her phone number. Get her email. Get her address. Take another vacation and go see her. Better yet, fly her to Nashville on an open ticket. The main point is this: get the hell away from Mallorca, Roman. You can keep an open line to the Goddess if you're smart about it.

So, it was settled.

Roman smiled as he lay there, unable to sleep due to his racing mind. *Screw you, well-dressed one-armed man. I'll leave Mallorca early and you'll be none the wiser until it's too late.*

A perfect plan.

Absolutely perfect.

Then it hit him.

His passport was in the hotel room.

* * *

By the time Roman finally controlled his panic over his missing passport, they exited the park and walked up the sidewalk of Avenue d'Antoni Maura. They viewed Roman's hotel from a distance. There were numerous police outside, along with the yellow tape of a crime scene. Thankfully, Sotinspector Reyes must have taken Roman's call seriously. Roman had once again worn his t-shirt on top of his head and also had on the Goddess's sunglasses, using the two items to camouflage his identity.

"Why don't you walk over there and just ask for your passport?" she asked.

"I would, but I don't trust the cops here. One of them leaked my identity to the killers and I'm afraid they'll do it again."

"How do you know they did that?"

"I'll tell you the whole story," Roman said. "But let's walk and talk. We need to get out of here before I get spotted. I can't risk it."

"What about your passport?"

"I'll think of something."

They'd continued inland, buying a bag full of toiletries at a small grocery. Soon thereafter, they found a city hotel in the bustling La Mission area with vacancy. Roman gave the Goddess cash for the room, eyeing her well-used passport as she paid. Her first name was Evangeline. He was disappointed in himself that he hadn't even asked.

Well, you have been a bit preoccupied, Roman.

Riding up in the cramped and musty elevator was a bit awkward—especially since they were two strangers heading to a room together.

"I'm Roman," he said, extending his hand to right his earlier wrong.

"Sorry," she said with a smile. "I'm Eva."

"Eva," Roman replied, matching her smile.

"You look like you're about to laugh."

"Sorry. It's just…after seeing you so many times, I'd come to think of you by one name."

"What do you mean?"

"Well, in my mind, I'd given you a name."

The elevator halted at the 6th floor. As the doors slid open, she asked to hear the name.

"The name?" Roman asked, unsure of what to say.

"Yes. What name did you give me?"

"Uh, Barbara," he lied.

"Barbara?"

Roman shrugged.

"Barbara," Eva repeated, seeming bemused over the choice.

They followed the corridor to the room. It was very basic, with two beds, a bathroom and, thankfully, a small window unit air conditioner. Eva turned on the air while Roman ripped into the toiletries, finding the ibuprofen. His ankle was looser now that he'd moved around on it for a while, but he still couldn't walk without a limp. And, of course, his head ached. He took four pills and stood in the middle of the room, his eyes darting nervously around. He didn't know what to do next.

"Why don't you go ahead and shower?" Eva asked. "I'll wait outside on the balcony."

Roman took her advice, showering and brushing his teeth with the new, stiff toothbrush. He donned his dirty clothes in the bathroom before stepping back out. Eva was sitting on the small balcony. Through the filmy curtain, he was able to see that she was smoking a cigarette. He wondered if she might be on the phone.

His eyes darted to the dresser. Her phone was sitting by the small television. The battery was still disconnected.

Eva turned and waved. She took a final drag on her cigarette and came inside.

"I hope I didn't take too long. Bet you were bored."

"I work inside for long shifts—being outside in the sun never gets old."

"I'm surprised that a nurse smokes cigarettes."

"Only on vacation," she said, crossing her heart with her finger. "And whenever I have too much to drink—which doesn't happen very often."

"Sorry about my dirty clothes," Roman said, gesturing at his shirt. "Maybe I can get some more later."

"We'll get you something at one of the nearby stores and I'll stop by my hotel later and change."

"Do you mind if I use your phone again?" he asked. She affixed the battery and gave him her code.

As he listened to Eva turning on the water, he dialed Delta Airlines and, of course, was told he couldn't board a flight back to the United States without his passport, even in the event of an emergency. Afterward, Roman used the local telephone directory—the first time he'd used a paper version in at least a decade. He called the hotel where he'd left his passport and, time and time again, was greeted by the answering machine message. After the beep, the machine informed him in English that the mailbox was full.

"What if that curly-haired asshole took my passport?" Roman said to himself. "What if I can't get it back?"

Searching again in the phone book, Roman was pleased to find a United States consulate right here in Palma, Mallorca. In fact, it was only about a mile from his current location.

He dialed the number and was greeted by a person with a mild accent. After a few questions, Roman was put through to someone else.

"How may I help you?" the man asked.

"I'm an American citizen in Mallorca and I need help."

"Please tell me the nature of your problem."

"Okay, get ready for a mouthful," Roman said. "I witnessed a murder, and the murderers are now after me. I realize that sounds crazy, but it's true. And, now, I've lost my passport—it was stolen, actually."

"Whoa, whoa, whoa. Slow down, okay?" The man let out a long breath. "You claim you witnessed a murder?"

"I *did* witness a murder, in El Arenal, the night before last." Roman briefly explained.

"Right…we were contacted by the locals about this," the man replied. "It's our understanding that there's no evidence backing up your claims."

"They're not claims—they're facts." Roman felt his temper coming up. "And maybe you should call the Hotel del Sol, just above the old city in Palma. I got a room there last night and one of the killers kicked in my door. I had to jump out of a second-story window to get away. Ask the owner—he saw the whole thing."

"You jumped out of a hotel room window?"

"Yeah. Sprained my ankle and knotted up my head. The guy had a gun. The cops are there, now. Ask them."

"Hmm," the man mused, sounding unimpressed. "We'll look into it. And now you say you've lost your passport?"

"No. It was stolen. Actually, maybe not stolen, but it was in the hotel room when I had to jump out of the window."

"Oh yeah…when the killer kicked your door in?" the man asked.

Roman knew when he was being patronized. "What's your name?"

"Frederick Kelley, sir."

"What do you do there?"

"I'm the General Services Officer."

"And who is your boss?"

"I report directly to the Consul General."

Whoop-dee-doo. "And who might that be?"

"Louisa Reynolds."

"May I speak with her?"

"No, sir. She's on vacation. I'm the acting Consul General."

"Then, Mister Kelley, I'd ask you take my situation more seriously, or I'll call the embassy on the mainland."

"I'm taking this seriously, sir. As I said, I've spoken with the police several times about your claims. They have no evidence, other than extremely peculiar behavior by you."

"Did they tell you my friend was murdered in Houston?"

Kelley paused. "No. I'm sorry about your friend, but *how* is that possibly related?"

Roman explained. As he did, he heard the water shut off when Eva finished her shower.

"So, you think these people who killed the man in El Arenal somehow got to your friend all the way in Houston, Texas…interrogated him…killed him…all simply to find out which Palma hotel you're staying in?"

"Damn right. How else can you explain it?"

Kelley was quiet for a beat. "Where are you now, sir?"

"I'm in a safe place."

Eva emerged from the steaming bathroom wearing her exact same shorts and shirt. There was a towel wrapped turban-like around her hair. Roman put a finger over his lips. She walked past him and stretched out on the far bed. Roman continued to stare at the wall as he spoke.

"Just what is it you'd like me to do?" Kelley asked.

"I want a passport so I can get the hell out of here before someone kills me. And in the meantime, I'd like your Marines there to give me full protection. There are Marines, there, right?"

"Yes, sir. The United States Marines are tasked with State Department security."

"That's what I thought. I'm a U.S. taxpayer in good standing, and I'm a veteran. Whether there's evidence of what I saw or not, I'm entitled to protection."

"I see." Kelley paused for a few seconds. "Would you mind holding for a

55

moment?"

Roman grunted and was greeted by elevator music. He turned, seeing his new friend stretched out on the bed. She'd bunched a pillow up under her toweled head and faced him.

"Having any luck?"

"Not really," Roman answered. "This is the U.S. Consulate and they're acting weird."

"Maybe you'll just be stuck with me for a few more days."

Roman opened his mouth to reply but only managed to chuckle.

What had he stumbled into with her, Eva, the Goddess? All those times he'd seen her, back before that dreadful night, had he missed out by not having the balls to simply approach her? Because, clearly, she enjoyed his presence. Just as he was about to say something, the line clicked.

"Mister Littlepage, are you there?"

"Yes."

"I just phoned the police."

"Sotinspector Reyes?"

"No, sir. It was his commander. He told me about what happened at the hotel. Where exactly are you right now?"

"I'm not telling you, Mister Kelley. Every time I tell someone where I am, somebody tries to kill me. And now my friend in Houston is dead," Roman said, feeling his voice cracking. "And my other friend who was also here with me, I can't find him."

"What's his name?"

"Michael Singleton of Columbus, Ohio."

"I'll look into it." There was a shuffling of paper. "Mister Littlepage, I'm sorry for all your trouble. You're right about being an American citizen who deserves protection. If you'll please come directly to the consulate, you'll be safe while we work on your passport issue."

"What do you mean *work* on my passport issue?"

"With your positive fingerprints, we can produce a temporary passport for you."

"Finally," Roman breathed.

"When can you be here, sir?"

"Maybe a half-hour?"

"Fine, sir. And for your own safety, I'd like you to use the rear entrance. There's a small road that runs parallel to Avinguda de Gabriel Roca. Follow it south from the side street Carrer de la Padrera. When you come to the high security fence, that's us, just keep coming. About twenty meters later there will be a Marine at the rear gate. I know you don't have I.D. Just tell him your name and tell him I sent you."

"I have my driver's license."

"Perfect."

"Thank you, Mister Kelley." Roman ended the call and unclipped the battery from the phone.

"What'd they say?" Eva asked.

"They're going to help me get a passport and get out of here."

"How long will that take?"

"He didn't say."

"That happened to my friend on our trip two summers ago and it took two days to get a replacement."

Roman frowned. "Seriously?"

"Is that what he said, that they would get you a new passport?"

"He said they'd get me a temporary."

"Hmmm."

"What?"

"When I first came out of the shower, you and he seemed to be sparring."

"You know, your English is as good as mine."

She sat up and shrugged. "Most young Germans know English as well as our native language."

"So, you're right, he and I were kinda arguing."

"Then, all of a sudden, he acts like he wants to help you," Eva said. "After he talked to the police?"

"What's your point?"

"I'd just be careful, Roman." She took the two phone components from him.

He ran his hands back through his damp hair. "Look, I'm as confused as I've ever been, but do you actually think those psychos could somehow get help from our consulate?"

"No," Eva said, shaking her head. "All I'd say is be careful. According to what you've told me, nothing here has gone the way you planned since you saw those men kill that other man."

Roman nodded. "Point taken."

"Tell me again about the killers."

"Why?"

"Because I'm going to watch out for them. I've seen the one with curly hair."

Roman relayed all he could remember.

"And which arm was the man missing?"

"Left arm. Missing flush with his shoulder," Roman answered, making a chopping motion on his own left arm.

"You know, if he's a well-known criminal, he shouldn't be all that hard to find, especially with the missing arm. We get cops all the time in the E.R. asking us to help identify suspects. They always look for some identifying feature— I'd say the missing arm is pretty conspicuous." She motioned to the bathroom. "Let me comb out my hair and I'll be ready to go."

"You're coming with me?"

The answer was a blissful kiss on Roman's cheek.

Ten minutes later, they hung the "do not disturb" sign on the door and departed the hotel.

Chapter Six

Today was the hottest day since Roman had arrived in Mallorca. Although the humidity was nothing like it was in Nashville, the temperature had to be hovering near 100 degrees Fahrenheit. Eva walked beside him, telling him about her two sisters after he'd asked about her family. Once again, Roman wore her sunglasses and his filthy t-shirt hung from the top of his head. Knowing he looked like an idiot—but a well-concealed idiot—he limped down the hills from the center of Palma, headed to the U.S. Consulate that overlooked the western edge of the bay.

To Roman's left, the massive sand-colored Cathedral dominated the skyline. To Roman's right and behind him, the nominal business area of Palma loomed, seeming slightly out of place against the old Spanish charm that tinted the remainder of the island. Tourists and locals swarmed on the streets of the old city. The cafés were full, filling the air with culinary smells that made Roman hungry. When they turned to the southwest on Carrer d'Espartero, the view below was splendid as numerous sailboats and yachts slowly swayed on the sparkling baby blue waters of the Bay of Palma.

The beauty of the day and the company of a girl he'd dreamed about buoyed him. But then, like a heavy door slamming on his thumb, the grim realities came back to him:

He'd seen a man murdered.

Mitch was dead.

Mike was unaccounted for.

Wendy and the kids were on the run.

And the one-armed man and his killers were out here somewhere, hunting him—this very second.

How did it get to this? All I did was go take a leak, and it turned my life upside down.

Roman had purposefully come down the hill to the northeast of the consulate. The service road that Mr. Kelley had mentioned ran perpendicular to the main bay road, behind the row of the bay front buildings. The base of the hillside had been cut backward, leaving just enough room for the buildings and the service road that ran behind them.

It occurred to Roman that, when he was on the service road to the consulate, he'd be bordered on his right by cliffs of rock, and by rows and rows of buildings on his left.

Why did Kelley want me to come in from the rear? He said it was for my own protection. When did he start showing concern for me? And did he think the one-armed man and his killers were outside waiting on me?

Roman was silent as they descended the last of the hill. He stopped when he saw the service road. It was just as he'd envisioned—confining.

"Roman?"

"You know, I was thinking about what you said, about Mister Kelley's sudden change." Roman gestured down the cramped service road. "Now that I see where he wanted me to go, I don't like it."

"What do you mean?"

"Look at it. Rock wall on one side, buildings on the other."

"Nowhere to go, if you have to run."

"Let's keep walking. I just want to walk out there by the bay and have a quick look."

They continued forward to Avinguda de Gabriel Roca, stopping behind a swaying palm tree. Back to the north, he could see the Hard Rock Café, the cathedral and the center of Palma against the white-blue summer sky. The consulate was several blocks south, about 300 meters away, in close proximity to the ferry terminal.

"Look over there," Eva said, pointing. Across the street from the consulate, in the ferry terminal parking lot, were four Mallorcan police cars. Judging by the dark silhouettes, there were several police sitting in each car.

"Why shouldn't the police be at the terminal?" Roman muttered, mainly to himself. "Could be unrelated."

A lace of smoke wafted from the window of one of the police cars. Smoking cops—sitting, waiting.

Adjacent to the row of police cars was a blue sedan, also with two silhouettes. Roman squinted, unable to see any detail. Rather than head toward the consulate, Roman crossed the street, walking toward the bay and keeping his head turned to the left. Though he was limping, he altered his gait even more, as if he'd been crippled. He held Eva's hand and whispered for her to follow along.

An Italian Ice vendor had parked his cart on the bayside walking path. Roman queued with several other people and peered at the sedan that was parked with the police cars.

He could see much better from this vantage point. And there, in the passenger seat, was Sotinspector Reyes.

Sonofabitch. What is all this?

Why would the Mallorcan police be lying in wait for him? Was this some sort of trap orchestrated by the State Department man, Kelley, at the consulate?

"Will you please tell me what's going on?" Eva asked.

"I think they set a trap for me," Roman whispered.

"You mean, all those police cars?"

"Yeah, but I've haven't done anything wrong. Why would they send that many cops?"

"Let's leave," she said, pulling his hand.

"Hang on."

"They're going to see you."

He scratched his chin. "Yeah, maybe, but I need to figure out what's happening."

"How are you going to manage that?"

"*Perdon,*" Roman said to the man in front of him, tapping him on his shoulder. "*Habla Ingles?*"

The man was probably in his early forties, waiting in line with two children. He replied that he spoke English.

"May I use your cellphone? It's a local call. You can dial it." Roman pulled out a 10-euro bill. "I'll pay for your Italian ice in return."

The man shrugged and told Roman he could dial the number. He handed him a very old, beat up iPhone.

"Watch the police," Roman whispered to Eva.

He dug Sotinspector Reyes' card from his pocket and dialed the number as he stepped out of hearing range of the man and his children. After a few rings, Roman observed as Reyes eyed his own phone before holding it to his ear.

"Reyes."

"Hey, Sotinspector," Roman said. "This is Roman Littlepage."

"It is? Where are you?" Reyes asked, his head whipping to the consulate.

"I'm inside the consulate, waiting on you. Mister Kelley said you guys are coming in?"

Reyes exhaled loudly as if frustrated. "Well...*he* was supposed to call us."

"Look, it's fine...no big deal. I'm willing to cooperate."

"I knew you would be, Mister Littlepage." Reyes got out of the car and motioned to his troops to cross the street.

"Just tell me one thing, Sotinspector," Roman said, watching the police as they waited for a break in traffic. "Am I being formally charged?"

"No, of course not," Reyes replied, hurrying across the eastbound lanes and waving his thanks to the drivers who had stopped. "We simply want to ask you some questions about it."

"About what?"

Reyes paused in the median and straightened. "Did Señor Kelley not tell you?"

"He did, but I want to hear it from you before I agree to talk."

Cocking his head, it appeared as if Reyes was considering what to say. "Well...Señor Littlepage...we need to discuss the murder of Señor Lomas."

"And who exactly is Señor Lomas?" Roman asked, wondering if that was the name of the man he'd seen stabbed.

Reyes' tone indicated puzzlement over Roman's question. "Señor Lomas, of course, is the hotelier from Palma."

The hotelier was murdered?

This wasn't happening. Roman felt as if someone had dumped a bucket of ice water down his back. "Are you telling me the old man from the hotel is dead?"

"Yes, señor. Didn't Señor Kelley tell you?"

Roman hung up the phone. Trying to remain calm, he walked to the railing at the bay and flung the iPhone into the water.

The owner of the iPhone yelled several well-known Spanish curse words, causing his older daughter to cover her smiling mouth with both hands. Apologizing, Roman dug into his wallet and handed the man 200 euro. Rather than slug Roman, the man stared at the money in bewilderment. He eventually nodded and slid the money into his pocket. It seemed he knew he was on the better end of the deal.

"What was all that?" Eva asked as they walked away.

Taking Eva's hand, Roman led her to a bench farther down the path. "Oh, my God," he mumbled, lowering his head into his trembling hands.

"What's wrong?"

Roman pointed to the consulate. "Watch."

The police stopped at the front gate of the consulate. Sotinspector Reyes was animated as he spoke to the two Marines at the gate. Soon after, a man in shirtsleeves and a tie appeared from inside. There seemed to be a great deal of confusion. The man in the tie held his hands open as he communicated with Reyes, then, after they realized what had happened, pandemonium set in.

Gesturing hands. Pointing fingers. Significant weeping and gnashing of teeth.

Score one for Roman Littlepage.

"Will you please talk to me?" Eva pleaded.

Roman felt nauseous. He took deep breaths, finally managing to swallow. "Something didn't sit right about that alley...about them having me come in the back door. You mentioned it, too. When we got out here and saw all the cops, I called the detective and told him I was already inside. I asked if he was coming in."

"That was clever."

"I wanted to confirm that they were there to take me in. Once they started heading inside, I asked if I was being formally charged."

"Charged for what?"

"I didn't know," Roman answered, "but obviously they didn't send ten cops just to chat with me."

"You tricked them."

"Yeah, I guess. But the joke's on me. The nice little man that ran the hotel, the one I jumped out of..."

"Yes?"

"He was murdered. And now the Mallorcans think I killed him."

"Are you serious?"

"That's what they said."

Eva glanced nervously around. "We need to go. Even though you threw the phone into the water, they might be able to figure out where that call came from."

"You think?"

"I watch a lot of true crime shows on my iPad. Cellphone tracking is basic nowadays, and nearly every police department relies on it because just about everyone has a mobile phone. Come on." Eva stood, taking Roman's hand and crossing the street. They hurried up the hill as fast as Roman could manage.

Two blocks above the bay was a small park. Children played in the shady grass. Several people lounged about with picnics. Knobby olive trees with copious leaves created a whispering canopy above. Despite the tranquility and beauty, Roman was in the deepest pit of his entire life. He wanted to scream. He wanted to cry. He wanted to give up.

She led him to one of the empty park benches and the two of them sat there, talking things through.

"I've never hurt a soul," he said to Eva.

"Why do they think *you* killed that man?"

He shook his head. "It's these people who are after me. They're brilliant. They're relentless. They're evil." Roman eyed Eva. "As much as I hate the thought, you need to leave me now. Go back to your friends and if the cops connect us, just say you never knew my name. When they tell you I'm a fugitive, just act puzzled and agree with them by saying I acted strange."

"I'm not leaving you."

"Yes, you are."

"No, I'm not." Eva crossed her arms and repeated the phrase in German, just for good measure.

"I'm in deep shit, Eva. I don't know what to do or where to go. They're going to find me and then I'm either arrested, or dead."

"Calm down, okay? Take some deep breaths."

Though he really wanted to keep panicking, Eva had an effect on him. He obeyed her.

"Good," she said. "Now let's think about this for a moment. Instead of trying to figure out who the killers are, what do you think they want with you?"

Roman stared at her. "What do you mean?"

"Why are they trying to kill you?"

"To shut me up, I guess."

"But you already told the police, didn't you? You gave descriptions and everything."

Roman frowned.

"Did you hear the killers say anything, you know…critical?"

"No. Just a bunch of yelling and a few threats I understood."

"Could they think you overheard something?"

"I dunno…maybe."

"None of them gave you anything, did they?"

"No. Once I saw what was going on, I hauled ass."

"And you didn't meet the person they killed beforehand?"

"No…I never even saw his face."

"At all?"

"They were on top of him," Roman explained. "Maybe I did meet him at some point?"

Eva allowed him to process his thoughts.

He shook his head. "No…I didn't. The only men we've met have been bartenders and servers in restaurants."

"Roman, I think we need to determine *why* they're after you. That's the most important thing right now. That's what could keep you alive."

"If they're after me, then what good would killing that little old hotel owner do?"

"You said the cops have a leak. Maybe they think they could get to you somehow once you're arrested."

"True."

"What else?"

He shook his head in frustration.

"Don't give up."

He straightened. "What if I call the consulate again?"

"Are you nuts?"

"I'm serious. I need them to know I'm innocent. They're supposed to support me as an American citizen. If I run, I look guilty as hell."

"But call them?"

"Hell yeah. And, besides, I feel like unloading on someone."

Roman and Eva chatted a while longer.

Ten minutes later they left the park and began searching for an old fashioned payphone—one with numerous avenues of escape.

* * *

"Hola, you've reached the Consulate General of the United States. Ingles or Espanol?"

"English. I want to speak with Frederick Kelley."

"I'm sorry, Mister Kelley is unavailable at the moment. Would you like his voicemail?"

"Tell him Roman Littlepage is on the phone. He'll take the call."

"Sir, he is very busy. I can put you through to—"

"I'm the person the police are after, lady. I'm the reason for all the commotion. Now, please, tell him Roman Littlepage is on the phone."

"Uh, yessir, one moment."

Long delay.

"This is Kelley. Is this Mister Littlepage?"

"You were going to let them question me for the murder of the hotel owner?"

"It's not that simple."

"I didn't even know he was dead until I called."

"I believe you, Mister Littlepage. But if you're innocent, why resist questioning?"

"Do they think I killed my friend Mitch, too? How do they explain that?"

"Mister Littlepage…Roman…I'm not passing judgment on your innocence or guilt. And I'm sorry about your friend. But look at it from the Mallorcans' point of view. You reported a murder of which they found no evidence. Then, you said your hotel room had been burglarized. No evidence of that, either. After some strange behavior on your part, the police discovered a hotelier, dead, in your hotel room and the only connection they have is you. It looks bad, sir."

"One of the murderers I first reported, the man with the curly hair, came to the hotel. He showed a credential—kind of like what FBI or Treasury agents carry—and then he came to my room with the owner of the hotel and kicked in my door. By the way, how do they explain the door being kicked in?"

"That's a good question."

"Well, you can ask them for me. And I have witnesses who can verify that the curly-haired killer chased me from the hotel."

"And who are these people?"

"Never you mind. When you guys figure out that I'm a victim, maybe I'll bring them around. Gotta go."

"Wait…wait…before you hang up, I just want to get all my facts straight…the door was kicked in, and you have witnesses who can verify that curly-haired man chased you?"

"Yes, and he showed some sort of official credential to the hotelier."

"How do you know?"

"Because I saw him from the stairs when he was in the lobby. I ran to my room and that's when he kicked the door in. I jumped from my window to get away."

"Where will you be, Mister Littlepage?"

"Seriously?"

"I have to ask."

"I'll be somewhere very private. Call my congresswoman and the State Department. I'm completely innocent. When that's proven, I'm going to barbecue your bureaucratic ass for not helping me, *Fred*." Roman hung up the phone and dipped his head.

"Okay, it's done. Now we need to get out of here," Eva said. "Quickly."

They walked north for a kilometer, turning right on a narrow cobblestone footpath that ran through the old city. The footpath was dotted with bars and restaurants. The area was very crowded. After another kilometer, Eva chose a restaurant and Roman donned his wrinkled t-shirt. Inside, Eva asked if they could sit upstairs. They climbed a narrow, winding staircase and seated themselves at a table by the open window.

"You okay?" she asked.

"Yes and no," he answered, playing with a sugar packet.

"You said you were going to 'barbecue his ass?'"

"It's a southern phrase."

"If he was going to help you, he probably won't now."

Roman shrugged. "Couldn't help myself."

The server arrived. Roman asked for a bottle of mineral water then glanced at the menu and shook his head. "You order," he said to Eva. She ordered a charcuterie plate along with some bread.

When the server had left, Roman said, "You really should leave me, Eva. If I get arrested, they might charge you, too."

"Will you *please* stop telling me to leave. And you've done nothing wrong."

"True, but I have to prove that."

"No, *they* have to prove you killed that man."

He tossed the sugar packet to the table, leaned back and vigorously rubbed his face. "I'm sure that curly-haired asshole set me up, somehow. I'm positive he did something that gives the cops damning evidence that I killed that poor little man."

"How would he do that?"

"Who knows? Maybe he stabbed the guy and somehow faked my prints on the knife?"

"I doubt that. I know this is scary, but you need to stay calm so you can think clearly."

A bout of silence prompted Roman to peer down to the cobblestone street. He remembered, just before he jumped, the hotelier had tried to open the chained door.

"Why did they have to murder that man at the hotel?" Roman asked. "He was just a kindly old fellow, not hurting a soul."

"Think back to the first murder—because that's the key to all this. Are you absolutely certain the man who was killed didn't give you anything, or tell you anything?"

"I'm a hundred percent certain. I never met him." He shrugged. "Maybe they *think* we met."

"Maybe. Right now, you need to eat and hydrate, okay? You'll feel better if you do. And if we talk about something else, maybe the reason will come to you."

He nodded and considered her. "You know, because of all this craziness, I really don't know anything about you. I keep getting smacked in the face by a question: as pretty and smart as you are, why would you want to derail your vacation by helping me?"

"Because I like you."

"That's it?"

She appeared mildly offended. "Do I need to provide other reasons?"

"No, it's just…I dunno…before I met you, you were always with your friends. And…gosh, when was it?...the night before last, when I saw the murder, there were four guys who you and your friends seemed to know."

She made a dismissive motion with her hand and rolled her eyes. "Oh, them. One of my friends kind of liked one of the guys. They're Dutch, and *not* my type. I guess we were humoring them for her. I didn't care for them at all. They were vulgar, always openly talking about earning their 'German flag.'"

"What's that?"

"I just learned the phrase this week. Supposedly, some guys use that phrase to describe sleeping with a girl from another country."

Roman grunted, finding little humor in the crass game played by those four—

He sat up straight and turned his head.

Why do I feel I'm missing something?

"What is it?" Eva asked.

"I feel like I just missed something important."

"What do you mean?"

"A clue."

"Something I said?" she asked.

He massaged his forehead. "I don't know…something about the restaurant, maybe."

"Think back to the restaurant…what else can you remember?"

He flattened his palms on the table, shutting his eyes, trying to recall the details of that night, despite the horror. "The men I saw were there after hours. They were having drinks together. Four drinks, meaning…the meeting must have started in a friendly manner. When I walked in, I thought the place was still open. Well…sort of. The door was partially locked."

"Partially?"

He shook his head. "The lock hadn't been turned all the way. But some of the lights were on, and the drinks were all on the bar."

"So, you broke in?"

"No. I pushed and the door opened. And I *really* had to go."

Just as Roman was getting to his point, the plate of meats and cheeses arrived, along with fresh baked bread and a bowl of olives. The server placed a large bottle of cold mineral water on the table and gave them both glasses adorned with a fresh lemon. Eva spoke Spanish, thanking the server and telling her they didn't need anything else. Once the server had gone back down the stairs, Eva leaned forward.

"So, what are you getting at?"

"They know each other," Roman said, his heart pounding.

"Who knows each other? The four men you saw?"

"They knew each other, too, but that's not who I'm talking about."

She frowned. "I'm so confused."

Roman didn't answer her for a moment. His mind was turning with too much speed. He poured a half glass of bubbly water and sipped it as his mind connected the dots. Finally, he looked at her and spoke.

"Sorry…when my mind races, I don't communicate well."

"I'm glad you're excited," she said, touching his hand. "Can you explain what you're thinking for me?"

"Sure. What if somebody at that restaurant let the killers in? Think about it. Someone unlocked that door for them, or left them a key. Maybe it was an employee, or maybe the owners. But someone at that restaurant definitely knows the killers."

"Don't you think the police have already gone through all that?"

"Maybe, but they doubted my story from the get-go. And they found no evidence and no one has turned up missing."

"So you want to learn more about the owners of the restaurant?" she asked.

"I do."

After they fleshed out his theory, Roman again tabled the subject—they could refocus on it later. They did their best to enjoy a long lunch, chatting mostly about Eva's 29 years in Germany. She'd grown up in a town outside of Cologne and now lived in Berlin.

Roman tried to find out more about her personal life. She said she'd never been married. When he asked if she had a boyfriend, she'd shrugged and shaken her head. It was the sort of body language that indicated to him that there was someone in her life, but it either wasn't serious or she was keeping her options open for something better.

"Do you have hobbies?" he asked.

"Work is my main hobby. I really love it."

"I've heard nursing is hard."

"It's grueling at times, but it's also my passion."

"If that's the case, why are you here on vacation?"

Eva pushed her plate away. "Everyone needs a holiday—even if they love their job. Those girls I'm with are my best friends from what you would call high school. We take a trip each year."

"I feel like you want to say more."

She chuckled. "I do enjoy my vacations, but I usually end up helping someone or getting diverted somehow."

"Like this?" Roman asked, feeling a bit crestfallen. So, he wasn't special. He was simply this year's project.

"No," Eva answered after a pause. She touched his hand again. "Never like this. You said it yourself: I could get in big trouble for helping you."

He eyed her.

"But it's more than just helping you…I like being with you," she said, her delivery quite sultry.

Roman guzzled water, feeling his face and neck splotching.

From there, the conversation turned to more mundane things. But Roman kept turning one idea over in the back of his mind: the restaurant owners, or someone from the restaurant, were the key to finding the killers.

And, suddenly, there it was: his plan.

* * *

That late afternoon was a busy one.

First, Roman gave Eva a wad of euros and sent her on a shopping trip. When she returned, he tried on his new clothing and eyed himself in the chintzy bathroom mirror. He wore a bright yellow ball cap backwards. On his face were wraparound amber sunglasses and he'd shaved his four-day stubble, leaving only a thin goatee around his mouth. On her brief shopping trip, Eva bought him baggy skater-style shorts and a gaudy wine red tank top advertising Dynamo Dresden. According to her, he now looked decidedly German and blue collar, like a working-class Dresdener who might purchase a bargain Mallorca package holiday with his friends.

He'd fit right in with the revelers of El Arenal.

Eva had also purchased Roman a six-pack of clean underwear. She'd winked as she handed the package to him, saying she'd "guessed on his size." They fit perfectly.

Eva's other big purchase was prepaid cellphones. She bought two, just as he'd requested. Roman set them to charging as soon as she returned.

While she'd been shopping, he used the hotel phone to call several scooter rental stores. One, in nearby Can Pastilla—which was where Eva's hotel was—offered to rent him a Suzuki Inazuma 250cc motorcycle. Though it was a kitten compared to Roman's 800cc bike back home, the Suzuki was far better than a puttering moped or scooter. If the people he planned to follow were to take the highway, he should at least be able to keep up. The rental company wanted only 50 euro per day for the Suzuki.

Roman arrived at the rental company around sunset. The clerk was wearing a Ramones t-shirt, prompting a conversation and, eventually, a challenge from Roman for the clerk to name all the members of the band, including the drummers. This bit of jocularity helped Roman build a bit of rapport. When the attendant finally arrived on the bike, it was time to pay and sign the forms. Roman pretended he left his wallet in his hotel room—which happened to be many kilometers away. When the punk rock-loving clerk waffled on the rental, Roman slid an extra 50 over the counter and that was that. The bike was rented to Michael Davis of Toronto, Canada—according to the form Roman filled out. Now he had wheels and relative anonymity, especially when wearing the full-face helmet they'd provided. Roman rode back to the hotel with the second helmet strapped to the seat.

Eva was waiting in the room. While he was gone, she'd taken a taxi to her own hotel and picked up some clean clothes.

"What did you tell your friends?"

"They weren't there," she said. "I left them a note."

"Will they be worried about you?"

"They'll be fine. They know I'm independent."

Roman checked his watch. There was quite a bit of time between now and the time the restaurant would close. Though he felt a tremendous desire to spend that time here in the hotel, with Eva, he was too shy to say so.

But what might happen if they did stay here? What would the coming hours bring? Would she make a move, or even drop a hint?

"We've got a good bit of time," he said.

"I know," Eva answered, looking at him.

"Any ideas?"

"We can do whatever you want to do," she said, her eyes drifting to the two beds.

There was tangible electricity in the room…

"How about a ride on the bike?" he blurted, immediately hating himself for asking such a wimpy question.

Eva didn't smile, didn't show anything when she answered with, "Sure."

You stupid sonofabitch, Roman seethed inwardly. *You should've stopped talking and kissed her. You're still a pussy. Always have been…*

"I…uh…got you a helmet," he said, grabbing his things.

"Great."

Once they were on the bike, Roman slowly relaxed. Though he'd rather be making out in the hotel room, it was nice to ride with no purpose. They cruised for several hours as Roman let the rush of warm evening air clear his mind. Though the 250cc engine struggled to accelerate with two passengers, the bike was adequate once they were up to speed. They rode to the south end of Mallorca, finding an abandoned lighthouse at the southern tip. Other than a few other sightseers, the setting was quiet save for a flock of birds settling in for the night. Roman and Eva sat on the ancient stone wall bordering the sea. Below them was a sheer rocky drop of at least 100 feet. Roman stood on the tiny rock ledge on the far side of the wall, looking down at the sheer cliff face. If he were to slip, he'd die a gruesome death on his way to a watery grave.

His current perch was metaphorical for the position he was currently in.

There was still plenty of sunlight—three hours to go. Eva tapped out a cigarette and Roman asked her for one.

"I didn't think you smoked."

"Used to but I don't now. Probably isn't going to affect my life expectancy, at least not at the moment."

They sat there smoking quietly as the water lapped at the rocks below. The sun slowly slid down toward the water on the western horizon. A catamaran slid silently by. Several people lounged in its center netting. They waved up at Roman and Eva.

"This is really nice," Roman said. "It's hard to believe I can enjoy myself in my current situation."

"The human body is capable of all sorts of things."

He looked at her. She drew closer.

What do I do?

Kiss her!

What if she pulls away?

Roman stood, stepping over the wall. "I guess, uh, we'd better start thinking about heading back. Gotta be at least thirty miles back to the hotel. Then another ten for me to the restaurant."

Eva stood without a word. Minutes later, they were heading north, back to their hotel.

When they first departed, Roman buzzed slightly from the cigarette. As his head cleared, he pondered his predicament. Just days before, he was a divorcee vacationer, kicking up his heels with his buddies, trying to make the best of his newfound independence.

Now, not only was he the sole witness to a brutal murder, but he'd been framed to look like the killer in a second murder. And this...this running, this hiding, this retribution—this wasn't Roman Littlepage. He came from an orderly life, where disputes were handled civilly. To Roman, it was unusual to even see two men get into a shoving match.

Several years ago, in the course of running his business, Roman had come up against a man who didn't play by the rules. In fact, the man was so ruthless he'd actually stalked several competitors and threatened them with physical harm. Roman didn't know how to deal with people like that. Thankfully, he and that other man rarely operated in the same space, so Roman had purposefully given him a wide berth.

Then, about a year ago, the ruthless man was found on the ground next to his car. He'd been severely beaten, losing several teeth and suffering a few broken bones. The entire business community whispered that he'd probably screwed over the wrong person.

The wrong person...

Roman lifted the visor on his helmet, allowing the warm air to blast his face. He wondered if he had it anywhere inside him to finally *be* that wrong person.

Do I have the balls? Can I make these people regret what they did to Mitch? Can I make them sorry they ever came after me?

A significant portion of him had his doubts.

They rode all the way back to Palma. Before she walked into the hotel, Eva kissed her index finger and touched it to Roman's lips.

The Suzuki floated to his next destination.

Chapter Seven

It was 11:15 p.m. when Roman cruised through El Arenal. The party was just beginning to hit its stride. There were revelers everywhere, the heavy crowd giving him the feeling of anonymity. Better yet, no one would take notice of a poorly-dressed Dresdener on an underpowered motorcycle. Once he'd negotiated past the throng, he motored up the street that fronted the Lemóni restaurant. Seeing the restaurant brought the same haunting images back to him. Pushing the horrific thoughts aside, Roman focused his thoughts on how to watch the restaurant without giving himself away. He circled around to the north and came back to the south via the back alley, stopping at the location where he'd hidden after the murder several nights before. From here, he could see both the front and back door.

Looking left, Roman determined he was behind a souvenir shop that had closed hours before. This was good. He backed the motorcycle into the darkest of the shadows up next to the cinderblock back wall and waited.

And waited.

And waited.

The owners of Lemóni didn't leave until nearly 12:30 a.m.

Over the balance of his surveillance, Roman saw exactly seven customers depart the restaurant. None were anyone he recognized and they all seemed to be normal vacationers who'd simply enjoyed a nice meal. Someone, though Roman couldn't determine who, locked the front door from the inside at 11:34 p.m and began the typical closing routine. The trash was taken out. The shadows through the amber dining room windows suggested someone was setting the tables for tomorrow.

By 12:15 a.m., the lights in the dining room were out and several employees filed from the back of the restaurant. Several women departed and walked north. Two men, probably cooks, walked directly by Roman but never looked his way. They were too busy smoking and laughing about something that must have been hilarious. A short time later, Roman saw the husband and wife owners exit the rear of the restaurant. The wife used her cellphone light to illuminate the back door while the husband used his keys to lock several locks. He then pressed his key fob and an older Mercedes in the alleyway blipped its lights as the doors unlocked.

Here we go.

Roman waited until they were several blocks away before he cranked the Suzuki and followed. The restaurant owners drove to the east, crossing over the highway as they continued farther inland on a two-lane road. Roman remained well behind, having no trouble seeing the Mercedes since there were few cars out at this hour. After 7 or 8 miles on the two-lane road, the brake lights shone and the Mercedes made two right turns. Roman held back. He saw the Mercedes stop, partially off the road. Roman pulled to the right and turned off the Suzuki, extinguishing its lights. Once his helmet was off, he could hear the grinding chain of an old gate opening. Moments later, with the crunch of grit and rock, the Mercedes eased into the driveway.

The open gate was only 50 meters away. Roman put down the kickstand and came off the bike.

Do I go in there? What if they have a dog? What if they have a motion alarm?

He gritted his teeth, angry with himself.

Remember your competitor who finally tangled with the wrong person? When, Roman…when will you be the wrong person?

Run, dammit. Get in there!

As best as his ankle would allow, Roman ran, following the long rock wall. He made it inside the gate when there were only a few feet remaining before it was fully shut. Flattening himself against the rock gatepost, Roman watched.

The Mercedes came to a stop in front of what appeared to be a modest home. The home was about 75 meters from the gate, situated behind two large trees with little vegetation on them. The house had an elevated wraparound porch. If Roman blinked, he might think he was looking at a rural ranch home in west Texas. There was a porch light on, allowing Roman to see everything that was happening. The couple was quiet as they walked to the house and, upon opening the front door, both began to talk in funny tones.

Seconds later, Roman saw the dog. He snaked through the couple's legs, obviously pleased that they were home.

Roman couldn't make the breed of canine out—all he could tell is the dog was medium to large and had a significant amount of hair. Once the dog had sufficiently greeted its owners, the man pointed to the yard and commanded the dog to do something—probably its "business." Roman watched as the dog descended from the porch and walked around the Mercedes. The dog hiked its leg up on the closest tree, outing itself as a male. As he urinated, he suddenly lifted his nose to the wind and sniffed.

While there wasn't much wind, it was, of course, blowing from the gate to the house.

After the dog finished his business, he moved a few steps away and straightened like a pointer…

Staring directly at Roman.

That lasted for only a moment, because the dog broke into a full run, running in a straight line to Roman.

Oh shit!

Roman remained flattened against the gatepost, squinting his eyes shut as he heard the onrushing dog's grunts.

Will he tear my hands off? Is he one of those breeds that latches onto a person's face? Paws on the dirt. Heavy breaths. Coming at full speed.

Maybe if I cry out they'll show mercy and call the dog off? Damn, getting my ass kicked in a Spanish jail cell sounds good right now.

Roman opened his mouth to yell as the dog reached him. The dog skittered to a halt, barely stopping in time.

There was a momentary pause, the two beings staring at one another, before the dog jammed his snout into Roman's crotch.

Roman had never been so happy to have a dog sniff his junk.

From that point, the dog followed his nose downward, smelling Roman's legs and feet. Judging by all the reddish-blonde hair, it seemed the dog was a friendly Golden Retriever anxious to meet a new friend. After inspecting him, the dog licked Roman's hand, nuzzling Roman to pet him.

The husband, probably blinded by the porch lights, looked all around and called after the dog. The dog's name sounded like *FUH-leeks*. After hearing the name several times, it occurred to Roman the dog's name was Felix and the husband simply pronounced the name in the Spanish dialect.

The husband continued to call and finally Felix let out a small whimper before he began to trudge back to the house. At one point, he stopped and looked longingly back at Roman, as if he wanted to play with his new friend.

Roman sagged with weakness. The spike of fear created by the onrushing dog, followed by the subsequent relief over the dog's friendliness left him soaked with sweat and feeling slightly nauseous.

At the front door, the husband playfully admonished the dog who went sulking inside, halting again to look back out to the gatepost. Finally, the husband went inside and could be seen walking through the house.

From what Roman could see, the husband did not pause to lock the door.

* * *

The wait was agonizing. Not only was Roman sleepy, he was also scared. What did he hope to find? What was his endgame? He tried to come up with excuses to talk himself out of this crazy stunt. He tried to scare himself. Even though the consequences of what he planned to do—like getting arrested, or shot—seemed horrifying, the alternatives were just as scary.

Don't start thinking about giving up, Roman. This is your best move. Be proactive. In the words of Mitch, "Do—not—be—a…"

The restaurant owners had been quite active for this first hour, judging by all their movement. Finally, Roman noticed the couple had changed into nightclothes. The husband walked around the house, shutting off lights and pulling drapes shut. Roman waited on the man to lock the front door but, as far as Roman could see, he never did.

Surely the door must lock automatically. Right? Do people sleep with their houses unlocked?

Roman remembered his father, who was now deceased, telling stories of his childhood, about how they never locked their doors.

And Mallorca, as Roman had learned, was nearly nonviolent. Sure, some crime occurred, but primarily it centered on theft from oblivious tourists. Why would burglars bother with a house way out here when a veritable theft smorgasbord existed around the Bay of Palma?

So, maybe the door *was* unlocked.

Roman started his stopwatch. Though he caught himself nodding off several times, he gave the couple a full hour to fall asleep. The night cooled grudgingly, still warm enough to cause Roman to perspire. When the hour was finally up, it was time to check the front door. In the event the door was unlocked, Roman was most concerned about the dog. What if he barked?

Second on Roman's list of concerns was a burglar alarm. He'd not seen the couple arm an alarm, but that doesn't mean they didn't have one.

Finally, Roman's greatest worry revolved around the couple. What if they weren't asleep? What if they were sitting up reading and the husband kept a loaded shotgun by his bed?

Is breaking into their house worth it?

No. No way.

Pussy.

Okay, I'm going.

Heading inside. Stay tuned.

That was the text message he sent to Eva. Her reply came in less than a minute. She told Roman to text her as soon as he was finished.

It took five minutes for Roman's leaden feet to carry him to the front door. The porch didn't groan under his weight—small favors. Using his shirt, Roman pressed down on the European-style door handle. It moved all the way down. Wincing, Roman gave the door a light push.

It opened.

There was no audible alarm, only a rushing sound similar to static from a speaker. It took Roman a moment to realize he was hearing white noise. The restaurant owners must have turned it on at night to aid with their sleep. After a moment of allowing his ears to adjust, Roman heard another sound, even over the significant white noise.

Someone was snoring quite loud.

More small favors.

He pushed the door almost shut and stepped inside, waiting on Felix. The dog didn't come.

Judging by the white noise and the direction the owners had walked as they'd turned out the lights, the bedroom was to the left. Roman's eyes had fully adjusted to the dark, leaving him to see everything in shades of blue and purple.

He was standing in a large room that would probably be described as a family room. On one end was a wide stone fireplace. At the back end a long dinner table and, closest to Roman, a sitting area of sofas and chairs. From what he could see, there were books and magazines everywhere and the house had the pleasant smell of cinnamon and years of good meals.

Roman looked to the right, beyond the fireplace. The kitchen was there, with openings into this room on both sides of the wide fireplace. Straight back were windows and a door that probably led to a rear patio. And to the left, the bedroom or bedrooms. It seemed to be the type of house tailored to two adults.

Holding his breath, Roman walked forward. As he grew closer to an opening on the left, he realized it was a doorway but the door was open. Creeping, he finally dared look in. His assumption was correct—the room was indeed a large bedroom. The couple slept in separate single beds and it seemed, based on the rise and fall of his chest, that the husband was the snoring culprit. Wherever the white noise machine was, the sound was quite loud in the bedroom. Roman finally saw the dog. He was curled up in his own bed, tucked against the outer wall at the rear of the room. Due to the white noise, Roman didn't think the dog would awaken.

Feeling slightly emboldened, Roman turned and walked to the kitchen. He would start there.

* * *

Fifteen minutes had passed since Roman had illegally entered the restaurant owners' home. He'd searched the kitchen, using the light from his cellphone that was currently in airplane mode to prevent any unwanted sounds. Other than a stack of open bills and correspondence at the corner of one counter— and those told Roman nothing—there'd been hardly anything to look at in the well-equipped kitchen. He removed the front page from the wireless bill, folding it and sliding it in his back pocket.

Off the kitchen, on the opposite end of the home from the bedroom, was a laundry room followed by a utility room. There'd been little to learn there, other than the fact that one of the owners possessed a fairly sophisticated set of woodworking tools. He checked all the cabinets and drawers, finding nothing out of the ordinary. Roman walked back through the kitchen and eyed the large living room.

Because of the open door to the bedroom, he was afraid to use his cellphone light in the living room for fear of waking the restaurant owners. There was a bit of light coming through the windows thanks to the moon. That should do for basic searching. But if he wanted to view anything in detail, he decided he'd carry it into the kitchen and use his phone light.

Roman started at the large table at the rear of the house. Other than magazines in a bowl at the center of the table, he found nothing else of interest. He did take note that not all of the magazines were Spanish. There were several in English and two or three in what looked like Greek. He moved on to the sitting area.

After rifling through books and magazines near the chairs and sofas, Roman eyed the various photographs on the tables and bookshelves. He quickly deduced that the restaurant owners were childless. Earlier, due to their age, he'd assumed, if they had children, they were no longer living at home. But now, after seeing only photos of the couple and their numerous dogs through the years, he decided they'd lived a life with no children.

Having found nothing even remotely helpful, Roman wished there were some way to search the bedroom. He tiptoed to the opening and peered in again. Nope. There was no way. Roman took a moment and scrutinized what he could see of the room. There were two far doors—probably the bathroom and closet. There appeared to be photos, a telephone and the noise machine on the night tables. Each side of the room had a tall chest of drawers and on the wall where Roman was, there was a wide dresser with mirror. To the rear of the house was a sitting nook with a chair and ottoman. Nothing in the room caught his eye as something he'd want to study.

Frustrated, he stepped back into the main living room and combed his fingers back through his hair.

This entire harebrained scheme had been a fool's errand. What had he been expecting to find, the murder weapon, still bloody and awaiting him in a Ziploc bag? Roman felt completely defeated. What would he do now? The Mallorcans wanted him for a murder he didn't commit. He had no passport. His cash was dwindling. And some far-reaching group had killed his best friend and now wanted Roman dead.

Ready to leave, Roman took a final look around, focusing on the wall of books outside the bedroom. He was unable to read the titles in the dim light. Most of the books were without book jackets and Roman was able to see glints of the titles in gold and silver leaf. Down at the bottom, however, were several massive books with no title. Upon closer inspection, Roman realized they weren't books—they were binders. He grasped one and carried it to the kitchen.

It was a photo album.

Ten minutes later, Roman retrieved his fourth binder. There was only one remaining after this one. Thus far, he'd viewed hundreds of pictures of the couple through the years. He'd seen at least four dogs they'd owned and dozens of friends and acquaintances—but nothing that had helped him beyond determining the couple's travels and friends.

He placed the binder on the kitchen island and eyed the refrigerator. He was quite thirsty. Though he knew he'd touched numerous things, Roman used his shirt to open the refrigerator. Searching top to bottom, he finally saw several bottles of water. He opened one and chugged half of it, feeling markedly better. Capping the plastic bottle, he shoved it into his pocket.

When he opened the fourth binder, he noticed the photos were much older than the others. After a moment, he realized the photos were from the 1960s. This was evidenced by the old Kodak photo paper with scalloped edges. The year of each photo was stamped along with what must have been the month on the yellowing film paper border. The first photos began in *"Ioun 61."*

Roman flipped through the pictures, eventually deducing these photos were of the wife and her childhood family. The setting was almost certainly different than Mallorca. It seemed more like somewhere in the Middle East, Greece or Turkey. Two photos displayed a church of some sort in the background. Roman felt like he'd seen it before—maybe on television or in photographs. The church was large, with two tall, narrow steeples. The steeples were topped with distinctive onion domes.

Where have I seen those steeples?

The wife had been quite attractive in her youth. There were dozens of photos with her and what must have been her brother and parents. Her mother, who was also pretty, smiled in most of the pictures. The brother was probably a few years younger than his sister. He and her father typically eyed the camera with stern ruggedness. The men were both rather handsome but serious looking. Roman flipped through the entire album, the years continuing to 1965.

As Roman shut the album, he was struck with the fear he was being watched. He slowly turned, seeing no one. Deflating in relief, he padded back through the living area, again peering into the bedroom. Both people were in their beds, although the wife had turned over and was facing the other way. Felix was still fast asleep, nestled in his bed. The noise machine still covered the house in white noise.

Everything's fine. Finish what you started.

There was one more album to view and, for whatever reason, Roman felt compelled to take the time to look through it. While tonight had been a failure thus far, his instinct told him there was something to be gleaned from these photos. He replaced the fourth album, wincing when it clunked against the back of the shelf. He didn't move for a full minute.

Nothing. No response from the restaurant owners or the dog.

He retrieved the last album, taking it back into the kitchen.

By the time these photos had been taken, it seemed the wife had departed her childhood home. There were a number of photos of her and her maturing girlfriends holding books, indicating that she might have been away at university. On the next page, the wife and her friends posed for a photo in front of a stone sign. The letters were Cyrillic, but it did indeed appear to be a college or university. Several pages later, by *"Okt 66,"* her younger brother appeared in several photos in a military uniform of some sort. While his father proudly flanked his son, the mother seemed concerned, grasping the boy's arm tightly as if she didn't want to let him go.

Roman continued on, eventually coming to pictures marked *"Ioul 67."* In these photos, the younger brother lay in a hospital bed. Despite the cuts and abrasions on his face, he was all smiles and flanked by his mother and sister. There were no photographs of the father with the son.

When he flipped the page, Roman heard piercing alarms all throughout the house.

Actually, there were no alarms, other than the blaring klaxons in his head.

He was staring at another photograph of the younger brother, still in the hospital, but taken from a different perspective. He'd lost most of his arm, the remainder of it bandaged with numerous tubes extending from the stump.

It was his *left* arm.

Roman held the camera phone's light close to the picture, drinking in the young man's features and applying them to his memory of the man he'd seen ordering the killing at the Lemóni. The nose. The eyes. The chiseled, distinct face. Yes, it was him.

The restaurant owner's brother was, indeed, the one-armed man.

Holy shit.

Roman was so consumed with drinking in every detail of the photo that he didn't notice the dog, Felix, until he brushed against his leg. Almost yelling out, Roman lurched backward, watching as the dog eyed him curiously.

Why is the dog awake? Did he hear me?

Roman turned off the phone light. Unsure of what to do, he noticed the dog alternating his view. His heart racing, Roman slowly turned.

The woman he'd just viewed in hundreds of photographs was standing mere feet away. It appeared she was as scared as he was, an empty glass in one hand, her other hand covering her mouth.

The glass hadn't even hit the hardwood floor before she let out a blood-curdling scream.

Holy shit, indeed.

Chapter Eight

Sprained ankle and all, Roman burst through the front door so fast he fell down the steps of the porch, sprawling roughly on the ground below. The water bottle that had been in his shorts pocket skittered off into the bushes and his prepaid cellphone tumbled onto the gravel in front of him.

Thinking he was playing some sort of game, Felix ran to Roman, barking as he urged him to get up and keep playing. By the time Roman was on his feet, he was bathed in light as floodlights came on all around the house. After grabbing the phone, Roman ran toward the gate, his ankle protesting with each step. Roman pressed on, fearful a bullet would soon strike him in the back.

The distance to the gate seemed ten miles. Felix was with Roman every step of the way.

When he finally reached the gate, Roman grasped the top of the adjacent rock wall and glanced back at the house. The man and his wife stood on the porch. The man was on the phone, pointing and frantically talking. Roman pulled himself up to the top of the wall. When he did, Felix jumped up on his hind legs, his front paws on the wall as he continued to bark, acting aggressive now that Roman was at the property boundary. Thankfully he didn't bite Roman's ankles.

Roman dropped to the other side, crumpling painfully on the gravel below as his ankle gave way. Flares of pain shot up his leg.

There's no time for discomfort, Roman. Someone's coming for you.

He brought himself to his feet and hobbled around the wall to the motorcycle. Roman sat on the bike, turned the key and pressed the starter button, resisting the urge to gun the engine. Unfortunately, there was no way to turn off the lights—they were always on for safety.

You're a beacon, Roman. And, either the one-armed man and his friends are coming. Or, it's the cops. Pick your poison.

Regardless of who was coming, Roman knew his best bet right now was creating distance.

Earlier, when he'd followed the couple to their house, Roman recalled a secondary, one-lane road that had veered off to the left about a mile before he'd parked the bike. Getting his bearings with the aid of the moon, Roman crossed the two-lane road and rode with abandon straight into the rocky desert landscape. He knew he was probably leaving an easy trail to follow, but he also knew if he drove back down that two-lane road he'd be an easy target for whoever was responding to the distress call.

When he'd gone over a hill, Roman flipped the headlamps to their highbeam setting and increased his speed. The ride was rough enough to jar his fillings loose, but Roman wasn't willing to let up. As he began to ascend a second hill, something from the left caught Roman's eye. He stopped, killing the engine and lights.

In the distance, two police cars raced up the two-lane road. They were coming from El Arenal, just as Roman had earlier. He waited until the cars were out of sight behind him before he cranked the motorcycle and continuing forward.

He went down into a shallow valley, accelerating rapidly up the other side. As he ascended, he realized the rocks here were larger and jagged in spots. Due to his speed, he wasn't able to react to a section of large rocks. He struck them with some speed and managed to slow the bike before falling to the left. The Suzuki was on its side, the rear wheel free spinning. Roman pressed the kill switch and moved his arms and legs. He felt okay, although his left arm now hurt, added to his ankle. He leaned forward, feeling the front tire. Flat. He'd gashed it on a rock.

He opened the prepaid phone, finding it inoperable. Chintzy and poorly made, it had broken when he'd fallen down the steps. The light didn't even work anymore. He slid the phone into his pocket and prepared himself.

Although he was in pain, Roman knew he'd done exactly what he needed to do. And from here, as much as it would suck, walking was probably his best defense against drawing attention. After giving his eyes a moment to adjust to the dark, Roman began trudging toward the dull lights that represented Palma in the northwestern distance. The city had to be ten or twelve miles away.

Though he didn't know it, the distance was fourteen miles. Over rough terrain. With a sprained ankle and a gashed arm. In the dark. With cactuses everywhere.

The walk was hell—but he made it.

* * *

He trudged into the hotel room at sunup.

"Oh my God, are you okay?" Eva asked.

"Water, please," he said, leaning against the wall and sliding down to a sitting position. He removed his sneakers and socks, wincing with relief as he wiggled his toes. His ankle was extremely swollen and his legs were scraped and filthy.

"What happened?" Eva asked, giving him a bottle of water.

He chugged half the bottle. "What a night. What a freaking night."

"You look like you walked all the way back."

He nodded, finishing the bottle of water.

After she refilled the water bottle two more times, he relayed the full story of his escape.

"You think the police know it was you who broke in?"

"They have to," Roman said. "I left fingerprints, and the couple had seen me in their restaurant when the police first went there after the murder."

"Your arm is cut."

"I fell off the bike and then I probably ran into ten cactuses on the way back here."

"Look at your foot."

Roman eyed his ankle. Now that he'd taken off his socks and shoes, and ceased moving, his ankle and foot had swollen tremendously. She handed him a bottle of ibuprofen and he took four with another swig of water.

"Do you want a shower?" she asked.

"In a little bit. I just want to rest for a moment."

"Did you find anything?"

He eyed her.

"You did," Eva said, reading his face. "Please, tell me."

"You're not going to believe it. I still don't believe it."

"Believe what?"

"Eva...I'm almost positive the one-armed man is her brother."

"The woman from the restaurant?"

"Yes, the wife."

Eva seemed astonished and impressed. "How'd you come up with that?"

Roman explained the photographs of the young man in the military and the subsequent hospital photos showing him without most of his arm.

"I can't believe you found that," she smiled.

"Me neither."

"What else?"

"He was a few years younger than her. There were lots of family pictures before she went off to college, and that's when he appeared in a military uniform. A few pages later, there he was in a hospital bed with numerous injuries. He'd lost three-quarters of his arm."

"Were they Mallorcan?"

Roman shook his head. "Wherever they lived, it looked Middle Eastern, but there was a lot of stuff in the house that looked like it was written in Greek."

"Greek or Cyrillic?"

He shrugged. "I don't know. I just glanced and I knew it wasn't our alphabet. But my first instinct told me Greek."

Eva pulled her hair back into a ponytail. "Roman, this is huge. You uncovered *the* connection. Despite all that's gone on, you should be proud of yourself."

"Yeah, thanks," he answered, grunting as he stood. "But what do I do with it?"

"We'll think of something. At least you know more now. As they always say, information is power."

"Yeah, well…*they've* never been in my shoes," he grumped.

Eva shrugged.

"I'm sorry, Eva," Roman apologized. "Thanks for saying so many nice things. I just don't know how to make these discoveries work for me."

"Take stock of yourself," she advised. "Your mind has gotten you this far. You're still alive, and you've not been arrested. I'm sure you're exhausted." She motioned to the bathroom. "So, why don't you get cleaned up and then get some rest? I bet you'll think more clearly afterward."

After discussing it a bit longer, Roman managed to take a long, cold shower, despite his ankle. Rather than don his filthy clothes, he wrapped the towel tightly around his waist and washed his clothes in the sink. He tied a hand towel around his arm. The gash was superficial and wasn't deep enough to require stitches. As he carried his clothes to the small balcony, he asked Eva if she'd slept.

"No."

"Go ahead and crash."

"What about you?"

"I'm gonna hang these clothes outside. As hot as it's been, they won't take long to dry. I'll come to bed in a bit. I just need to wind down for a while."

"Are you sure?" she asked, cocking her head.

"Don't take this the wrong way, but I need a quiet hour to process everything. I couldn't really do it during the walk because I was just so determined to get here."

"Okay. Oh, by the way, I went down and paid for another night in the room. We don't need to worry about checking out," Eva said with a smile. "So, when you feel like it, come inside and rest."

"Thank you."

Roman turned away as she began removing her clothes. He didn't know how far down she'd take her disrobing and the very thought of it put a lump in his throat. So, out he limped to the small balcony with two bottles of water and his clothes in a bundle. Using the safety railing, he hung his clothes in the sun. As he placed his soaked jeans over the rail, the gold coin plopped out and bounced on the concrete balcony. Roman stamped his foot on top of the coin, preventing it from rolling off the edge. He stepped back inside, placing the coin beside his Chapstick as he retrieved the second prepaid mobile phone. Eva was under the sheet.

"You sure you're okay?" she asked.

"Yes. Sleep well." He walked back onto the east-facing balcony and pulled the drape and the door shut.

Despite the early hour, the summer sun was ascending rapidly and shining directly on him and his clothes. The lighter items would probably be dry in short order. Shutting his eyes to the glare, Roman stretched back in the chair and propped his bad ankle on the railing. The warm sun felt good on his clean skin. He leaned his head back and drank water, pondering what he knew.

Assuming Roman hadn't made a bad assumption, the one-armed man was the female restaurant owner's younger brother. He'd been in the military, though Roman didn't know where, and lost his arm in 1967. Of course, Roman knew the Vietnam War had occurred during that time. He also knew the 1960s were a tumultuous decade, but he couldn't name all the other wars and conflicts. He'd check later.

Roman wondered if the sister had been complicit with her brother using her restaurant. Did she allow him and his "friends" to stay after closing time? And because of that, did she know who the murder victim was? Did she know the cruel-looking man in the leather jacket? Did she know the knife-wielding man with the curly hair?

The gravity of what Roman had unearthed struck him. That woman could blow this investigation wide open with her testimony.

With her testimony…key phrase. Would she cooperate?

The biggest question right now involved this investigation—was it even an investigation at all? To the locals, and the U.S. Consulate, Roman was a murder suspect who'd reported another murder in which there was no evidence whatsoever. He couldn't turn to them for help—they'd simply detain him as they investigated the slaying of the hotelier.

What about the woman's brother, the one-armed man? What organization was he a member of that had enough reach to kill Mitch in Houston, Texas in a matter of hours? If the man had been 18 years old in 1967, he had to be at least 68 years old in 2017. That's not elderly, but he was no spring chicken, either. Assuming he was a member of some dastardly group, why was he still active at such an advanced age? And whose side was he on?

And who died on the kitchen floor of the Lemóni?

A spike of recollection came to Roman. The wireless bill! He dug into the pocket of his soaked jeans, hoping he hadn't destroyed the printed words with the shampoo and water. He relaxed when he unfolded the water-logged paper, still able to read the name and address:

```
Christopher Manakos
Cami de la Ladera 201
07629 Randa, Mallorca
```

Manakos? It sounded Greek.

But that was the husband's name, not hers…

Roman rubbed his temples. He knew he was forgetting something. Something critical. What was it, Roman? Think…

The flag!

That was the damned clue he'd missed yesterday at the restaurant in the old city. Eva had told him about the Dutch guys hoping to earn their "German flag." Though it didn't occur to him at that moment, it was the flag out in front of Lemóni that was in the back of his mind. And last night, he was parked in the alleyway on the other side of the restaurant, so he couldn't see it from his vantage point.

What country did that flag represent?

Roman unlocked the prepaid phone. It was some sort of generic touchscreen device. Though, like its twin, it was probably cheap as dirt, it worked just fine before it was dropped, operating like an iPhone with a less sensitive screen.

He navigated to the browser and typed in "national flags."

The search produced dozens of images. He clicked the first set of flags, which was nothing more than ten rows and ten columns of major flags from around the world. He searched for the white flag with the orange blob but didn't see it. Though it was trivial, Roman realized how prevalent red and blue were in the makeup of national flags. He went to the subsequent search results, still not seeing a flag with an orange blob.

Next, recalling the Middle East-like pictures he'd seen in the Manakos household, he searched "flags of the Middle East." Still no results with the first hit. But after paging through several of the links, he saw it.

The flag was white, with the shape of what looked like an island and crossed olive branches below.

Cyprus. The restaurant was Cypriot.

Lemóni…

Roman typed the name of the restaurant into Google Translate's auto-recognize feature. Lemóni came back as Icelandic? Of course, the name meant "Lemon." He then typed "Lemon" into Google Translate and asked for the Greek translation. It came back as "Λεμόνι." Sure enough, down below, in the English alphabet, was the word Lemóni.

Greek, once again. He looked up Cyprus, discovering that 81 percent of Cypriots spoke Greek. To Roman, this nearly confirmed the Cyprus origin of the restaurant owners—at least of the wife.

Roman stretched out in the chair again. He could hear the water dripping from his drying jeans. He shut his eyes, calming himself, doing his best not to force his thoughts.

Slowly now…slowly…

Who would care about any of this information? The Houston Police? That asshole, Kelley, at the Consulate? Sotinspector Reyes?

No.

Who would care?

Who would care?

Who did the one-armed man kill? And why? Somebody's missing that dead man. Somebody's worried right now.

So, who cares about the dead man? Whose side was the dead man on?

The one-armed man was wounded in 1967. Start there.

Roman opened the browser again. His Google search for "1967 wars" returned ten hits on the first page, all dealing with one subject: The Six-Day War.

Though he was vaguely familiar with the conflict, Roman didn't know all the specifics. In his recollection, Israel had repelled a much larger force in less than a week, hence the name. That was about all he remembered. He clicked on the top link, reading with interest, especially when it came to the belligerents: Israel versus a number of Arab nations.

So, was this the conflict where the one-armed man lost his arm and, if so, which side was he on? At the very least, the year and region indicated to Roman that he'd pinpointed the correct war.

Roman thought about the one-armed man. If he was cold-blooded enough to kill the man at Lemóni, then somehow murder Mitch in Houston, it meant two things: First, he was absolutely ruthless. And second, he didn't want to be found. He and his people were willing to kill innocents without compunction.

Who are they? Whose side are they on? Why do they want me dead?

Roman performed a number of searches concerning one-armed men, one-armed killers, one-armed Arabs and a host of other related terms. He found nothing useful. There was far too much to sift through, especially on a chintzy phone.

Who else might want to know? These killers are big time…they have the ability to reach around the globe through their network.

Who else is looking for them?

On a whim, Roman searched the browser for the Central Intelligence Agency. He went to the contact portion of the mobile page, seeing a red button with "Report Threats" in bold. He pressed it, finding a web form along with several phone numbers. It was 6:30 in the morning here in Mallorca, meaning it was just past midnight in Washington D.C.

"Who cares?" he muttered. This was definitely an emergency. Roman pressed the screen to call the international number, reminding himself he'd chew through the prepaid minutes four times as fast on an international call.

He was greeted by a voice menu. He pressed zero. There was a brief delay and a series of clicks before another menu. Pressed zero again. This time there was one click before a man answered—*a human being!*—his voice slightly slurred as if he'd been asleep.

"I'd like to report a threat," Roman said.

"We have numerous menu options for this, sir. You can either email us or leave a voicemail that will be—"

"This is an emergency," Roman interrupted.

"An emergency? Then you should probably dial your local authorities."

"It's a threat, possibly against national security."

"I see. May I have your name?"

"I'll tell you at the end of the call," Roman said, afraid that the wireless signal could be compromised. He wanted to make sure the CIA planned to help before spouting off his personal information.

"What is the nature of the threat?" the man asked, his tone about as excited as a server at a fast food joint asking Roman if he wanted mayo on his sandwich.

"I witnessed three men kill another man, and now they're after me. There's more to it, of course, but that's it in a nutshell."

"For that type of crime, you'll need to contact your local law enforcement about—"

"Hey," Roman said, cutting him off. "I'm calling you from Mallorca, Spain. And I have contacted local law enforcement, okay? This goes way beyond that."

"So, if you're overseas and have already talked to the host country's law enforcement, then I'd suggest you call the United States Embassy or nearest consulate. One moment." Roman heard keystrokes. "Okay, I've done you a favor and searched the State Department's website. There's actually a consulate located approximately 3,100 meters from where you are."

A chill went down Roman's spine. "You can tell where I am?"

"I can tell a number of things, sir."

Don't get scared. Don't give up. The CIA is not your enemy.

"Sir, listen to me. I'll be as brief as possible." Roman leaned back in the chintzy plastic chair and forced himself to relax. "I witnessed a murder." Roman told the entire story of the Lemóni murder in detail. The CIA man didn't respond.

"You still with me?" Roman asked.

"The server is recording all this," the man replied over papers fluttering, probably perusing the newspaper in his boredom.

Roman then relayed the story of Mitch being killed. He told about the hotel owner's murder and how the killers had orchestrated everything to frame Roman.

"Hmm," the CIA man replied, more pages fluttering.

Fighting the urge to get angry, and wanting to get all of this recorded in the hopes that someone with some pull might hear it, Roman continued. "With nowhere else to turn, I decided to go after the restaurant owners."

"Restaurant owners?"

"The murder I saw happened in the kitchen of a restaurant, after hours. After a number of dead ends, I began to wonder if the restaurant owners might know the killers. Turns out, I was right. I found out that the one-armed man is the brother of the female restaurant owner. And I'm almost positive he lost his arm during the Six-Day War in 1967. They grew up in Cyprus."

"Unless I'm mistaken, Cyprus had no role in that war." The CIA man spoke this in an amused tone, as if he were debating someone over beers at the local pub. "I'll have to Google that, but I'm almost certain."

"I'm telling you what I know. Look, he could be some sort of wicked Mossad or Arab agent and he kills at the drop of a hat. And he's *here* for the taking, don't you get it?"

Silence.

"Are you there?" Roman asked, his voice trembling.

"I am. Is that everything?"

"Yeah, isn't it enough? Were you listening? This one-armed guy is the ringleader. I figured he was on some most-wanted list and you guys would know exactly who he is."

"Sir, we're seeking thousands of people. Though I have a rather broad mental capacity, it's not easy to memorize each one."

"So, this call is for nothing?"

"No, sir, it's not. I've logged it and recorded it. We'll speak to the State Department and to the local authorities there. Now, if you will please give me all your information, I'll see if I can get you some assistance at the consulate."

"The consulate. You're going to get me help at the consulate?"

"Yes. It's three-point-one kilometers from you."

"Do you care about anything I said, about the potential threat to the U.S. from the one-armed man and his organization?"

"What exactly is this so-called threat against the U.S.?"

"He killed my friend, an American, and now he's trying to kill me. That not important enough for you?" Roman asked, realizing he'd yelled the question.

"As I told you, sir, this call has been recorded. Tomorrow, one of our analysts will hear all about your one-armed man and the Cypriot eating establishment named for a citrus fruit. Now, is there anything else I can help you with?"

"You can help me by taking me seriously."

"I'll pass the call on," the CIA man said perfunctorily. "Your name and U.S. address?"

Seething, Roman said, "My name is Johnny-go-fuck-yourself. And I live at one fuck you avenue."

After touching the red button on the phone, he removed the battery from the phone's back before he buried his head in his hands, nearly overcome with frustration.

He had no idea what to do now. No damned idea.

His frustration gave way to his exhaustion. Within five minutes, he was fast asleep.

Chapter Nine

Roman awoke two hours later, the sun scorching his skin as the memories of the futile call with the CIA flooded back to him. Rubbing his face vigorously, Roman was disappointed with himself for losing control at the end of the conversation. Sure, the CIA man was being insensitive, but Roman knew better than to take the conversation to the gutter. Oh well, what was done was done.

His lips and mouth were parched. Roman knew he needed to rehydrate with more than just a few bottles of water. In fact, he needed lots of water, nutritious food, and true rest.

Not just a nap, either...we're talking 12 hours of uninterrupted sleep. Maybe even extend this hotel room for a few more days in the event they track—

Panicked, he shot to his feet.

The man at the CIA had known *exactly* where Roman was due to the prepaid phone's signal. He knew Roman was 3,100 meters away from the consulate. He also said he'd reach out to the State Department and the Mallorcan Police.

The police...oh no. Please tell me he didn't do that.

Still wearing the towel, Roman gathered his now mostly-dry clothes and limped back into the room. He managed to get his underwear on before Eva turned, shading her eyes at the harsh light.

"What's going on?" she asked, her voice scratchy.

"I've got to leave," he said urgently. "They might know where we are."

"How?" she asked, propping up on her elbows.

"I called the CIA to report all this and the guy was able to read the phone's signal. He knew exactly where I was, right down to the meter."

"You called the CIA?" she asked, sitting all the way up. "That shady American intelligence agency?"

"That's them," he said, tugging on his socks.

"What'd you tell them?"

Roman waved his hand dismissively. "It was after midnight there. The guy I spoke with was an uninterested asshole."

"But you told them everything?"

"Pretty much," he said, slipping on his shoes.

"How did you leave it?"

"I got frustrated. Said some things to him I shouldn't have said." Roman walked back onto the balcony and retrieved the prepaid phone and its battery.

When he came back inside, Eva stood from the bed, wearing only a bra and a thong. She was every bit as delectable as he thought she'd be. There was a tattoo of some sort down below her belly button and off to the side. Feeling his heart lurch into his throat, Roman turned away.

"If you're leaving, I'm coming with you," she said, pulling on her shorts.

"No, you're not," Roman replied, facing the harsh light from the split in the drapes. "Listen, I realize you think you're doing something noble by sticking with me, and you are. But in the eyes of the police, you're going to be an accessory. Don't make my problems yours."

She pulled her shirt down over her head and eyed him. "That's my decision, isn't it? Do you not want me with you?"

He turned to face her. "I do...it's just..."

"You don't want me to get arrested?" Eva asked.

"Exactly."

"I understand, and it's a risk I'm willing to take. Besides, I'm a nurse. I can just tell them I was worried about you after your fall." She tossed him his wristwatch. "Finish getting dressed."

"I don't even know where we should go."

"You just know we need to leave here, right?"

"Right," he said with no confidence.

She slid on her sandals. "So, let's go. We'll figure it out together."

Roman plopped down on the side of the bed and rested his head in his hands. "I don't know what to do, Eva."

She rested a hand on his shoulder. "Do you really think we should leave?"

He shut his eyes for a moment, pondering the question and deciding to go with his instinct. "Yes, I do. I think...somehow...our location will get leaked to the killers."

"Then let's trust your instinct and get moving."

Roman looked up at her. "Thanks for all of this."

"You can thank me later," she answered with a wink.

They departed the room 4 minutes later.

* * *

After a quick appraisal of the long hallway, Roman discovered there were three traditional outlets from their floor. The elevator, which would deposit them in the lobby, was a bad idea. The better options were the stairwells on both ends of the hotel, plus there was nothing on either door indicating the risk of setting off an alarm if the door was opened. Roman reasoned that, if anyone were watching, they'd probably be focused on the stairwell near his and Eva's room. He suggested they use the stairs at the opposite end of the building. Eva concurred. After walking the hall, through the door they went.

Contrasting sharply with the bright paint and carpet of the hallway, the stairwell was as drab as could be. The stairs were concrete. The walls were concrete. Everything, other than the black handrail, seemed to be some shade of gray. At the bottom landing, Roman gestured to a tool tray sitting in the middle of the floor. Maybe the hotel's maintenance worker had left it there. Accidentally kicking it would cause quite a racket.

He carefully opened the interior door and peered down the hallway of the bottom floor. There were hotel rooms on the left and right, leading to the lobby. He could hear two male voices in the lobby but he couldn't see anyone. Eva listened to the voices and shook her head.

"That's the clerk talking to a hotel guest. They were discussing breakfast hours and nearby restaurants."

Roman closed the door. "Speaking of breakfast, if we can get out of here cleanly, I'd really like to pig out."

"Pig out?" she asked.

"Eat a lot of food. I'm starving."

"Ah," she said with a knowing smile. "*Überessen.* I understand, and I'll join you. I'm hungry, too."

He walked to the steel fire door on the opposite side of the stairwell. "Here we go," he said, squeezing his eyes shut as he braced for the alarm. He pushed the door open, pleased to hear only the singing birds in the trees outside the door.

"Come on." He took Eva's hand, walking onto the small green lawn at the side of the hotel. Directly in front of him was the parking area. Across the parking lot was a secondary street, fronted by a row of shops and businesses. There was a decorative garbage receptacle next to the door. Beside it rested a white bag with slightly bruised fruit that someone had thrown out.

Using a squatty palm tree as cover, Roman peered around the building to the left, looking at the front of the hotel. There were no visible police and no obvious surveillance. He walked to the opposite corner, using a stand of bushes as concealment to take a look at the rear of the hotel. He saw no one there, either. Just as he was ready to lead Eva away, he noticed someone in the distance sitting in a compact Mercedes. What drew Roman's eye was a lace of smoke ascending from the car.

He focused on the silhouette of the person who was smoking. It looked like a man and he'd parked at the far end of the lot with the Mercedes backed in to give him a straight-on view of the hotel. The car was parked in the heavy shadows under the trees and the cherry from the cigarette glowed as the driver took a drag.

Roman recalled the stairwell at the opposite end of the building, where their room had been. The man in the Mercedes was perfectly positioned to eyeball the door on that end of the building. Roman glanced around, making sure no one was watching this door. He saw no one.

"There's someone in the car at the far end of the lot," he whispered.

Eva peered around the building. "Bet he's watching the other door. Good call using this stairwell."

"Damn it," Roman breathed. He peeked around to the front of the hotel and scrutinized the cars and scenery. There were five cars in the parking lot, all appearing empty. There were also two motorcycles, parked. Roman made a mental note to call the motorcycle rental store and tell them where their motorcycle was.

He could hear his explanation now. "Yeah, your bike is in the desert about fifteen miles east of Palma? Where? I dunno…in the desert, near some hills and a bunch of rocks and a shitload of cactuses."

Yeah, that would go over real well. Maybe he'd better just leave it alone and let the owner get paid by his insurance company.

Roman continued to scan the nearby area…

Beyond the front parking lot was a busy street and, on the other side, a row of restaurants. Roman eyed the people sitting outside of the restaurants, halting when he saw *him*.

It was the curly-haired killer. He wore tan slacks and a button down shirt with the sleeves rolled up. He sat at a covered table at an Italian café, his back against the glass of the building. He held a newspaper, but it was just low enough for Roman to see the curly hair. In front of him was a small espresso cup. The newspaper and the coffee were just for show—he was watching the hotel and could see both the main entrance and the area near this door from his location.

After scrutinizing the curly-haired killer's position, Roman stepped back and explained to Eva what he'd seen. As she peered at the curly-haired killer, Roman walked back to the rear. He eyed the man in the Mercedes. Finally, he decided the two men couldn't see one another. They'd chosen strategic locations to spot Roman when he departed the hotel.

"Are you sure the CIA knew you were here by the signal of the phone?" Eva asked.

Leaning against the building, and feeling mildly surprised that he wasn't more scared, Roman nodded.

"No sign of the one-armed man?"

"No," Roman answered. "I haven't seen him since that first night."

"I bet those two know where he is."

"Yeah. I'm more pissed about the idiot from the CIA calling the Mallorcans."

"And you think there's a leak in the police department?" Eva asked.

"Doesn't this prove it?" he replied with more heat than he wanted. "Sorry, but I'm just so sick of being chased."

"It's okay," Eva said, touching his arm.

Roman looked at both henchmen, making sure they were staying put. "Whoever has loose lips got word to these murderers that my signal was coming from this area. My guess is the CIA's signal reader was good enough to tell that we were on the south end of the hotel. That's why the one guy camped out down there."

"I wonder if they tried to find out which room you're in?" Eva asked. "If so, it's a good thing you didn't book it in your name."

"Thanks to you."

Eva pointed north. "If we duck down behind the bushes, we can get across the parking lot without the curly-haired man seeing us. Then, we walk straight behind the sign and go up that alley right there. If we do that, I don't think either of them will see us unless they move."

Roman checked the angles. She was correct, although the curly-haired killer might get a brief glance at them when they crossed the street, but he'd be looking at their backs.

"Yeah...but..."

"But, what?" Eva asked.

"There's one thing about all this that's bugging me."

"What's that?"

"I don't know...it just seems a shame to let these assholes do this." He gestured angrily in both directions. "They're both right there, within reach. And every answer we need to get out of this is in their tiny brains. Why should *we* run? Why shouldn't *they* be scared of *us*?"

"Look at you," she said, amused. "I haven't seen this man before."

"I'm just pissed, Eva. This is bullshit. I've done nothing wrong. These pricks are playing with my life."

"Shhh."

"Yeah, I know," he groused.

"You could call your consulate," she said, not sounding at all like she meant it. "Maybe they'd send those soldiers up here."

Roman removed the phone and its battery from his pocket. He eyed the two items for a moment before sliding them back into his jeans. "I would but they don't even believe I saw a murder. So, why would they come help me? Hell, they'd probably come arrest me and take me to the Mallorcans."

Roman walked to the corners and eyed both men again. He pulled the stairwell door back open, staring at the tool tray on the floor. His wheels turning, he gnawed on his bottom lip.

"What is it?" she asked.

"I'm going to throw an idea out there," he said, "and you can say no and it won't bother me."

She narrowed her eyes. "Say no to what?"

"First, hold the door open, please." He walked to the bushes at the rear of the hotel one more time, then eyed the alleyway across the street. "Yeah," he said to himself. "It'll work."

"What will work?"

"This." He explained his plan.

As he spoke, Eva's frown built into a wily grin.

Roman produced his prepaid phone and the battery. "We'll need to use my prepaid and your regular phone."

They mated the batteries to the phones, powered them on and set them to vibrate.

"Are you sure you want to try this?" she asked.

"Fuck it."

Perhaps—just maybe—Roman could seize back some modicum of control with this incredibly risky plan.

If only he felt as confident as he sounded.

* * *

Roman Littlepage had never been more scared than he was at this exact moment. Sure, there'd been periods of prolonged fear. When he was a child, he went through a phase when he was absolutely certain there was a monster under his bed. And that monster had a friend—an even bigger, scarier monster—who lived in Roman's closet. Each night, the very second Roman's parents departed his room, both monsters went active. Over time, Roman developed what he thought was a unique system for dealing with the monsters: provided he kept his eyes squeezed tightly shut, and the covers up over his head, the monsters were powerless. It was his own little force field, utilized by children the world over. Sometimes Roman would awaken, discovering he'd come out from under his force field while sleeping. Panicked, he'd immediately dive back under the covers.

It was a good system. It kept him alive.

Roman religiously employed his system for a full year and the monsters never devoured him. For all he knew, the two beasts eventually gave up and moved on to some other unfortunate kid up the street. Roman had always secretly hoped they'd made their home in that bully, Joe Horab's, house. Maybe that's why Joe's family up and moved to Upstate New York. It wasn't long before the hidden monsters were supplanted by a cache of tattered Playboys. As the years passed, a completely different nighttime game took place after Roman's door was shut. And locked.

Back to the fear at hand...

As Roman hurried to the buildings opposite the hotel, he tried to recall the last time his personal anxiety had reached this level—and he couldn't do it. He'd had jolts of fear before: nearly getting in a car wreck; seeing his children take a bad fall; going over the highest obstacle way back in basic training. And more recently...

Jumping out of a hotel window due to a gun-wielding murderer...

But never protracted fear such as this.

This terror resonated from deep in his gut, and it was made worse by the fact that Roman could end it at any time. He didn't have to go through with any of this. And though Roman had no experience with this sort of thing, making an uneducated guess, he put his odds of survival at 50/50.

Before he'd made the plan with Eva, he'd reasoned it out with himself:

These people are going to kill you, sure as shit. If you think you'll continue to elude an organization that has the resources to quickly kill Mitch Cardell in Houston, you're being naïve. They're going to find you, and when they do, they're going to jam that knife in and out of your belly. And, chances are, they'll take their sweet time letting you die.

Okay, Roman agreed, *but if they're so damned resourceful, why are the same two men here hunting me? Why haven't they brought in more thugs? If they can reach out to Houston and kill someone in less than an hour, why isn't Mallorca crawling with killers? Why is it these same two psychos?*

And where's the one-armed man?

Roman couldn't answer any of these questions, but what he could do, what he mustered every ounce of inner persuasion to do, was convince himself to go through with the plan.

Do not be a pussy. Do not chicken out. Grab your balls and do this. If you don't, you will die. Yes, it's a bit of a paradox, Roman. If you do this, you may very well die—now. But if you don't do it, you will die—either now or later.

Such an appealing menu of choices.

By this time, Roman had reached his mark. He'd ducked down and walked across the north end of the parking lot without incident. Across the way, he peered back at the curly-haired killer. He hadn't seen Roman. Now Roman wended his way around the block. After a two-minute walk, he was standing between two buildings, about half a block from the parked Mercedes where the cruel-looking man sat smoking, his back to Roman as he continued his surveillance on the south end of the hotel.

Roman recalled the cruel-looking man. His head was shaved and he had an angular face with a downturned mouth. Roman remembered the icy blue eyes and the way the man had spat on the murder victim.

This is who you're getting ready to ambush, Roman. You against a professional killer who spits on fresh corpses. Are you fucking mad? He's going to gut you like a pig and eat your liver with a rusty spoon. He's going to anticipate your every move and counter them viciously and brutally. This is a mismatch if there ever was one. Him beating you is like a vicious hunter clubbing baby seals. He's going to—

Stop it!

Your life's at stake. And it's worth your getting out of your comfort zone.

To hell with thinking about it any longer.

Roman slid the prepaid phone from his pocket and sent the text message that would act as the signal.

Then he slid the box-cutter knife from his pocket and extended the blade.

Roman eyed the blade. The box cutter was typical of one found in a toolbox. It had a long blade with score marks, made that way so the user could break off each section as it dulled. After taking it from the tool tray in the stairwell, Roman had broken the blade. He viewed the sharp, unused portion of the blade.

Do you have the balls to slice a man's skin with this knife? Could you hold it up against the man's neck and rip it across with all your might, cutting skin, slicing through his jugular and then feeling the blade scratch across the man's hard larynx?

Do you have that in you, Roman?

Do you?

You better.

* * *

Eva had let her hair down. Though it was wavy and unkempt from being bound in a hair band, it bounced in its blonde brilliance as she walked—strutted actually. She carried the paper bag of fruit, having shooed all the fruit flies from the bag. And now she paraded through the parking lot, heading directly in front of the Mercedes parked at the lot's corner. She pretended to be on the phone, which made her grip on the bag precarious.

When she was in full view of the cruel-looking man in the Mercedes, Eva dropped the fruit, sending oranges and pomegranates rolling. Still pretending to talk on the phone, she began to gather the wayward fruit, bending over with her derrière, hardly concealed by her short shorts, up in the air and on full display for the cruel-looking man whose surveillance had hopefully just taken on a new subject.

From his vantage point behind the Mercedes, Roman could see the driver straighten upon seeing Eva bend over. The man sat up, peering over the steering wheel as he drank in the image of the blonde beauty.

Though petrified, Roman began to move.

He crept forward while Eva put on her show, slowly picking up the fruit one piece at a time while speaking German into her phone.

Roman had reached the rear quarter panel of the Mercedes. His mouth was dry. His face twitched with fear. Each breath came in short bursts. He squatted low, peering under the car, able to see Eva gathering the last of her fruit. After saying a silent, five-word prayer, Roman lurched upward. He thrust each arm into the open window of the Mercedes, earning a grunt of protest from the cruel-looking man.

Using his dominant right hand, Roman grasped the top of the man's head and yanked it backward. Using his left, Roman pressed the blade tightly against the man's throat.

Roman had now passed the threshold. He was at a critical juncture.

He wanted to say something threatening, the way they always did in the movies, but his tongue was too swollen to speak. He could barely make a sound. Thankfully, the man didn't fight back in any way. He sat there, letting Roman hold the blade the way a customer allows an old-fashioned barber to shave his neck.

Eva was done with her ruse and joined Roman at the driver's window.

"Put your hands at the top of the steering wheel," she commanded in English.

The cruel-looking man was a cool sort. Though he made no sudden movements and complied with her command, he seemed unaffected by having a blade to his throat.

Speaking of the blade, Roman saw a dot of blood from underneath, realizing he was pushing so hard he'd cut the man.

"Hurry," Roman rasped, feeling his knees shaking. A small rivulet of blood now trickled downward from his blade.

Eva stretched the long white zip-tie she'd taken from the toolbox around the man's two wrists. "If you touch that horn, he's cutting your throat," she warned as she cinched the zip-tie tight. "Now, slowly move your hands down between your legs and keep them there."

The man's icy blue eyes, a serpent's eyes, flicked to her. His mouth ticked upward as he complied, pressing his hands between his legs as he tilted his head back even farther, as if inviting Roman to slice it open.

"Who are you?" Roman wheezed. He was on the verge of hyperventilation.

The man said nothing. Roman asked again, his voice recovering slightly as he expanded on his query. "Who are you and who do you work for?"

Nothing.

"Cut him deeper," Eva said, sounding every bit the experienced surgeon in a busy operating room.

Roman whipped his head around, his eyes wide.

"Just gash him so he knows you're willing to do it," she whispered.

Upon hearing these words, Roman felt queasy and faint. He could feel a gathering of saliva in his formerly dry mouth, the way he always did just before he threw up.

While Roman did all he could to maintain his position, Eva leaned down and used her own hand to press the knife further into the man's neck skin. "Where is the one-armed man?" she asked, lightly sawing the utility blade back and forth.

The cruel-looking man grunted in pain. And that was all it took.

The next thing Roman knew, he'd fallen to his side, viewing the undercarriage of the spinning Mercedes as the orange utility knife clattered down in front of him.

Actually, the Mercedes wasn't spinning—it was simply Roman's equilibrium. And he'd banged his head on the asphalt when he'd fallen, thankfully not in the same spot as last time.

Roman noticed Eva's arm take a swipe down to grab the knife. It had fallen and tumbled under the car; she wasn't able to reach it. He rotated his eyes upward, seeing her arms reaching into the Mercedes. She seemed to be struggling with the driver.

Roman was so woozy that none of this registered properly. He knew he should be worried but his thoughts were actually quite serene.

It kinda feels good here on the ground—so little pressure. Maybe I can just close my eyes for a quick nap. No worries down here. No more worries…

He shut his eyes. Opened them.

What is that annoying sound?

"Come on!" Eva yelled, tugging on his left arm, trying to get him to stand.

That sound again. And again. Alarm clock? Fire alarm?

"Get up!" Eva implored. "His partner is probably on his way."

Then it hit Roman—the cruel-looking man was sounding the car horn.

Chapter Ten

By the time Roman regained his senses, he was up and moving, limping on the sidewalk with Eva urgently tugging his hand. His level of consciousness was similar to how one feels in post-op, when you're awake but you know you probably won't remember anything later. His legs were working but everything seemed fuzzy or blurry.

"Come on, Roman," Eva said, continuing to tug him. "Are you okay?"

He saw a sidewalk sign. With a great deal of concentration he was able to see the sign was advertising food and coffee. Whoever had drawn today's specials had done a nice job depicting a cup of java next to plate of over-easy eggs.

"*Los huevos y café?*" he asked aloud. Roman had taken three years of Spanish.

Eva gave his arm a tremendous yank. "Roman, wake up!"

He looked all around, seeing the small alleyway that led to the hotel parking lot.

"Look at me, Roman," Eva said. "We're in big trouble. I need you to focus."

Then, it all came back to him. *The curly-haired killer. The cruel-looking man. The knife. The blood. The danger.*

Roman remembered having just come through here, on his way to the Mercedes. He remembered everything, up until the part when he collapsed. From there, his recollections were jumbled—nothing more than still-frame snippets.

"Did you kill him?" Roman asked, pulling her hand to stop her. He felt nauseous. "I'm gonna be sick."

He walked into a gap between two buildings.

"Deep breaths," Eva said.

Roman leaned against one of the buildings, taking massive breaths as his nausea subsided. They were at a street corner, the late morning sun beaming down on them both. A number of people walked the sidewalks, blithely going about their business, having no clue of what just happened less than a block away.

"Eva, tell me the truth, did you kill him?"

"No. You dropped the knife. I tried to keep him from honking the horn but he was too strong."

"That's right," Roman said, recalling. He still wasn't thinking clearly. Then a sudden spike of fear hit him. "Did he get out of the car?"

"I kept looking back and he did get out the car just as we turned on this street. But his hands were bound and he ran in the other direction."

"I'm sure he was running to his partner. We've got to get the hell out of—"

Roman was cut off midsentence by the look of sheer horror on Eva's face. Her mouth opened wide and she let out a short chirp. The entire sensation was strange because, at that exact moment, Roman was twisted around to his left as if someone extremely strong had thudded into his ribs with a lowered shoulder.

What hit me?

A fraction of a second later, he heard the report echo between the buildings.

Gunshot.

Few people, even those in distress, expect to get shot—especially when on a city street. And when one doesn't see it coming—and lives through it—it can take a moment to process. In this case, it took Roman a hair under two seconds. He turned, seeing the curly-haired killer running toward him, coming from the direction of the hotel. In his hand was a black handgun. Just behind him was the cruel-looking man, his hands still bound by the zip tie.

They were no more than 50 meters away.

Eva shrieked and shoved Roman around the corner.

"He shot me," Roman mumbled. He held his right hand over the wound. It was well below his heart and off to his side.

By this time, everyone in the nearby vicinity had stopped and stared at Roman. While Roman and Eva had certainly heard the report of the pistol, the sound hadn't been much louder than a backfire and it didn't seem many people realized Roman had been shot. All they saw was a man with a bloodstain on his shirt and his lady friend screaming.

But Eva wasn't screaming anymore. Now she looked determined as her head whipped all around.

"Hay un francotirador allí!" Eva shouted, pointing in the opposite direction from where the gunshot had originated.

Her exclamation certainly garnered a reaction. Translated, it meant, "There's a sniper over there!" In the modern climate of mass shootings and terrorism, no one seemed to question her statement—especially since Roman was dripping blood.

There were approximately 40 people in the vicinity of the intersection and, upon hearing her words, nearly all of them ran screaming down the street. Due to Eva's quick thinking and misdirection, the civilians headed straight toward the onrushing killers.

Her smokescreen was effective.

"Come on," Eva yelled, grabbing Roman's hand and pulling him into the nearest store. It was one of the many small convenience stores that dotted the island, selling drinks, snacks and sunscreen to the endless sea of vacationers.

Eva spoke in rapid Spanish to the woman behind the counter as she led Roman straight through the store and into the stockroom in the back. There, Eva snatched a stocking apron from a pegboard. Biting her bottom lip, she glanced around before seeing an open box of white Hefty kitchen bags. Her hands moving feverishly, she yanked a bag from the roll and tore it in several places.

"Here," Eva said, placing the neck string of the apron over Roman's head. Next, she folded the bag over several times and pressed it against his shirt.

"Use your left elbow to hold the bag and the apron over the wound."

Roman obeyed and hissed from the contact pain.

"The pressure will help. Trust me." Eva glanced back to the front of the store. She could see the store clerk speaking to someone at the door and pointing to the rear.

"Let's go," Eva said. She took Roman's right hand and exited the back door. They turned left into the back alley.

As he attempted to run, Roman waited for a bullet to the back but it never came. He'd forgotten about the pain in his ankle, but it was still affecting his gait. Much more pressing was the searing agony on his side. After passing several buildings, Eva led him into an alleyway and dead ahead was the cruel-looking man's Mercedes.

"Hey!" Roman protested. "I don't want to go back there again."

Eva didn't stop to speak. She simply tugged him along.

Before Roman knew it, she'd yanked open the passenger door of the Mercedes and eyed him urgently.

"Get in."

"Are you serious?"

"There's no time." Eva shoved him and he grunted as he sat. Sitting made the pain worse, as if someone was holding a smoldering piece of steel to his ribs. He clenched his teeth, amazed at the way the pain pulsed through him in waves.

Eva ran around the car, hopping into the driver's seat. She pressed the starter button as the Stuttgart product roared to life. Ten seconds later, they'd exited the hotel parking lot on the opposite side from where the killers had shot Roman. Eva doubled back to the north and settled in at a slow cruise on a side street.

"How'd you know the keys were in it?" Roman grunted.

She lifted the chunky key fob from the center console. "I saw it when we zip-tied him."

Using the button to his right, Roman reclined his seat just a bit.

"You okay?"

"I don't know."

"Do you feel faint?"

"Not while I'm leaning back."

"Okay. Keep talking to me and keep pressure on that wound. As long as you don't lose too much blood, I think you'll be okay. Show it to me."

"I don't want to."

"Do it now."

Roman gingerly removed his hand from her makeshift pressure bandage. She reached over and yanked his shirt up, making him yell out.

"Sorry," she said, touching her own side. "Let's see…left side has a lung and the left edge of your stomach." Eva looked at the wound again. "Too high for a kidney. You breathing okay?"

"Hurts."

"But no bubbling sound? Does it feel wet when you breathe?"

"No."

"Okay. Cover it back up. You might have gotten lucky. Do you feel bones clicking?"

"No."

"If it missed ribs, then we're talking incredibly lucky. We'll have to wait and see on that and the stomach. Resume pressure."

"Where are we going?"

"I don't know…but we have to ditch this car soon. They might be able to track it." She merged onto a wide ribbon of highway.

"Eva…"

"Yes?"

"You saved my life back there."

Eva eased the car into the center lane as the mountains loomed. "All I did was help you run away."

"But when you yelled what you yelled in Spanish, and all the people started running…"

She allowed a tight grin. "I said a sniper was across the street. But I pointed in the opposite direction."

"Right, to impede those psychos' progress. But how, Eva? How would you possibly know to do such a thing?"

She looked at him. "Back in Germany, after all the terrorist attacks across Europe, it's the public's biggest fear. I've seen terror panic even strike the E.R. before."

Roman reclined his seat even more. He turned and eyed the blonde beauty as she drove. Perhaps she'd be better as a surgeon than just a nurse. If he made it through all this, perhaps he should repay her by sending her to medical school.

Feeling the yearning of sleep, Roman shut his eyes. "Eva?"

"Yes?"

"What kind of nurse are you?"

"Trauma…I told you that."

"I know…just making sure." He paused. "Eva?"

"Yes?"

"Am I going to die?"

"Not on my shift, you're not." She popped him on the leg. "Stay awake, Roman. We're getting ready to get out of this car."

"Then what?"

"We're going to take a train."

"A train? The island's only like twenty miles across."

"There's a train. Goes through a long tunnel under the mountains. I know because my friends and I took it."

He looked at her before looking down at his bloody shirt. "How will I pull that off looking like this?"

"We'll think of something."

* * *

Shortly after lunch, Roman Littlepage and his friend Eva boarded the Ferrocarril de Sóller at the small Palma Railway Station. Neither person looked like they did 30 minutes before. If someone were to see them, they would mark them as two construction workers of some sort, heading to work. Both wore jumpsuits, hardhats and wraparound sunglasses. In fact, Eva's hair was so expertly tucked up into her hardhat, and her jumpsuit so baggy, that it was difficult to determine her gender.

Once seated at the rear of the primarily tourist train, they removed food from their lunch pails and had a quiet lunch as the train chugged north, first over the Palmanyola plain and then through the 13 tunnels of the Serra de Tramuntana. Above their heads, up and down the sides of mountains, were some of the steepest and curviest roadways on the planet. The roads were so steep and curvy that many of the world's top cycling teams trained in Mallorca. But the tunnel below was straight as an arrow and cool in its center, and the cool provided a brief respite for Roman.

The cool was welcome because, despite managing to eat half of his lunch, he felt as if he were on the verge of death.

Earlier, Eva had parked the Mercedes in the basement of an under-construction concrete parking deck that was nearing completion. The bottom of the deck was in use and she tucked the car up against the back wall. Parking there was Roman's idea. His hope was the concrete would obscure the car's anti-theft locator—if it even had one. Eva had then snatched the jumpsuits and lunch pails from a nearby work truck. She'd left a small wad of money in the truck and, jumpsuits on, Roman and Eva walked—limped, in Roman's case—several hundred meters to the train station, where they purchased their tickets to Sóller. While they'd waited 15 minutes for the train, Eva visited a nearby pharmacy. Back at the train station, she went to the bathroom with Roman, locking the door and applying a dressing to his worsening wound. Though it wasn't bleeding profusely anymore, the wound had begun to redden at its edges.

Preventing infection would be their greatest challenge.

As the crowd at the station had grown, Roman had shut his eyes and leaned the hardhat over his head. To most people, he looked like a worker dreading the afternoon ahead. But in reality, he was gritting his teeth, counting the seconds as the waves of pain radiated through his body.

And now, at Eva's urging, he'd managed to eat almost half of the worker's lunch. Whoever the man or woman was, they'd packed some sort of chicken roll up that any other time Roman would have found tasty. He swilled the entire bottle of accompanying water and tried his best to take in the view as the train made its way directly through a picturesque town.

"This is Sóller," Eva whispered.

"Till you mentioned it, I hadn't heard of it," he grunted.

"It's an old port town. Most regular tourists head to Palma, El Arenal and Magaluf. Sóller, however, is mainly for the wealthy. There are all kind of spas, resorts and multi-million euro estates nearby."

"How's that gonna help us? I'm pretty much out of cash. If I use my credit card, they'll know where we are."

"They won't know if I pay. They don't know who I am."

"Not yet," he gasped, "but give 'em time." Each word was a struggle.

The train slowed as it approached the station. Roman removed the hardhat and pressed sweat from his hair. He wasn't sure how he was going to walk.

"Eva, even though we parked underground, they're going to find that Mercedes. And when they do, they'll get your fingerprints and they'll know who you are. Then, they'll run your credit card and, bam, we're caught."

"Who said I was going to use a credit card?"

He looked at her, watching as she went inside the jumpsuit and came out fanning 5 or 6 of 50-euro bills.

"Where did you get that?" he grunted, glancing around.

"When I went to the pharmacy, I visited the ATM and took out three-hundred euro."

"I don't want you to use your own money."

"It's okay."

"I'll pay you back," Roman replied, not having the energy to protest. He looked at Eva, watching as she gathered both lunch boxes now that the train had stopped. She really was amazing and, despite his injury, he was well aware of just how lucky he was to have met her.

"Come on," she said. "You can do it. Just get up and get moving. It'll hurt at first."

After he'd groaned and grumbled his way off the train, Roman stopped her. "Eva, I know enough to know that I'd be dead now if I hadn't met you."

She adjusted a few wisps of escaping hair, tucking them back up under her hard hat. "Come on," she said. "You can thank me later."

They headed south, towards the charming center of Sóller, following the streetcar-like tracks that the narrow gauge train had just taken through the town's center. From the distance, Roman could see a rustic stone church near the middle of town. There were mountains towering over three sides of the attractive Spanish port, framing the picturesque locale in a setting suitable for a skilled oil painter.

And though he was viewing a scene ready for canvas, Roman Littlepage limped toward the town in a worker's jumpsuit. He was covered in odorous sweat and down his left side leaked his own sticky blood from a gunshot wound. Roman knew he was probably concussed, and he also had a sprained ankle, a gash on his arm and a collection of bruises and scrapes.

But his physical condition wasn't his worst predicament—it was his situation. There was an evil organization bent on killing him. And despite all he and Eva had done to evade them, Roman knew they would soon find him. They'd found him before and he was certain they'd find him again.

Unfortunately, Roman was correct.

Chapter Eleven

Eva chose a small hotel on the edge of Sóller. Before she went in to arrange for a room, she led Roman to a nearby plaza surrounded by a teeming flower garden. Roman sat on a park bench and watched Eva as she removed the jumpsuit and used a few items from her bag in an effort to make herself presentable. After toweling off her face with a wet wipe, she used a bit of powder and lipstick. She worked on her hair for a moment before shrugging and muttering something in German.

Roman dipped his head and grunted.

"Are you okay?" she asked.

"Just hurts like hell."

"I'll be as quick as I can."

Roman watched as she hurried across the street and up the stairs into the hotel. He eyed the outside of the building, counting five floors. The brass plaque at the front of the hotel advertised 3 stars. In Europe, 3 stars typically indicated much higher quality than 3 stars in the United States. On both corners of the hotel, Roman noticed surveillance cameras. He began to look around at the streetlights and buildings of the charming old town, counting a staggering seven cameras just from his vantage point.

Leaning his head all the way back, Roman shut his eyes and tried to make sense of his future. What was his end game? Would anyone help him or was the goal at this point simply surviving the next hour?

Each hour is a victory. I remember guys who'd made it through Ranger School telling me that. Their ultimate prize was graduation and the coveted Ranger tab on their left shoulder. My ultimate prize is a heart that continues to beat and a mind that still functions.

Let's just say for a minute that I turned myself in to the Mallorcans. Surely I could get a good enough attorney to disprove the murder charges related to the old hotel owner. Because the attorney would beg the question, what was my motive? Why would I kill someone? And now that I know the connection between the restaurant owner and the one-armed man, I'd imagine that the murder I reported could be delved into further—despite a lack of evidence.

So, am I making a mistake by running? If I just stop now and turn myself in, maybe the State Department will actually intervene and we can all work together to straighten the whole thing out.

Right?

Two orange and black birds landed in the nearby grass, scuffling. He couldn't tell if it was two males, fighting over territory—or if it was a male and female and this was some sort of precursor to their mating. Was it a fight, or was it love?

Roman kept watching, applying their conflict to his own situation.

There's just no way to tell. Yes, if I turn myself in, it's possible that everything would come out in the wash. Sure, there'd be some red tape, but in the end I'm absolutely innocent. That always comes out, right?

Wrong.

What if it doesn't come out in the wash? What if that curly-haired killer left damning evidence proving that I killed the hotel owner? What if they charge me with murder and the U.S. State Department washes its hands of me? What then?

"Dammit!" he yelled aloud, making the two scuffling birds take wing.

Feeling reckless, Roman unzipped the jumpsuit midway down his torso. He reached his right hand inside, finding the soaked bandage that Eva had taped on. It felt like a washcloth soaked in warm oil.

A different voice filled his mind: *Are you alive, Roman? Are you still with us?*

He gritted his teeth and pressed away the bloody gauze, pushing his index finger into the wound.

Ahhh, there it is. A nice little hole.

Roman could feel the ribs and cartilage and gristle. He scraped his fingernail back and forth, yelling out in pain as he burrowed his finger further in, causing his body to spasm as flares of pain jolted his torso.

"Stop!" Eva yelled. "What are you doing?" She'd just been walking back. Grasping his shoulders, she shoved him to a straight sitting position and eyed him in horror.

"Why were you doing that?"

Roman felt nauseous. The pain of what he'd just done now began to register in waves, just like they'd done soon after he'd been shot. He leaned forward and vomited up the small amount of food he'd eaten.

Eva waved off an Asian couple who were obviously asking if Roman was okay, but doing so in what sounded like Mandarin Chinese. She leaned down and faced him. "Roman, talk to me."

"I'm screwed, Eva," he said, a string of spittle hanging from his lower lip. "I'm absolutely and completely screwed. If I run, they find me. If I turn myself in, I go to prison."

"So, you combat it by reinjuring yourself?"

"Pain's the only thing right now that feels real. Everything else is a bad dream."

Eva pulled his jumpsuit open and winced. "You opened it up wider than it's been."

"Yeah," he grunted, pressing his elbow down over the wound. "Hurts so good."

She held up a key. "I got the last room. We're going up there and we're going to get your side fixed up." Eve handed him a few towelettes from her bag to clean the blood from his hand. "Don't give up, Roman. Stay with me. This isn't over."

"Feels pretty close."

She tilted her head. "What were you thinking about while I was gone? Why have your thoughts turned dark?"

"Other than you, Eva, I feel like everyone else, and everything else, is against me. No matter what I do, it just gets worse."

She seemed exasperated. "Can you at least walk?"

"Yeah."

"Just keep that outfit on and go around the back of the hotel. It slopes down and there's a service door around back. I'll go through the hotel and let you in down there."

She wadded a ball of clean tissues from a plastic packet. "Use your elbow to press these against the wound."

After obeying her latest order, Roman stood, retching dry heaves onto the cobblestone path. He then began to totter toward the hotel.

"Can you make it?"

"Piece of cake," he muttered, keeping his elbow clamped to his side.

She went in through the front of the hotel and was waiting at the utility entrance by the time Roman staggered around the corner to the shady rear of the hotel. The elevator was small, suitable for only two people. He could barely stand as they ascended to the top floor. Eva led him to the room down a short, carpeted hallway. Inside, she turned on the shower and told him to get in and to clean himself liberally.

"You want to give me a minute?" he asked.

"No time for privacy," she replied, snapping her fingers and sounding like she was on shift in the emergency room.

Roman unsteadily stripped naked and accepted her help to get into the stand-up shower. The water burned as it coursed over the wound.

"Move your arm," she commanded.

Once the wound was fully soaked, it stopped hurting so badly. Roman used the bar of soap on his matted head of hair first.

"Use soap on the wound," she said. "I know it's perfumed and not ideal, but we need it clean."

He hissed as he washed the injury. Glancing down, he saw the wound clearly for the first time. It consisted of two holes, several inches apart. The area between the holes was quite red and both holes burped blood with every beat of his heart. The exit wound, at the rear, was worse. It had tiny pieces of flesh hanging off like bits of cheese from a hot pizza. Just seeing it made him feel faint.

"You okay?" she asked.

"Almost done."

He washed the remainder of his body, even while the bathroom began to spin. He gripped the shower door handle for stability.

"Roman?"

"I'm good," he muttered. "I'm just…feeling…tired…"

"Roman, that door won't hold you. Roman, give me your hand. Roman!"

"I…I…I aaaammm gone beeeee okaaaaaay."

The world went topsy-turvy.

Slip. Slide. Clunk.

Black.

* * *

"Roman? Wake up." A shake. "C'mon, Roman."

Roman opened his eyes, squinting due to the bright light and the dry, scratchy sensation under his eyelids. His mouth was dry and pain emanated from several areas of his body. He was growing used to waking up like this. Surprisingly, he felt only a slight tugging pain around his gunshot wound. Eva stood over him, alternating her vision between both of his rapidly blinking eyes.

"My eyes feel like they have sand in them."

"You're dehydrated, but not for long. Just keep blinking and they'll lubricate."

"Is it okay if I move?"

"Yes, but be careful."

Roman felt a tugging on his arm and noticed a clear tube running to the top of the bed. He turned his eyes upward, seeing a nearly full bag hanging from the bedpost. "Where'd you get an I.V.?" he asked.

"That's actually your *second* bag."

"How'd you get that?" he asked, scooting backward as she propped several pillows behind him.

"After I cleaned you up, I went back out into the square. I learned that there's a fire department about a block away. I walked over there and convinced a fireman that I'm a nurse and my best friend had a dangerous hangover. I guess I flirted a little bit and convinced him to give me two bags of Ringers and a fluid admin set."

Roman nodded, dumbfounded. "How long was I out?"

"An hour maybe? It was a combination of pain and exhaustion. You barely even stirred when I stuck your arm." She winked. "Got you on the first try, too. You have nice veins."

Again Roman looked up at the I.V. "Thank you…I don't know how to…"

"To what?"

"Express my appreciation. You've saved my life."

"I didn't, actually. The hydration will give you more energy. And bandaged, that wound will eventually clot over. You're just lucky he wasn't using hollow points."

He touched his side. "Feels a lot better."

"You got off about as easily as any gunshot victim could. The bullet really never went below the dermis. If it had been a hollow point, it would've mushroomed and really torn you up."

Roman glanced under the sheet. He was naked.

"May I have a towel?"

Eva went to the bathroom and returned with a fresh bath towel. He placed it over his midsection and took stock. Even when he moved, the bullet wound felt pretty good. His entire midsection was tightly wrapped with tape and bandages. The pressure on the wound was what seemed to do the trick.

"If we get you the right kind of shirt, no one will be able to tell you're bandaged."

"Did you sew me up?"

She shook her head. "Medical tape. Gauze. TipStop compression bandage. Bought it all at the *farmacia* around the corner when I went down for the I.V. I even loaded your wound with an antiseptic that burns like hell and you didn't even wake up. That's how exhausted you are."

"Don't I need stitches?"

"You'll be all right for now. As long as you don't get infected, I don't see those wounds giving you much trouble."

Roman looked around, seeing several hand towels with blood on them.

"What will we do about all the blood?"

"If we stay here a day or two, I'll distract the maid and you can grab some towels off her cart. We'll toss these."

Roman relaxed into the stack of pillows. "What time is it?"

"Two in the afternoon."

"I've got to get in touch with Wendy."

"Wendy?"

"My ex-wife. While I was out, I had this terrible dream…"

"Didn't she go somewhere safe?"

"Yeah, but I'm still scared for her and the kids, especially after all that's gone on."

"Calling her could be dangerous."

"If she went where I told her to go, then I can call there and not her cell. They wouldn't know to tap that phone."

Eva raised her eyebrows. "It's a big risk, but I understand."

"Okay. Maybe I'll wait a little while." Roman felt intense hunger. "Is there any way you could get us some food?"

"Sure. What do you want?"

"Anything. So hungry."

"There's a pizza place nearby. I also saw a bistro near the flower plaza."

"Seriously, I'll eat anything. I'm starving. And can you grab me a t-shirt?"

"Yes. I'll go now. Despite the I.V. I want you to drink that entire bottle of water before I get back," she commanded, referencing a liter bottle by the bed. "If you feel faint, move those pillows and lie flat."

"Thanks for everything, Eva."

She smiled from the door. "Remember what you said earlier, about everything going against you?"

"Yeah."

"Do you still feel that way?"

"I feel better," he answered, "but I still don't know what to do."

"Let's eat, then we'll decide what's next."

"Good idea."

Eva departed. Roman eyed the door, watching the "do not disturb" tag swing in her wake. There'd been something odd about their exchange just now. It was a slight distance of some sort, as if Eva were miffed about something.

Was it the mention of Wendy? Maybe Eva's a little jealous?

He shook his head.

That couldn't be it, could it? Eva was stunningly beautiful and Roman still had a hard time understanding what she saw in him. Why would she be jealous?

He touched his wound, appreciating her skill.

You got lucky with this one, Roman. Jealous or not, she's been a literal lifesaver, no matter how she tries to minimize the wound.

After swilling water, he eyed the room phone. *There's no way they know where Wendy's hiding.*

Screw it.

Using his calling card, he dialed U.S. directory assistance and phoned the Page's river house. The phone rang six times before voicemail answered. He looked at his watch.

Seven in the morning…they're still sleeping.

Roman decided to try Mike again.

Grunting slightly, Roman swung his legs off the bed and sat on the side of the mattress. He looked at his swollen ankle, seeing flecks of blue and yellow on both sides from the bruising. He tried to move it, greeted with pain and stiffness.

Roman lifted the receiver and again went through the lengthy sequence of numbers. He eventually reached the AT&T access number and from there he dialed Mike's cellphone number. Finally he was greeted with a U.S. ringing sound and, after only two rings, Mike answered the phone. The smile on Roman's face actually hurt it was so wide.

"Mike, where the hell have you been?" Roman asked, suddenly realizing he'd probably have to break the bad news about Mitch.

"Is this Roman?"

"Yeah."

"Roman, this is Jason."

Jason was Mike's younger brother.

An ominous bell tolled in Roman's mind. Something was wrong.

"Jason? Why are you answering Mike's cellphone?"

"We've been trying to reach you, Roman." A delay. "I'm afraid I've got some awful news. We found Mike last night. He'd been—"

Roman dropped the phone as if it were diseased.

There was no way. There was simply no way! This had to be a nightmare. Had to be.

No...God, no. Please!

Jason's voice was tinny from the dropped phone. "Roman? Roman?"

Taking deep breaths, Roman lifted the phone back to his ear.

"Roman, you there?"

"Jason..."

"Did you hear what I said?"

"Could you please say it again?"

Jason paused, struggling to get the words out. "We found Mike here in his condo. He'd been murdered, Roman. The police suspect a robbery but we're not so sure. One of the detectives told us, off the record, that it looks odd for a homicide. Listen, I know this is a sudden blow but I have to ask...do you have any idea of any enemies Mike might have had? Since my kids were born, I didn't talk to him as much as I should have. I'm sure you spoke with him more often and we know you'd just gone on vacation together. We're hoping you know something."

"Jason, I have to get off the phone right now." Roman licked his lips. "This sounds crazy, but I need you to tell the police that our friend Mitch Cardell was also murdered, but in Houston."

"What? When?"

"Right after he got back from our trip. I'm still here in Mallorca. Jason, please...tell them to call the Houston Police, then to report both murders to the State Department and also the CIA."

"Wait...Roman...what the hell are you talking about?"

"Listen to me, Jason! Do everything I said. Something awful happened here," Roman said, his voice breaking. "And I think the people involved murdered Mitch and Mike because of it."

"That's crazy."

"I know, and I agree. Please, do as I say, Jason."

"Have you guys been mixed up in something illegal?"

"No. Nothing like that. I witnessed a crime and now the people who did it are trying to find me. I have to go, have to get off this phone. Remember: Mitch Cardell, Houston, State Department, CIA. All of it's related." Roman dipped his head. "I'm sorry about your brother, Jason. He was the first friend I made in the Army and one of my best friends on earth."

Roman replaced the hotel phone in the receiver. He reclined onto the bed and lay there, painfully unable to cry.

It was the blackest moment of his life.

Chapter Twelve

After five minutes of silence, Roman rolled over and stared at the phone. He wanted to try Wendy again but he was afraid. Afraid to find out the truth. Afraid to find out what might have happened. Afraid of his worst fears realized. Was his family even at the Pages' river home? Were they safe? Were they just sleeping in? Or had the one-armed man and his organization found them? Had they found Roman's family and then…

Oh, God, please…no.

He sat up, bolstering himself.

You have to call, Roman. It's either happened or it hasn't. Your awareness of it changes nothing. C'mon…man up…dial the numbers. This isn't the monster under your bed. Face your fears.

Roman obeyed his inner voice, going through the same process as before. He'd not written the number down so he had to call directory assistance once again. After several false starts, he finally reached an AT&T operator and asked him to look up the Page household on Cobb Hollow Road, in Ashland City, Tennessee.

"Yes, sir, I have the number."

"Excellent. Please give it to me," he requested. After he'd written the number down, he provided his calling card number and asked the operator to ring the phone. He listened.

The phone rang a number of times before voicemail kicked in again. After a moment, the AT&T operator told Roman there was no answer.

"Try it again, please."

"Hold on." A moment later, the operator returned. "No answer, sir."

Roman again looked at his watch. It was still quite early in Nashville—there was a good chance they were sleeping. He thanked the operator and hung up. He again reclined on the bed, his mind awash in thoughts of his family and Mike.

I hope they're okay. I hope the reason they're not answering isn't because they're all—

The phone rang, startling him so badly he flinched. The flinch caused a jolt of pain to go through his side.

Roman stared at the phone. His first instinct was to *not* answer it.

But why not answer it? Maybe it's Wendy.

How could it be Wendy? Caller ID won't work on an operator-assisted international call.

Or does it?

I have to speak with my family. I have to take the chance.

Roman lifted the phone. "Hello?"

A woman's voice. "Mister Roman Littlepage?"

"Who is this?"

"If you're Roman Littlepage, I need to verify your identity. Please give me the full names of both your parents."

"Wait a minute...who the hell are *you*?"

"Apologies. I'm Special Agent Blasowich with the Central Intelligence Agency." The agent's accent was indistinct and seemed to have a tinge of British intonation.

"The CIA?"

"Yes, sir."

"How do I know you're with the CIA? And how'd you get this number?"

"There are ways we could verify my identity and role for you, sir, but there's not enough time."

"So, you want to verify me, but I can't verify you? To hell with that."

"Mister Littlepage, we listened to the recording of your distress call to us and we need to speak with you about it."

"Then, let's just trust each other, okay? I'm Roman Littlepage. No games. Now, again...how did you get this number?"

"We traced the call you made to your friend, Michael Singleton."

"So, you know he was murdered?"

"We do. And just as you theorized, we believe both your friends were killed in an effort to find you."

"I wasn't theorizing—it's pretty obvious why Mitch, and now Mike, were killed."

"It certainly appears that way," Agent Blasowich agreed. "I need you to help me fill in some blanks, sir."

"Before I do that, I need to know about my family."

"Excuse me?"

"I sent my ex-wife and children into hiding. Where are they?"

"You sent them to Ashland, Tennessee, correct?"

"Yes. I sent them to a friend's vacation house."

"That's been handled by a different team. One moment." She clicked off but was back in seconds. "We've safeguarded your family," the agent answered.

Roman slumped with relief. "Are they okay?"

"I'm sure they are but I'm not a part of the group who has them," she said, impatience evident in her tone. "Again, sir, we need you to fill in some blanks to help us."

"Here's one that's not a blank: one of the one-armed man's psychos shot me this morning, right after I recorded that call to you guys."

"You've been shot?" the agent asked. Roman could hear other voices murmuring in the background.

"I got lucky. The bullet grazed me. But these assholes are stopping at nothing to kill me. Why? Why do they want me dead?"

"Listen, Mister Littlepage, we have several people on their way to see you right now. Before they get there, I need you to cooperate with me."

"Wait, are they here on the island?"

"No, they're flying there from central Europe. They should be there in…less than an hour."

"I hope you haven't involved the local cops. They've got a leak."

"We won't. Believe me, we want this to be absolutely quiet."

"So, what is it you want me to do?"

"I need you to stay right where you are and do not leave your hotel room. Don't make any more calls. Don't use your identification and do not tell a soul you're American."

"They don't even know I checked in here. I had a friend do it."

"A friend? Who?"

"Don't worry about that. She's trustworthy."

"Have you spoken to anyone since you've been in the hotel?"

"No one other than my friend."

"Good. Stay inside, close your curtains and don't answer the door."

"Makes sense."

"Mister Littlepage, you should not trust a soul other than the agents who are coming to help you. The man…" The agent hesitated.

"What is it?"

"I'd rather not put this out over the air, but suffice it to say that the one-armed man you saw is extremely dangerous."

"No shit, lady. You think I don't know that by now? Who is he?"

"I can't get into that over the phone."

"Is his sister the restaurant owner?"

"Sir, I cannot discuss that."

"Tell me this: Is the one-armed man notorious, like those Al-Qaeda and ISIS leaders?"

"Not at all. He's very elusive and not much is known about him."

"What do I do if they find me before your people get here?"

"Your job is to stay put and stay quiet," she said, a bit of ice in her voice. "If you do that, they won't find you."

He could hear the key in the hotel room door. A moment later, Eva appeared with a large pizza box, a plastic bag with several bottles of water, and another paper bag. Roman held a finger over his lips. She motioned to the door, as if she should leave, but Roman shook his head.

"Ex-wife?" Eva mouthed, removing a white souvenir t-shirt from the second bag and placing it on the bed.

He shook his head then pointed to the phone. *"CIA,"* he mouthed back. Eva's eyes went wide.

"Mister Littlepage, are you there?"

116

"Yeah."

The agent plowed ahead. "Mr. Littlepage, we believe you're telling the truth. If you cooperate with us, we're willing to help you. Do you understand?"

"Yeah."

"Now help me understand a few things—did you speak to the man they killed in the restaurant?"

"No. I didn't even see his face. Who was he?"

"He was an ally to the U.S. and was working in conjunction with our people."

"Working on what?"

"I'm sorry, but that's classified."

"Of course it is. In case you haven't realized, I'm kinda in the middle of this thing. I'm not sure anything should be classified to me."

"Listen carefully, Mister Littlepage. Did the man who was killed give you something?"

"No. He didn't give me anything. I told you, I never met him."

"Are you certain?"

"Dammit, yes."

"The man who was killed was supposedly in possession of something quite important. It is currently unaccounted for."

"What is it?"

"That's classified."

"You're a real piece of work, lady."

"Mister Littlepage, it seems you have something your pursuers want. Desperately. Are you absolutely certain the man who was killed didn't give you anything?"

"No. How many times do I—"

Roman halted himself in midsentence and slowly turned to the dresser. Next to the flat screen television and his ever-present Chapstick rested the battered gold coin. He eyed it.

"Sir?"

"Sorry, I thought I heard someone," Roman said, still staring at the coin. "I told you, I never met the man. He—didn't—give—me—anything."

"Understood. Like I said, our agents will be there soon. Please just stay put and cooperate when they get there."

"Cooperate how? You're putting me on a private jet and getting me out of here, right?"

Eva was standing before him, listening to him while chewing on a fingernail.

"Mister Littlepage, I simply ask that you cooperate with their plan."

"Plan?" Roman narrowed his eyes. "The best plan I know is called *haul-ass-immediately*."

"One moment." Agent Blasowich could be heard covering the phone.

After a considerable delay, she said, "We'd like you to participate in the apprehension of the men who are after you."

"What does that mean?"

"Essentially, we'd like you to reveal your location at a carefully controlled time and place, and then we'll apprehend the men."

"Bait! You want me to be bait? Are you insane? I watched these guys stab a man over and over and over. They killed a kindly old hotel owner. They shot me on a crowded street. And now you want me to be their bait?"

"Not bait, Mister Littlepage. This will be a controlled activity and—"

"Activity?" Roman yelled. "What, like a fourth grade field trip? Sorry, lady, but hell no. The only way I work with your people is if they get me the hell out of here. I'm not anyone's bait."

"We're not a rescue organization. If you'll just be reasonable."

"Me be reasonable? Me?"

"Mister Littlepage…"

"I'm not helping you by being your bait."

"Mister Littlepage, if you'll please—"

"I'll call the CIA hotline number again soon. Keep my family safe." Roman hung up the phone. He then took it off the hook.

"What was all that?" Eva asked.

He eyed her, then eyed the coin.

"What is it?" she asked. "Was that really the CIA? Why were you so angry and talking about being their bait?"

"Unplug this I.V., please. It's just about done, anyway."

Eva removed the tape and catheter from his arm, placing a bandage and a piece of cotton over the puncture mark. "Hold your finger over the bandage," she said.

Roman was silent for a moment, deep in thought. Eventually, he slid his underwear and pants under the sheet and pulled them on. Then he stood and began walking. He moved all around the space, testing his side and ankle, limping back and forth over the length of the hotel room.

"Roman?"

"That *was* the CIA, and they're on their way here. But they're not coming to get me out of here."

She furrowed her brow but said nothing.

"They want me to lure that one-armed asshole and his friends out so they can nab them. That's why I was yelling about bait."

"Who is he?" she asked.

"The agent said he's desperately wanted but very elusive. She wouldn't say more. I got the feeling they don't know much about him, or don't want to tell me."

"Did she give you his name?"

"No." He motioned to the dresser. "Grab your things. We're getting the hell out of here."

"Roman, are you sure you want to expose yourself again?"

"Yes. Bring the pizza and those waters, please."

Roman pulled on the new t-shirt along with his socks and shoes. He slid the gold coin back into the watch pocket of his jeans, wondering if the coin was what they were after. It couldn't be, could it? How the hell could an old coin be worth so much?

They took the elevator to the basement and left the way they came in. "How much did you pay for the room?" he asked.

"Two-fifty."

"Doesn't leave us with much."

Because of that, they walked back near the central plaza and visited an ATM located out in front of a small local bank. Since his cover was already blown, he decided to go for broke. Knowing the ATM had a camera, he told Eva to stand off to the side. He guessed his accounts were frozen, but figured he may as well try. Surprisingly, the machine allowed Roman to withdrawal 300 euro, giving the couple a grand total of 350 euro to work with.

That should keep them afloat for a while. Together, they walked to the northeast. He ate pizza on the walk out of town. The food, the fluids, and the shot of adrenaline from the CIA gave Roman just enough energy to limp out of Sóller.

Chapter Thirteen

They'd walked about a mile although, to Roman, it felt like 10. The afternoon was stifling hot, made worse by a dull breeze that blew seaward, heated and dried after journeying over the hot rocky landscape of interior Mallorca. They were on a small secondary road that tracked with the coast but climbed. Down below them was the main coastal road. The road they'd chosen, which had very little traffic, had already climbed several hundred feet up the side of the mountain. On the left side of the road was a rough, knee-high rock wall, guarding against the sharp drop down to the coastal road. On the right were gates to exclusive homes tucked back into the hills. Though he'd done okay at first, Roman began to weaken as the road steeply ascended. They'd ditched the pizza after Roman had three slices.

"I wish I'd have stayed in the room," Roman grunted. He felt dizzy and nauseous.

"These people who are after you—do you think they'll find out you used the ATM in Sóller?"

Roman plopped down on the rock wall and swilled the remainder of his water. "Yeah, they'll find out. And I'm sure the CIA already knows."

Eva looked back at the Port of Sóller. "There are a few roads that come in from Palma. Then one road that heads down the coast. Then, these two roads that run up the coast. A one chance in five that they could come this way and find us."

"Not bad odds."

She shrugged. "What if they split up? We're taking a big risk right now— especially by not moving."

"I've got no energy. Maybe I'll get lucky and next time they'll shoot me in the head so it's all over with quickly."

"Don't talk like that," Eva admonished.

"Sorry. I'm just tired…and weak."

"Just rest for a minute." Eva lit a cigarette and sat next to him, dangling her feet the opposite way, giving her an ocean view. Down below was a steep rocky face, the orange earth dotted with cactuses and scrub trees. She turned and studied him. "What was the CIA asking?"

"The agent was positive the killers believe the man who was killed gave me something. That's why they're chasing me."

"Why would the killers believe he gave you something?" Eva asked.

"I have no idea." Roman dug into his watch pocket and held the coin in the palm of his hand. "I never really thought about it, but right before I saw them kill him, I found this."

Eva took the coin and examined both sides. "Found it where?"

"In the bathroom. It was kind of hidden on top of the hand towels."

"Kind of hidden?"

"I pulled a hand towel and the dispenser fell open. The coin was sitting on top of the stack of paper towels."

"Why didn't you tell me?"

"Until they mentioned why I was being chased, I just thought it was a cool old coin. I didn't think it could possibly be worth enough for them to go to such awful lengths to get it." He gestured to the coin. "What's that language?"

"It's Japanese and it's *extremely* old."

"What the hell would they want with an old coin? It couldn't be worth that much, could it?"

Eva clamped the cigarette between her teeth, scrutinizing the coin from every angle. She flipped it back to him. "That's not what they're looking for."

"How can you be certain?"

She shrugged. "I'm not, but like you said, I can't imagine a group like this cares about a coin, even if it's ancient and worth a million euro." She crushed the cigarette out and flicked it down the hill.

"Regardless, I think the CIA is right. The killers think the man they killed gave me something."

"And by wanting you to act as bait, the CIA thinks the one-armed man is still here?"

"Apparently."

They grew quiet for a moment.

"What if the dead man gave you something, but nothing tangible?"

"What do you mean?"

"What if he simply gave you information?"

"Good point, but I *never met* the man."

She turned her head to Roman. "Did I hear you say something about your family?"

"The CIA has them, thank God." He frowned. "The agent sounded a little…I dunno…unsure about it, though. She kept saying she wasn't involved with their safeguarding."

"Well, you obviously didn't trust her or we wouldn't be up here on this road."

Roman groaned. "I'm so sick of all this. Sick of running. Sick of bureaucracy."

"Sick of me?" she asked.

For the first time in a while, Roman smiled. "Definitely not."

"Ditto," Eva agreed. "Let's move a little farther," she said, gesturing up the road.

"I can't," Roman said. "I don't mean to sound like a wimp, but I've got no more strength." He lifted his hand, watching it tremble. "Eva, am I going to be okay?"

"Yes, but you need rest. Since this began, you've only had a few hours of sleep. Add to that all your injuries, blood loss, lack of nutrition, and heavy stress...and this is what happens."

"If I could just lay down," he replied, shutting his eyes.

"Stay here." Eva stood and crossed the road. Forty meters to the left was an expansive cobblestone entrance flanked by dual columns and guarded by a heavy gate. She touched a button at the intercom and waited. When the intercom squawked to life, she spoke Spanish, giving a broken apology as if she were looking for a friend's house.

"What are you doing?" Roman yelled.

"That house is no good. Don't move," she answered back to Roman, continuing up the road. He watched her repeat the process at another gate before she disappeared around the bend.

Roman sat there and studied the coin. He slid it back into his pocket, wishing he knew what it was the one-armed man and his friends were after. As he waited, two cars passed, the occupants paying him no heed. Twenty-five minutes later, Roman heard a humming from the left. He turned, watching as a new looking golf cart rounded the bend. Eva was behind the wheel.

"What the hell?" Roman asked as she scraped to a halt.

"Get in."

"Where'd you get that?"

"Our new hotel. Get in."

Roman obeyed, holding the forward roof support as she slowly wheeled through a U-turn. "What new hotel?"

"I started checking these mansions, to see if anyone was home. Finally, I came to one where no one answered. So I hopped the gate and went up to the house."

"Are you shitting me?" he asked as the cart ascended the steep road.

"No."

"What'd you do then?"

"I've always been a little crazy, Roman...as if you didn't already know that," she said with an impish grin. "So, when I didn't see anyone, I broke a window at the back and waited on an alarm. No alarm sounded, so I opened the window and went inside. Still no alarm. This golf cart was in the garage, plugged up."

"What if the owners are just out to lunch?"

"Could be, or maybe they recently left and went back to Germany."

Roman could think of hundreds of questions. He started with the stupid one. "How do you know they're German?"

"Because all their books and magazines and mail are in German. They could be Austrian, too, or maybe Swiss. But I'd bet they're German judging by the Bavarian paraphernalia littered throughout the home."

Roman ran his hand back through his hair and yelled his question. "Holy shit, Eva…you actually broke into someone's home?"

"You did, too. Remember?"

"Touché."

She turned into a comparatively modest entrance. After traveling fifty feet up the driveway, she produced a device that looked like a garage door opener and pointed it back at the gate. When she touched the button, the gate slowly creaked shut.

"You're wanted for murder, Roman, and I'm your accomplice. I think breaking and entering pales in comparison to everything else, don't you?" She mashed the gas as they ascended the steep hill to the Frank Lloyd-style home perched on the side of the mountain.

* * *

It took ten minutes, but Eva eventually convinced Roman to go inside and get off his feet. Obviously the slices of pizza hadn't been sufficient. Roman gorged himself on crackers while Eva continued to insist that their current crime didn't add on to their predicament. And in case someone came home, they'd simply feign confusion and leave. According to Eva, the closest police were many kilometers away and she and Roman could be long gone before the authorities arrived.

"What if the owners have a gun?" Roman asked.

"Good Germans with a gun in Spain? Highly doubtful." She gestured all around. "So you might as well eat, drink and sleep. It's the only way you're going to have a chance to somehow pull out of this tailspin."

After a bit of cajoling on her part, Roman agreed to stay the night. Once he'd ingested a surprisingly tasty microwave breakfast from the freezer, he had cheese, more crackers, stale bread and a chocolate-covered ice cream bar from the freezer. Now sated, he allowed Eva to douse his wound in rubbing alcohol—he howled like a lonely beagle—then he chose the darkest bedroom and slept. When he last looked at the clock, it was 3:31 p.m.

His sleep was deep and dreamless.

When Roman opened his eyes, he could see the sky outside was dim. The clock read 6:25. The house faced roughly to the east and his bedroom was at the rear of the house, meaning the sunset should be beaming through the gaps in the closed blinds.

Maybe it was cloudy or even raining.

He rubbed his eyes and eyed the bedside clock again. 6:25 a.m. Holy shit. *I slept 15 hours.*

Suddenly, solely based on the knowledge he'd slept so long, he felt better. Woozy and disoriented, but better.

He stood with some difficulty, stretching his legs as he pondered his environs. Though he'd hardly taken time yesterday to appreciate the home, today he noticed the preponderance of wood in the house's construction. The floor was hardwood, partially covered in an area rug. The walls were made of vertical wood tongue-and-groove slats—probably some sort of pine judging by the knots. And the ceiling was made of similar slats but more narrow, painted black. The effect was quite nice and provided the house with a nautical flavor.

Limping to the door, Roman pulled it open and smelled cooking sausage and coffee. But the best smell was that of baking bread. Moving slightly better with each step, he made his way down the narrow hallway to find Eva in the kitchen, a number of items cooking in front of her.

"How do you feel?" she asked brightly.

"Confused, but better. Can't believe I slept that long."

"You needed it."

"No sign of the owners?"

"Just me, you and a pesky fly I can't seem to kill." She handed him the fly-swatter. "Maybe you'll have more luck."

"Will my nurse allow me some coffee?"

She laughed. "So, you're treating me like your real nurse, aren't you? Sure, you can have coffee. You can have anything you like." Eva poured him a mug. "Do you know how long you actually slept?"

"Yeah. About fifteen hours and I don't think I even rolled over." He lifted his shirt. The rubbing alcohol had made his bandage loose. He peeled it aside, peering in at his wound. Eva looked, too.

"Looks about the same and doesn't appear infected. How's it feel?"

"Hurts, but more dull now."

"Good. Although early healing is easily undone, it's critical. During sleep, that's when all those tiny fibers in your body begin the slow process of knitting back together as skin and muscle and scar tissue. That long segment of sleep you got was critical."

He sipped the strong black coffee and walked to the front window, looking out over the precipitous drop down to the shore. Beyond the rocky coastline was a sea of blue that stretched out in all directions. Several miles to the north, a large ocean liner headed west, though it seemed to be sitting still.

When Roman turned back to see Eva still working in the kitchen, he noticed she was wearing no shorts—just a long t-shirt and a pair of light blue panties.

His reaction was immediate, so he looked away.

"Do you like eggs?" she asked.

"Any way you want to fix them," he said, lifting a three-day-old newspaper. "Have you figured out where the owners are?"

"Judging by the clues I've found, I think they left Mallorca two days ago. I found a calendar inside a cabinet that seems to show when family members and friends will be here. Someone named Curt von Berg, and his friends, are to arrive in three days."

"And the owners are indeed German?"

"Yes. The family who owns the house is from Rosenheim, which is in the southernmost part of Bavaria. Whoever they are, they're quite wealthy. Even though this place isn't quite as palatial as the others nearby, it's pretty easy to see that it's made extremely well." She rapped on the pan she was using. "All this kitchen equipment is top drawer. And did you notice all the wood in the house?"

"I did."

"Find a nail."

"I'm sorry?"

"Find a nail. Look at the wood."

Roman searched the floor, wall and ceiling nearby. There wasn't a single nail mark to be seen. "No nails."

"I slept about ten hours myself. When I got up this morning, I was bored and started poking around. Every single fastener is hidden to the naked eye. When I found some in closets and such, I could find only wood screws. Do you know the skill needed to manage that over an entire home?"

"I'd imagine having it built that way is expensive."

"Extremely. Okay, your *Frühstück* is ready. Sit," she commanded.

Roman took a seat at the dining room table, allowing her to serve him breakfast. She placed a hot croissant near his placemat.

"This looks so good."

"Breakfast is easy."

He tore into the croissant. "Hearing you talk about this wood, you sound as if you have some sort of experience with home building."

"My papa and his brothers are carpenters. It runs in the family."

Next she brought a large plate with sausage, scrambled cheese-eggs and a sliced, slightly bruised banana.

"Sorry about the banana. It was all they had left."

"How did you make croissants?"

"They had a tube in the refrigerator. So they're not homemade, but they smell good."

He jammed the rest of the croissant into his mouth. "Tastes good, too."

Finally, Eva brought over a pitcher of orange juice. "Frozen from concentrate, but better than nothing. Eat everything in front of you. There's more."

Roman stuffed egg into another croissant. "You already eat?"

"I had a little something earlier."

Roman ate for a moment. "When did you decide to be a nurse?"

"Pretty young. Can't remember exactly when but I do know it was in my teens."

"Is the schooling difficult in Germany, to become a nurse?"

"I guess. I always did pretty well in school."

"You know, my ex-wife was a nurse. Still is, I guess, but she let her certification lapse. She worked in the NICU...you know what that means?"

She shook her head. "I know English quite well, but I struggle with all the acronyms."

"It's the neonatal intensive care unit."

"Oh, yeah...that's hard work. Takes a special type of person, too. I can handle adult suffering...but children..." She shook her head.

"You mentioned you work in the ER. Wendy always said the toughest part about any hospital nursing job was—"

"Roman? Two favors?"

"Yeah?"

"Can we stop talking about my work, and about your ex-wife?"

"Sure."

She winked at him. "Even though I know it doesn't seem like it, I'm still on vacation."

He chuckled and took a large bite of his loaded breakfast croissant. "Yeah. So am I."

Chapter Fourteen

As the day wore on, Roman and Eva took inventory of the critical items in the house. There was plenty of food and basic medical supplies to keep them afloat until Curt and friends arrived in a few days. Eva suggested they take the rest of the day to continue to recover and ponder their next move. There was no rush and no point in leaving. At some point, Roman needed to call the CIA. He was desperate to know that Wendy and the kids were safe, but surely they were, right? That was his primary tenet for cooperating with the CIA. But if he called too soon, they would get a bead on him and pressure him to act as their bait. Roman's hope was they'd find the one-armed man and his thugs in the meantime. Because Roman had zero desire to be anyone's bait.

Although he felt as if he had a safe hanging over his head, Roman was able to force himself to relax. He and Eva went outside to the pool, making sure all sightlines were blocked from the neighbors. Turns out it was completely secluded, located in the midst of a sprawling rock garden and surrounded by tall evergreens on the inside of a stone wall.

They relaxed at poolside, chatting about a number of things before learning they both liked a great deal of the same music. Their choices in books were rather different, but their taste in movies was almost identical. After a half hour, Roman began to perspire under his bandage.

"I better go back in. It's burning."

"Do you mind if I stay out for a bit?" Eva asked. "I really love being in the sun."

"Take your time," he answered. "I'll go inside and watch some TV."

He found nothing on television that he wanted to watch. After a half-hour of puttering around in the house, Roman grew quite bored. He walked to the sliding door and looked out at Eva. She was in the same position, leaning back and reading one of the homeowner's German magazines. Roman glanced around the house, wondering what he might do next.

Earlier, as he'd explored all rooms of the house, he'd seen a desktop computer located in the study. Roman sat at the desk and turned on the power, watching as the computer came to life. He was pleasantly surprised that the computer required no password.

After the computer was up and running, Roman checked the Internet connection. The computer was online and ready to surf at high speed. Was it possible that the search for him was so intense that all Mallorcan outbound Internet traffic was being monitored? He shook his head. There was no way, right? On an island as populous as Mallorca—there must be millions of Internet queries per hour, right?

To hell with it.

He opened Google Chrome, watching as the Yahoo.de home page appeared. Roman navigated to Google and began performing various searches: 'one-armed criminal', 'one-armed terrorist', 'world's most wanted criminals.' He tried more than a dozen combinations, scanning the results afterward. Just like last time: nothing.

Roman leaned back and closed his eyes. *Think, Roman. What do you know about him?* He recalled the night of the killing, recalling how nicely the man's suit had been tailored. He remembered finding the man calm and distinguished. Roman even recalled the way the man had viewed him with a peculiar expression of sadness, perhaps exposing the tiniest thread of decency in his otherwise despicable being.

None of that matters, Roman. What do you know that might help you find him?

He's almost certainly from Cyprus. Then, Roman recalled: *Six-Day War.*

He began performing new searches and, on the fifth try—'lost his arm in the Six Day War terrorist'—Roman got a hit. It was an article from the BBC in 2007:

...however, the man behind the bombing is believed to be Andreas Konstantinou. Though authorities believed Konstantinou dead from a 1994 bombing in Tel Aviv, new surveillance footage from a Mayfair restaurant indicates Konstantinou is still alive and met with the chief suspects four days prior to the blast. Although the video is low resolution, sources inside MI-6 and the FBI agree that the one-armed man in the video is probably Konstantinou, who lost his arm during the Six-Day War in 1967. Other intelligence sources indicate that Konstantinou likely flew into London by helicopter, though the origin is unclear.

Konstantinou was born a Cypriot, enlisting in the Syrian military when he was 17 years old. After losing his arm in the Six-Day War, he attended university in Germany and France. His ideology swung wildly through the tumultuous years of the 1970s, as Konstantinou was linked to the far left Red Army Faction as well as several French and German right wing terrorist groups. Initially thought to be a foot soldier, Konstantinou was eventually identified as a skillful financier for criminals and terrorists. In 1988, *Le Point* published an exposé on Konstantinou, describing him as having grown wealthy through his aid to terrorists. Although he's repeatedly been tied to the International Bank of Damascus, officials from the bank have denied any connection to Konstantinou.

The lack of one arm makes Konstantinou easily recognizable and is almost certainly a detriment to his anonymity. But, according to numerous sources, Konstantinou refuses to wear a prosthetic. Several world agencies have accused the United States and other NATO nations of working with Konstantinou on occasion—a claim the United States denies. At the time of his alleged death, Konstantinou was rumored to live in an exclusive and private Mediterranean enclave.

"Andreas Konstantinou," Roman whispered. His first order of business was reading the Le Point exposé. The article seemed to paint Konstantinou as an opportunist and mercenary, with allegiance to one thing: Money. Roman then spent a half-hour scanning for newer information. The trail went cold after 2013, when Konstantinou was spotted outside of Sydney, Australia with a well-known Australian billionaire rumored to be connected to organized crime. Since then, Roman could find nothing about Konstantinou other than casual mentions. One blog run by an obvious nutjob—who claimed to have been unjustly fired from the CIA—asserted that Konstantinou was currently an unnamed prisoner of the United States at Guantanamo Bay.

"I wish," Roman said, standing and stretching. He walked to the rear of the house, looking outside again. Eva had bunched her shorts up and removed her top and bra. She was lying there, perfectly still—the Goddess he'd dreamed about. Roman gaped for a moment before reminding himself he'd seen at least a thousand sets of tits on this trip. European women think nothing of removing their top while tanning. Still, it was all he could do to pry his eyes away.

He touched his side, realizing it wasn't really hurting at the moment. All this rest seemed to be helping. After filling a glass with water from the front of the refrigerator, Roman removed the coin from his pocket, thinking about the story on Konstantinou, and how he was involved in the money end of terrorism.

Back on the computer, Roman searched for the world's most valuable coins. According to several websites, the highest value placed on a coin was just over $10 million dollars, for the 1794 flowing hair silver dollar. Roman scanned numerous lists and could find no coin similar to the one in his possession.

He went back to the magazine article, from 1988, which estimated Konstantinou's net worth at more than $200 million.

And that was in 1988...

Would he be in such a twist over a coin, even if it were worth $10 million?

I think not.

Roman rolled the chair over to the study window, examining the coin in the daylight. Like any old coin, it was worn and nicked. The raised areas of the image on both sides of the coin had been smoothed by centuries of use. The letter marks around the rim of the coin were nearly illegible. The images and detail seemed consistent with old coins Roman had seen in collector's shops over the years. He was just about to slide the coin back into his pocket when something caught his eye.

On the rear of the coin were two tiny indentations—ultra small depressions. The coin was so battered he nearly didn't notice them. But what Roman found odd was the two tiny indentations were directly across from one another. Though it was nearly impossible to see with the naked eye, Roman felt like there was the tiniest of gaps between the rear face of the coin and the edge. He studied the coin for a moment before carrying it to the garage where the golf cart was parked with an old Jaguar that had a flat tire.

On one wall of the garage was a wide wooden workbench. Roman found a metric tape measure and determined the distance in millimeters between the two holes. He then used a nail to make indentations on the wooden workbench the exact same distance apart. Finally, he plugged the cord drill into the outlet and used the smallest bit to drill narrow pilot holes through the bench. Roman searched until he found two long drywall screws. He traded the drill bit for a cross-tip screwdriver bit and, squatting down, he drove both screws straight up through the workbench. Roman then slowly backed each screw down until just the very tip protruded through the workbench.

He placed the coin on top of the two screw tips, watching as one tip slid into the small indentation on the coin. The other tip was a millimeter off position. Roman took a hammer and a chisel off the pegboard. He placed the blade of the chisel against the tip then tapped it with the hammer. After three efforts at adjusting the screw, the coin's two notches slid perfectly down on the screws. This held the coin fast. Using his fingers, Roman tried twisting the coin counter-clockwise. It wouldn't budge.

Using a thin strip of silver duct tape, Roman wrapped it around the edge of the coin—a trick learned from many basic do-it-yourself plumbing projects. He then gripped the outer, tape-wrapped edge of the coin with channel locks and again twisted counter-clockwise.

Nothing. Shit.

Roman went into the kitchen and retrieved a wad of paper towels, using them to wipe his dripping face. His bullet wound began to sting as he was sweating all over. He drank water and tried not to look outside at the topless Goddess. When he failed, he realized she had rolled to her stomach, her firm butt poking slightly up into the air.

Despite the exquisite display by the pool, Roman's mind continued to go back to the coin. He walked back to the garage and again gripped the coin with the channel locks. This time, he attempted to rotate the coin clockwise. He used slow, steady pressure and…

Holy shit.

It turned.

Roman lifted the coin, satisfied that the lower half had remained still on the screw tips. He couldn't believe he'd figured it out. This coin wasn't a coin after all.

After removing the tape from the edges of the tiny device, Roman pressed it between his two thumbs and unscrewed one side from another. He held it over the workbench when he felt he was getting close, and just as he prepared to separate the two pieces, the door to the house opened. It was Eva. She'd donned her t-shirt and eyed him curiously.

"What are you doing?"

"It wasn't a coin."

"What?"

"Look." Roman held the coin where she could see it and rotated both sides. "Whoever made it, milled the threads in the opposite direction. Do you know how precise the milling had to be to create a false coin like this? This is far smaller than the thinnest Swiss watch."

"Have you opened it?" she asked, breathless.

"Not yet."

"Do it, but be careful."

Roman obeyed, completely unscrewing the two pieces. He carefully separated them, nonplussed with what he saw.

In the bottom half of the coin was a minuscule rectangular compartment. Held in the compartment by two hair-like wires was a rectangular black and gold object no bigger than a match head.

"How did you know to do that?" Eva asked, studying the other half of the coin.

"I don't know. I was just trying to figure out what those men wanted, and my mind kept coming back to the coin."

"Wait a minute." Eva searched the workbench before going inside. He could hear her rummaging in the kitchen. Moments later, she returned with a heavy magnifying glass.

Roman placed the bottom half of the coin on the bench. They held the magnifying glass above it, pulling it backward for maximum magnification.

"Is that a super tiny microchip?"

"Yeah, or something like that," Eva answered. "It probably plugs into a flash drive. There could be gigs of data stored on that little device."

"Gigs? Seriously?"

"You wouldn't believe how small implanted devices have become. I went to a continuing education class and learned that they've invented smart particles that can flow through your bloodstream and send back data."

He touched the lower half of the coin. "So, this is it?"

"You figured it out, Roman."

Roman straightened and opened his arms to the heavens. "Finally!" he yelled. "And to think, I've been carrying this in my pocket with my Chapstick. I had no idea. What if I'd lost it?"

She gave him a hug. "But you didn't. This is big."

"What do you think's on the chip?"

"Could be anything," Eva answered. "I honestly wouldn't know."

"Do you think they can track it?"

She shook her head. "If they could, you'd be dead by now. And it's so tiny that I don't see how it could transmit anything, especially not very far."

Regardless, Roman went into the kitchen, searching until he found a cast iron skillet. He returned to the garage and covered the two coin pieces with the skillet. In the event the microchip could be tracked, perhaps the heavy iron would obfuscate its signal.

Eva stared at him with narrow eyes, a hint of a grin on her face. "I'm amazed that you figured out how to open that fake coin."

"Wait till I tell you what else I know."

"What are you talking about?"

"Hang on." He led her back into the kitchen, getting two Beck's beers from the refrigerator. After pouring them into tall Weissen-style glasses, Roman slid one beer to Eva.

"*Pröst,*" he said, clinking his glass with hers.

"What are we toasting?"

He sipped his beer and joined eyes with her for a moment. "I know who the one-armed man is."

"Seriously?"

"Very seriously."

"How?"

"I used the desktop computer in there. Started doing various searches about one-armed terrorists and the Six-Day War. His name is Andreas Konstantinou. He's a shadowy type on the money side of terrorism, worth hundreds of millions of dollars."

Eva appeared worried.

"What's wrong?"

"I hope your searches didn't give us away."

He shrugged. "If they did, they did. But knowing gives us more power."

"What do you mean?"

"That little microchip out in the garage is our safe ticket out of here."

"You think you can somehow use it to bargain for your freedom?"

"*Our* freedom."

"How?"

"I don't know...yet."

Roman and Eva talked for a full hour. At times, their conversation was spirited, but never heated. They talked through a half-dozen ideas. After boiling everything down, much of their discussion centered on Konstantinou's rumored involvement with the International Bank of Damascus.

* * *

The clock chimed 10 p.m. as Roman pushed his plate away. Eva had made good use of the frozen chicken and vegetables from the garage freezer and had proven herself to be rather deft in the kitchen. She cleaned the plates from the table.

"Want another beer?"

"I'm fine, thanks. That was really tasty."

"I like cooking."

"Do you cook for yourself back home?"

"Not too often. I used to cook three or four times a week."

"No more?"

"I don't like cooking for myself."

"Did you have a roommate?"

"No," she said, seeming to hesitate a bit.

"Who were you cooking for?"

"I had a boyfriend. He'd come over and I'd cook for us."

Roman felt the prick of jealousy in his gut but responded cheerfully. "Well, you certainly are a good cook."

Eva placed the plates in the sink and brought Roman a glass of tap water. She placed four orange pills in front of the glass.

"What are these?"

"Ibuprofen."

He slid them back. "I'll take them in the morning. I'm probably going to crash soon. I feel pretty good, actually."

"Take them now. I'm the nurse."

Roman shrugged and tossed the pills to the back of his throat, chugging the water afterward. "Won't those make me bleed?"

"That's aspirin. You'll be fine. Listen, I need to be direct with you about something." Eva eyed him intently. "I'm not so sure I feel good about the plan we discussed."

"I don't feel good about it, either, but I don't know what else to do."

"I was thinking about what we came up with. The basic premise is rather good, but if we want to make it off this island alive, I think we have to meet Konstantinou face-to-face."

"What's to prevent them from killing us on the spot?" he asked.

"We don't take the microchip with us. We meet Konstantinou and his men. We make our deal for them to let us walk away. *Then* we tell them where the chip is."

"Why would they agree to that?" Roman asked.

"If they don't, then they won't get their precious chip." She stabbed a finger in the air. "But know this: the very second we call them, we're exposing ourselves. The plan might be flawed from the start."

"We've got to try something. We can't stay here forever, and now the CIA's here on the island, too. We're going to get found, probably sooner than later."

They chatted further about how to reach Konstantinou and the rendezvous location they would demand. They both agreed that they must control all facets of the meeting.

"Let's give them no more than one hour from the time we hang up," Eva said. "No more. If we give them longer, they'll have time to prepare an ambush."

"Think they can get there that fast, even if they're in Palma?" Roman asked.

"On this island, you can get nearly anywhere in an hour. And giving them such a tight timeline will show we mean business."

"I can't believe my life has come down to this. A meeting with cold-blooded killers, all over a microchip that's as small as a piece of rice?" Roman leaned forward and rested his elbows on the table, using his hands to hold his forehead. He shut his eyes. "You can't come with me tomorrow, Eva. Too dangerous."

"Roman, don't start this."

"Start what?"

"Panicking."

"I'm not panicking. But I can't let you get killed."

Eva disentangled his left hand from his hair, gripping it in her own. She stood, tugging at him.

"What?"

"Come on."

"Where are we going?"

She didn't reply, just continued to tug until he stood. Eva led him through the house to the large bedroom at the end of the hallway. She walked to three spots around the room, lighting candles. When she came back to him, she kissed him.

It was wonderful.

Next, Eva carefully lifted his t-shirt over his head. Then she worked on the button to his jeans.

"Eva, the kiss was nice, but we probably shouldn't—"

Her hand moved to his mouth and she pressed an index finger over his lips. Then she knelt, getting his jeans undone and pulling them to the floor.

"Eva…"

"Shhhh." She tugged his underwear down.

Eva remained on her knees in front of him. Roman was aware of his own heavy breathing as she gripped his lower back, pulling him to her. Then, when it was obvious she needn't go on any longer, she stood and disrobed. She took his left hand and placed it on the side of her breast while moving his right hand to her hip. They kissed again.

It suddenly occurred to Roman why she'd insisted he take the ibuprofen.

After a blissful moment of standing, she led him to the bed and situated him on his back. She sat astride him and started slowly, obviously gauging his reaction to see if he was in pain.

If he was, he didn't notice.

When it was apparent Roman was managing just fine, Eva slid her feet forward, allowing her to squat and move with vigor. She leaned forward, so her face was mere inches from his as her sounds grew more intense. The noises and sensations inflamed Roman and within a minute the two of them were grunting and gasping before Eva collapsed next to him, catching her breath.

Her right hand made its way to Roman's hair, playing with it as she spoke to him in her native tongue, saying, *"War das gut?"*

Roman knew enough German to answer honestly, saying, *"Sehr gut,"* three times in a row. After a minute, Roman said, "You know, you did all the work."

"When you're healed, you can climb on top," she answered with a wink.

They enjoyed two beers each by the pool before doing it all over again. At midnight they slept, both of them well aware that this fine evening might have been their last.

Chapter Fifteen

At 4:41 a.m. Roman awoke and stood from the bed. His ankle felt markedly better. The activities of earlier seemed to awaken new pain from his side, but it didn't feel critical—just sore. Thankfully the knots on his head had cleared up completely. He quietly departed the bedroom and made his way to the office at the front of the home. Using the dim light of the floor lamp, Roman searched the office and located three flash drives in the top right drawer. He carried the three drives to the garage. Once the door to the house was shut, Roman flipped on the work lights and set about prying each of the flash drives open with a small knife.

When he saw the guts inside the tiny devices, he was disappointed. Though he was pretty handy with mechanical repairs and the like, microchips certainly weren't Roman's specialty. And though the flash drives had circuit board similarities, each was different and contained a radically different architecture.

Roman slid the coin microchip into view, examining it in relation to the interior of the three drives. There was no match that was even close.

He'd hoped the microchip would simply snap into a flash drive to be accessed. But seeing the guts of the flash drives made Roman realize that the coin microchip probably only mated to one specific type of flash drive, and that flash drive was probably custom-made to accept this tiny chip. Or maybe the coin chip didn't even belong to a flash drive. Maybe it went inside a phone, or a—

"What are you doing?"

He whipped his head up. Eva was standing in the doorway, wearing only her t-shirt.

"Jeez, you surprised me," Roman said.

"I woke up and you were gone."

"Sorry. I was thinking there might be a way to know what's on this microchip."

"Why?"

"It might give us a clue that would give us more leverage."

She stepped down the stairs and leaned against the old Jaguar. "Roman, I understand your curiosity, but I also think neither of us wants to know what's on that chip."

"Why?"

"This one-armed psycho, Konstantinou, deals with terrorists, so I can only imagine what sort of information must be stored on there that's got him so eager to kill."

"Exactly," Roman said, perhaps a bit too forcefully. "And maybe, just maybe, it's so damning that I should destroy it right now. What if it's the layout of the water system of Los Angeles, or the plans and access points to a nuclear reactor in Germany? That's worth me dying for, right?"

"Roman…"

"But if it's just the bank codes of this sonofabitch's hidden money, then I'd rather not die for it. But I would like to *know*, so then I can make an informed decision."

Roman realized he had yelled nearly every word.

"You're so upset. What's happened?"

He dipped his head. "I'm not upset with you."

"Come inside."

They sat at the kitchen table with the lights out. There was no talking for several minutes—just quiet. Finally, Roman spoke.

"I don't know if I have the guts to go through with this," he said. "I guess I was looking for a way out by figuring out what's on that chip."

"You do have the guts."

"Okay, assuming we get lucky with the bank, and assuming I meet with Konstantinou…and assuming he doesn't kill me…what if I'm giving him something damning on that microchip?"

"Roman, please stop worrying about that. He'll be caught in hours."

"I just wonder if I should just give in and call the CIA."

"Go ahead." She leaned forward. "But you said you didn't trust them, that they wanted you to act as bait."

"By going through with our plan, I'm doing almost the exact same thing."

"But you're not trying to trap Konstantinou and his men. They didn't get where they are without being smart, believe me. They'll know you and I are working alone."

"Meaning, they may kill us."

"True, Roman, they might try. But I'm willing to gamble that they'll want their microchip and, in the end, this Konstantinou is a businessman. He'll make a business decision and we'll walk away."

Roman didn't reply for a moment. "I guess you're right, Eva. I've just never…"

"Been shot? Been chased? Been accused of murder?" she asked, an ironic smile forming on her lips.

"Yeah. It's been a pretty rough week."

"Think you'll ever come back to Mallorca?"

"Everything was great until all this happened."

"At least we met. In my book, it's been worthwhile."

"That, indeed, is the silver lining."

Roman stood and offered his hand. He led Eva back to the bedroom. This time, they did not make love. They lay there, close to one another, until the sun came up.

Neither slept.

As the sun rose, Roman went out by the pool to be alone for a bit.

* * *

At 2:49 p.m. local time, a female employee of the International Bank of Damascus answered the phone in a pleasant, singsong Arabic greeting.

"Good morning. Do you speak English?" Roman asked.

"I do, sir. How may I help you?"

"I need to speak with the highest ranking bank officer. This is an emergency."

"That's Mister Al-Palmyra. I'm sorry, he's in a meeting right now."

"Interrupt his meeting, please. I can assure you he'll want to take this call."

"I can hand him a message as soon as his meeting is over, sir. Will that be sufficient?"

"No. Hand him a message *right now*. Tell him I have an urgent communication for Andreas Konstantinou."

"Sir…"

"Lady, I'm not misleading you. Mister Al-Palmyra will want to speak with me, immediately. I guarantee it."

She paused a moment. "Please say the man's name again."

Roman spelled Konstantinou for her and was put on hold. After five solid minutes, a man with a heavy Arabic accent came on the line. "This bank does not have, nor has it ever had, any association with Andre—"

"Are you Mister Al-Palmyra?"

"Yes. And as I said, this bank—"

"Stop talking and listen," Roman replied in a calm voice, having practiced these lines ad nauseam with Eva. "Mister Al-Palmyra, I'm not a cop and I'm not a reporter. I'm the man who has the Japanese coin that Konstantinou desperately wants. Are you recording this?"

Al-Palmyra was clearly taken off guard. "A coin? I don't know what this—"

"Record this because I'll say it just once. This is a matter of life and death."

"Sir, I cannot—"

"I will absolutely tell Konstantinou that it was *you* who refused to take the message. He will be *very* upset with you. Now, record what I have to say."

"One moment, please." The phone clicked one time. There were a few bumps and muttered words. Finally, "Sir, you're now on speaker and I'm recording with my mobile phone. Please speak loudly and slowly."

"You tell Konstantinou I have his coin and I know there's something hidden inside it. I haven't opened it or damaged it, and I will give it to him in exchange for two things. First, his man with the curly hair has to confess that

138

he killed the hotel owner in Palma, Mallorca. And second, Konstantinou simply has to let me and my friend go free."

"Sir, this is extremely—"

"Stop talking, Al-Palmyra, and just keep recording. Andreas Konstantinou, at precisely 1500 hours Mallorca time, you and your two men will meet me on the *westernmost* edge of the beach at Cala Tuent. That's *Cala Tuent*, in Mallorca. Come alone. If you kill me, you won't get your coin. Konstantinou, if you do not come, you won't get your coin. I want *your* assurance, not that of your two men. You have to meet me, your man has to give me a useable confession, then you have to let me go. Then, and only then, will I give you what you seek. This is the only way I will do this. I have evaded all authorities in order to keep this between me and you. The American CIA is here in Mallorca and I am not working with them—I've remained on my own so you and I can make this deal. After this, we all go on living and I'll never speak another word of it. 1500 hours...be there."

When he was finished, Roman—feeling a bit like Clint Eastwood—asked Al-Palmyra if he got it. Roman then heard his own voice as the Syrian banker pressed play on his recording app.

"Call him this very second, Mister Al-Palmyra. I guarantee you he will be extremely interested in that recording." Without waiting for a response, Roman ended the call on his remaining prepaid phone and handed it to Eva. She nodded at his performance before pitching it from the cliff, watching it tumble into the ocean.

"Think that'll work?" Roman asked.

She clicked the timer on her watch. "Assuming Konstantinou is still here, like you think he is, then someone from the bank is probably calling him, or calling someone who knows how to reach him. How long do you think it'll take to get the message to him?"

"Ten minutes, maybe. Then, Konstantinou has to decide if he wants to take the chance to get his precious coin. If he does, he'll have no time to come up with a trap."

"Won't he think it's a trap?" she asked.

"I don't think he will. I'm just hoping he doesn't have some sort of ace up his sleeve."

"Like what?"

Roman shook his head. "Who knows? But when you look at all they've done thus far, we'd be crazy to underestimate them."

With an hour remaining before the meeting, they walked back to the golf cart. Roman was silent, wondering if he'd be alive at sundown.

Chapter Sixteen

Situated about five miles from Sóller, Cala Tuent was a secluded and enclosed beach on Mallorca's sparsely populated northwestern shore. It was rather isolated and, because of its coarse sand and rocky outcroppings, not incredibly popular with tourists other than naturists and nudists. Roman and Eva parked the golf cart at the beach overlook, arriving 45 minutes prior to the deadline.

Staring out over the water, Roman could see why Eva had suggested they meet here. The coastal road provided a narrow strip of access to the parking area at the overlook. The beach itself was twenty feet below the road and U-shaped, providing a shallow but protected harbor approximately 250 meters across at its widest point. The rocky shore was suitable enough for sunbathing and the water in the cove-like beach was baby blue and clear as a bell in the shallowest areas. The outer area of the beach, leading to the sea, was dominated by jagged cliffs on both sides, topped by trees and vegetation. The net effect was an incredibly secluded beach and an area accessible only by sea or the one entrance at the main road.

There were about 20 people scattered on the beach, most of them wearing nothing at all. The largest group was an older foursome milling about in the shallow water on the eastern edge of the beach. The western edge, where the meeting was to take place, was dominated by large, knee-high rocks. Because there was little flat ground on that side, no one was sunbathing nearby.

"Where should we put the coin?" Eva asked.

"I'll hide it."

"Do it quick, just in case they get here early."

Roman and Eva picked their way down to the beach. They walked to the western shore, eyeing the area around them. Behind the rocky coast was a tall and jagged cliff. At the base of the cliff were several gnarled olive trees—a familiar sight in Mallorca. Roman walked to the middle tree and carefully placed the fake Japanese coin beneath a rock at the back of the tree's base.

Eva had walked to the water's edge, peering left and right.

"See something?" he asked.

"No. Just checking the depth here." She held his hand. "You okay?"

"Ready to be done with this."

"Want to go through everything one more time?"

They discussed every contingency they could think of. When they were finished, Eva's fingers played with Roman's as she asked, "So…how was last night?"

He chuckled. "Last night was pretty amazing."

"I agree," she said, biting her lip. "I hope you'll see me again after this."

"Are you kidding? Why wouldn't I?"

"Well, assuming we both get to leave, it's just going to be strange having an ocean between us."

"The one thing I've got plenty of is frequent flier miles. It's one of the few assets my ex-wife didn't take from me in our divorce."

Eva tapped out a cigarette. Roman asked for one. She lit them both and put one between Roman's lips.

"How long?" he asked, smoke escaping his mouth with his query.

She checked. "Thirty-seven minutes. Be firm with them, Roman. And just remember, you *have* what they want. Don't give that up, no matter what, until you get what you want."

"Thank you, Eva." Despite his nerves, he managed a smile. "I can't believe you spent your vacation running with me."

She smiled and squeezed his hand. "It's been better than a vacation."

"You might want to reserve judgment on that until we're done here." Lightheaded from the cigarette, Roman tilted his face to the sky. "I can't believe I'm doing this. I can't believe I'm wanted for murder. I can't believe I've been shot." He lowered his eyes to hers. "I'm just a normal guy, Eva. How'd all this happen?"

"You're going to make it out of here. We both are. And just think of the stories you'll have to tell to your children and their friends."

He couldn't help but chuckle. "My son will think this is the coolest thing ever to happen to us." His smile dissolved. "But only if I make it back."

"You will." She kissed him on his cheek. "When do you want me to hide?"

"Let's give it a bit more time."

"Where are you planning to stand when you talk to them?"

"How about down there," Roman said, pointing to a triangular section of rocks that jutted out a bit farther than the rest of the beach.

"That's too far from where I'll be hiding. I won't be able to hear." She walked back to the trees and high grass, eyeing the waterline. Eva came back and pointed. "Stand to the right of the point. See over there, right in front of that darker area of water?"

"Will do," Roman said, eyeing the spot.

She checked her watch. "Thirty-two minutes."

When 20 minutes remained, Eva hid herself. From that point on, Roman stood there sweating, his fear multiplying exponentially with each passing minute. He kept hearing something behind him.

"Are you talking?" he hissed back at her at one point.

"Yes. Sorry…just repeating the plan to myself. Don't be nervous," she answered. "And please don't look over here or they'll know."

"Don't be nervous," he muttered to himself. "Yeah…right."

* * *

At exactly 2 minutes before the deadline, Roman heard the distant crunch of gravel. He turned and watched as a silver sedan pulled into the parking area up at the overlook. The distance from where he stood—which was exactly where Eva suggested—was about 150 meters. Roman's heart lurched because the first man who exited the car was the curly-haired killer. He stood by the car for a moment, staring through a set of binoculars and talking on a mobile phone. Once he'd eyed Roman for a bit, he tossed the binoculars back into the car and slid the phone into his pocket.

No one else exited the car. What the hell? Why was he alone?

The curly-haired killer made his way down to the beach and took his sweet time as he ambled in Roman's direction.

Roman's hands shook. The tips of his fingers tingled.

This is it, Roman. You might not be alive in five minutes. Who are you, anyway? Why are you standing here? Are you crazy? Turn and run. Go now!

Shut up. Just shut up. You've held me back my entire life. For once, shut the hell up.

Roman refocused.

"See him?" Roman hissed over his shoulder. Eva was well concealed in the sparse tree line just behind him, tucked down behind clumps of sea grass and the olive trees.

"Why's he alone?" Roman asked.

"Look left," Eva whispered in return.

Roman turned to see a boat entering the protected cove. The boat was modern, flat black and shiny red and looked very fast—probably a 28-footer. It had an inboard engine and sat rather low in the water. Roman watched as the bow came all the way down when the boat slowed. At the helm was the cruel-looking man, his wraparound black sunglasses hiding the ice-blue eyes that had previously bored into Roman's soul. A cigarette dangled from the man's lips as he edged the boat out of the current and into the gentle eddy in front of the steep rocky beach where Roman waited.

It occurred to Roman that Konstantinou might have a yacht and this boat was his launch. Perhaps he'd been sea-based all this time. Roman recalled the article he'd read. Konstantinou had been seen in London and Australia, but no one knew how he came or went. *Who gives a shit?* None of those things mattered now—the meeting was happening. All of this insanity will be over soon.

Roman trembled. He clenched his fists in an effort to conceal his fear. He wasn't confident that he'd even be able to speak.

Glancing to his right, Roman could see the curly-haired killer was now only 100 feet away.

"Stop," Roman said, holding out his palms to the curly-haired killer and the boat. "You," he said, to the curly-haired killer. "Walk out and pull their boat in, and then the three of you walk to me together."

The curly-haired killer shook his head and spoke English with a light accent. "You don't give the orders."

"I do if you want your coin."

The curly-haired killer did nothing to suppress his nasty grin. "We have your *family.*"

Though the sky was crystal clear, Roman heard the rumble of thunder.

We have your family? Did I just hear that correctly?

And it was the way the curly-haired killer said it—so conversationally. He'd said it with the same concern that he might if he was telling Roman that there wasn't much of a breeze on the beach today.

"What did you just say?" Roman asked, mostly out of reflex.

"Your family, we have them. Your wife, Wendy, and your two children." The curly-haired killer's eyes sparkled. "They're unharmed, for now. Your two friends, Mike and Mitch, however, are no longer with us. They'd be unharmed, too, but they were both highly uncooperative."

Roman felt his knees beginning to buckle. "You don't have my family. I was told…"

"Told what?"

"I was told they were safe."

"Whoever told you that was lying. They're not safe…not at all."

"I…uh…I don't believe you."

"I don't care."

Sonofabitch…this can't be true. It can't! Roman fought the urge to turn and look at Eva.

The cruel-looking man spoke in a foreign language to the curly-haired killer, who nodded. The curly-haired killer then pointed beyond Roman.

"Too many people over here. Start walking. Walk around the mouth of the bay, there. On the other side is a pool, protected by the rocks, out by the sea. We'll talk there."

This time Roman looked around, trying his best to conceal his eye contact with Eva. She shook her head frantically, signaling him not to go.

"Start moving. I'm not asking," the curly-haired killer threatened. "Go now, or my people back in Nashville will go to work on your family. You don't want that, believe me."

Holy shit. This is so bad. And if they somehow find out about…what I've done.

Roman was convinced he'd bungled this entire operation.

With no choice rather than obey, he followed the rocky shoreline and wondered if Eva could somehow follow from inside the scant tree line. If these people truly had his family, Roman didn't care at this point if he lived or died. He'd gladly give his life for his family's freedom. But he didn't want Eva to die in the process. He hoped she stayed put so he could settle this alone.

But there was one key point that was bothering Roman—the thing that he'd done this morning.

It was big. It was colossal.

He prayed they didn't somehow find out. If they did…

* * *

Just as the curly-haired killer had indicated, the unseen coastline to the left of the rocky point contained a protected pool. The pool was several hundred feet wide and appeared rather deep at its center. Clear water swirled inside the pool, but gently enough that the cruel-looking man was able to easily navigate the boat in through the opening. After reversing the boat several times, he navigated it aft to the shore. He tossed a grapnel anchor from the stern and tugged the craft close to the rock line. He threw another anchor from the bow, pulling the boat taut in an effort to keep it moored off the rocks.

Roman then saw his chief nemesis, Andreas Konstantinou, stand from the rear of the boat. He flicked a cigarette into the water and considered Roman for a moment before making his way up and onto the deck at the stern. The curly-haired killer waded into the water but Konstantinou waved off his assistance. Using his one arm to support himself, Konstantinou descended on the aft ladder and waded up to the beach. When the cruel-looking man had done the same, the threesome walked up together but remained separated by several feet each.

This time they wore clothes more appropriate for Mallorca, but still out of place for the beach. Both henchmen wore black slacks and muted golf shirts. Konstantinou wore all black, and once again Roman noticed the long sleeve silk shirt was cleanly tailored where his left arm should be. The only thing slightly telling about the man's disposition was his shirt—it was unbuttoned halfway down, exposing a deeply tan chest and a thick gold rope with a medallion of some sort.

This was the first time Roman had seen Konstantinou since the murder. He wasn't a large man, probably around 5'7". He was lean and his one arm was straight and thin. But the angles of his face, and the confidence of his manner, told an entirely different story than his lack of imposing size. This was a leader of men who'd taken a wrong turn, fueled by greed and an absence of scruples.

"How do I know you have my family?" Roman asked, the very thought sickening him each time he focused on it.

"Do you have my coin?" Konstantinou countered. His voice scared Roman. The tone and intonation took Roman back to that fateful night in the kitchen of the Lemóni, listening as Konstantinou calmly ordered a man stabbed again and again.

Roman struggled to wet his mouth. "Before we talk about your coin, I want to know about my family."

Konstantinou gestured to the curly-haired killer. "Call the States. Tell them to kill one of the children. Use a blade."

"Wait!" Roman yelled. "Please, don't hurt my kids. Yes, I have your coin."

"Give it to me," Konstantinou said, holding out his hand.

"I don't have it with me."

After muttering what must have been a curse, the cruel-looking man lurched forward and grabbed Roman's shirt. He pulled back his hand to punch but an almost inaudible grunt from Konstantinou stopped him. After a second more, the cruel-looking man released Roman, leaving his t-shirt wadded at the center of his chest.

"You'll pardon us for being irritable," Konstantinou said with a polite smile. "Normally, I enjoy Mallorca. But this trip hasn't been pleasant. You've made our lives most difficult, Roman Littlepage. Now...*where*—is—my—coin?"

"Let my family go. Do it and I'll get the coin."

"Where is it?"

"Not until my family is free."

"You're in no position to bargain," Konstantinou snorted.

"If you hurt any of them, you won't get the coin. I'll die before I tell you."

The three men chuckled.

"I do have a question," Konstantinou mused. "How did the coin end up in your possession? This is of critical importance to the well-being of your family."

Roman shrugged. "The night I saw you guys...you know...in the kitchen, I'd first come into the restaurant just to use the bathroom."

"The restaurant was closed," Konstantinou said, shaking his head as if he didn't believe Roman.

"It's the truth. The door wasn't locked all the way. I gave a small push and it opened. The deadbolt was only halfway out. I had to piss badly so I went to the bathroom. The coin was hidden in the paper towel dispenser. I took it."

"If it was hidden, then how did you find it?"

"I washed my hands. When I pulled a towel, the paper towel dispenser fell open. The coin was sitting there."

Konstantinou turned to the curly-haired killer. The two again spoke in a language Roman couldn't place. Perhaps it was Greek. Konstantinou nodded and turned back to Roman.

"The man who we met with did use the restroom when we first arrived."

"I told you, I'm not lying," Roman said. "I just want my family to be safe."

The cruel-looking man eyed Roman as he muttered something in their language. Given the way he looked at Roman, he was probably suggesting they kill him. Konstantinou shook his head.

Roman decided to get on with it before things went south. "If you want your coin, just let my family go free. *Please.* But I have to have proof they're free. And I need something to prove I didn't commit that hotel murder."

"Your demands are considerable," Konstantinou noted.

"Like I said on the phone with the bank, the CIA is here looking for you. They wanted me to help them trap you. I evaded them in order to meet with you, no strings attached." Roman measured Konstantinou's face, surprised when he showed no concern.

"Roman, your CIA pays me more, each and every year, than any other organization on earth. Believe me, they don't care about you any more than I do."

"That doesn't make sense," Roman stammered. "Why would they have suggested the trap?"

"They want the chip that's inside the coin and they'd rather not pay me for it. I'm in business, Mister Littlepage, same as them. While I often work with them, they'd rather not pay me what I'm owed." He bit his bottom lip, his smugness radiating around him. "And they desperately want that chip."

"What's on the chip?"

"Is it nearby?"

"I'm not telling you anything else until you let my family go and give me my confession."

"You actually believe you can hold out, don't you?" Konstantinou asked, narrowing his eyes.

"It scares me, but I do," Roman said through clenched teeth, trying not to imagine the torture they might inflict. "And I don't even know that you have my family. The CIA told me *they* had them."

Konstantinou shook his head. "Well, the CIA lied. That's what they do, Roman."

"Still…until you do as I asked, I'm not giving you shit."

"You've made a grave error by attempting to bluff a player who has already stacked the deck." Konstantinou turned to the curly-haired killer. "Make the call. Do both kids, then the wife."

"Wait! Please…don't." Roman's face contorted. "I'll get your coin."

"That time has passed. Make the call," Konstantinou maintained.

The curly-haired killer lifted the phone to his ear.

Struggling to maintain his equilibrium, Roman threw up a final Hail Mary. He made his tone respectful and obsequious. "Sir, please, I have the coin. It's undamaged. I'll give it to you. And then you can kill me, if you want. But, please, don't harm my family. They've done nothing wrong. I beg you, sir. I'm at your mercy."

Konstantinou stared at Roman. It was as if he were divining Roman's soul. Then Konstantinou murmured a brief phrase to the curly-haired killer who, in turn, spoke briefly to the person on the phone and hung up.

"Alright, Roman Littlepage," Konstantinou spoke. "You have one final chance. Where's my coin?"

"It's in Sóller," Roman lied, thumbing his finger down the coast.

"Why is it there and not here?"

"I thought it was wise not to bring it. I'm sorry," Roman answered, his eyes darting all around. When he looked right, he saw Eva. She was hiding behind a group of rocks on the hillside just above the point. She gestured to Roman. He couldn't tell exactly what she meant, but it seemed she was telling him not to look her way.

"Where in Sóller?" Konstantinou asked.

"Uh, down by the sea."

"Where by the sea?"

"I'll take you to it," Roman said. "But, before we go, please let my family go."

"No deal."

Roman shut his eyes for a moment. He knew what he was about to say were the weightiest words of his life. But he also believed it was his family's only chance.

"Let them go and I will take you straight to the coin. Please, sir," Roman said earnestly. "But if you don't let them go now, I won't take you, and I won't tell you."

"You're right back to where we were earlier. By holding out, you're killing your family."

"But you'll kill them once you get the coin," Roman countered. "I'm simply trying to bargain with you in good faith. Do with me what you want, but please let them go. Please, sir…I'm begging you."

The cruel-looking man produced a switchblade knife and opened it with a snicking sound. Konstantinou stopped him with a shake of his head. Then, surprisingly, Konstantinou's tone changed when he spoke to Roman.

"Despite all the trouble you've caused, you've shown respect." He nodded. "And to someone like me, that carries weight."

Konstantinou spoke to the curly-haired killer who pressed two buttons on the phone. After a moment, the curly-haired killer had a rapid conversation in the same foreign language.

As he did, Roman looked all around and managed to glance at Eva. This time she pantomimed as if she were touching her watch and then slowly motioned downward with her palms.

Unless Roman was wrong, he'd guess she was telling him to go slowly, though he had no idea why.

The curly-haired killer said something to Konstantinou, who nodded. Konstantinou gestured to the phone.

"Take it. Talk to your wife. They're free. And the only reason I'm doing this is because I have *you* in my possession. And killing your family wouldn't sit well with my biggest client, your CIA."

Roman accepted the phone with his trembling hand. He stared out at the deep blue sea and spoke Wendy's name. All he could hear was murmuring then shuffling. He heard footsteps on wood, followed by a scratching sound. Then he heard his children asking questions.

"Wendy, are you there?" Roman asked.

Breathless. "Yeah, I'm here."

"Are you okay? Are you hurt?"

"We're running down a dirt road."

"Wendy, are you okay?"

"Yes. They kidnapped us, Roman! They knew where we were."

"I know, Wendy, I know. Are you okay? Are they following you?"

"No. I'm looking back. No one is following us. I can hear a highway somewhere up ahead."

"Where are you?"

"We're not far from the Pages' river house. They kidnapped us right when we got there. They blindfolded us."

"Did they hurt you or the kids?"

"No. They locked us in a room but they didn't hurt us."

"Are you sure?"

"I'm positive. Hold on." Roman could hear her speaking to the kids. "Yes! There's the highway. We're okay, Roman. Where are you? Are you alright?"

"I'm fine."

Konstantinou snapped his fingers and held out his only hand for the phone.

"Wendy, go down to the highway and flag down a ride. I've got to go."

"Roman, are you sure you're okay?"

"I'll call soon. Tell the kids Daddy loves them. I love them so much," Roman said, his voice breaking as the words left his mouth.

He knew those were the final words his children would ever hear from him.

Konstantinou snatched the phone from Roman's hand. "There, I've done my good deed for the year—and it also proves to you that the CIA lied about having your family. They don't give two shits about you, Roman Littlepage. So, let's go get my coin and end this."

The cruel-looking man shoved Roman toward the boat.

Chapter Seventeen

With dripping pants and shoes, Roman stood aboard the speedboat, watching as the cruel-looking man produced a set of handcuffs from a black duffel bag. He spun Roman around, cuffing his wrists behind him, cranking down the cuffs far too tightly. The cruel-looking man shoved Roman into the aft-facing seat behind the starboard side cockpit. Though the man didn't say anything, he pointed a crooked warning finger at Roman.

The three men spoke in their native language. The curly-haired killer must have wanted to drive because he knelt in the cockpit and cranked the large inboard motor, leaving it idle as he stepped aft to bring in one of the anchors. The cruel-looking man was at the bow, tugging at the forward anchor. As the big inboard burbled and rumbled, Konstantinou sat on the rear bench seat, eyeing Roman.

"No one will ever be able to say that you didn't have balls," he said to Roman, though it didn't sound like a compliment. It sounded more like a death knell, a final compliment in the last few moments of Roman's life.

And it *would be* the last few moments of Roman's life, because he'd lied through his teeth about the coin being by the sea in Sóller. The coin wasn't there and once Konstantinou realized it, he'd start the torture that would only end with Roman's death.

But, now that he'd secured his family's safety, he hoped he could do the same for Eva. If she had any sense, she'd go to the police or simply run away.

His manner languid, Konstantinou crossed his leg and removed his cigarettes, checking to see if they'd gotten wet. When he realized they were dry, he tapped one out.

"May I have one?" Roman asked.

"Hell no," Konstantinou sneered. "This isn't a movie."

The cruel-looking man now had his anchor free and was pulling it in. The curly-haired killer was struggling with his, but now that the forward anchor was free, he was able to use some slack to wrangle it from the rocks.

Konstantinou was saying something but Roman didn't pay him any attention. He didn't pay attention because he realized this was his final chance to help himself. He'd saved everyone else's life—now it was his turn. Only his chances were extremely slim.

But why not try? You owe it to your children. They're free Roman. The only life you're gambling with is your own, and it's going to be over in minutes.

Roman pondered kicking Konstantinou but immediately thought better of it. All that would do was garner a violent reaction from the other two. No,

Roman needed the upper hand. Because he was facing aft, he was able to see the shore. Though he couldn't see Eva anymore, he had to risk exposing her by somehow making the three men look to shore.

With a risky plan in mind, Roman stood and stared back at the point that led into the protected beach of Cala Tuent. He made his face scared and panicky. "Holy shit, how did they find us? I swear I didn't tell anyone where we were meeting."

That did the trick. The two henchmen were still reeling in their anchors. Konstantinou was lounging and smoking. When they heard Roman's words, all three turned to look at the point.

Roman used that moment to whirl around to the cockpit. He kicked forward with his wet right shoe, striking the single lever throttle and jamming it forward. The throttle had a silver push-button that had to be depressed in order to move from neutral. But the force of Roman's kick broke the mechanism, sending a few pieces of broken black plastic tumbling to the deck.

Mission accomplished. The boat roared to life.

The curly-haired killer had been on the rear deck and fell immediately overboard as the speedboat lurched out from under him. Unfortunately, the anchor he'd just freed fell into the water with him. It would come back into play a mere few seconds later.

The cruel-looking man fell, too, but he remained on the craft, sprawling roughly onto the deck in the keel aisle and splitting open his chin in the process.

Also suffering the effects of the sudden acceleration, Roman stumbled backward, unable to catch himself due to his handcuffs. He had enough presence of mind to adjust his fall slightly to the right, thudding directly into Konstantinou.

The impact earned Roman a satisfying grunt from the one-armed terror profiteer.

Through it all, the powerful speedboat lurched forward, propelled by a 500 horsepower motor that pushed the lightweight boat back toward the opening that led to the Mediterranean.

His arms behind his back, Roman struggled to get off of Konstantinou. Aiding Roman, Konstantinou managed to use his one arm to push Roman backward. With no hands available to fight, Roman pulled back his head and smashed his forehead into Konstantinou's face.

The man's nose exploded blood.

Roman turned to see the cruel-looking man. He'd scrambled to his feet and rushed aft as he dug his pistol from his waistband. He let out a kamikaze shriek when he brought the pistol around to shoot.

Then, the cruel-looking man was thrown forward, along with everything else in the boat.

The aft grapnel anchor had found another rocky purchase.

They were near the far side of the large pool. The anchor tethered the roaring boat, sending it wheeling starboard like an unbroken colt willing to injure itself just to be free.

The sudden stop had thrown Roman off of Konstantinou. Roman was now on the deck, aware that the bloodied Cypriot was stomping with his wet loafers, striking Roman in his face and neck. Having no other recourse, Roman opened his mouth and attempted to bite Konstantinou's thrusting ankles.

Still pin-wheeling to the starboard, the thrust of the boat broke them free when they were aimed back to the shore. The anchor had held fast until the boat came around nearly 180 degrees. When it came loose, the effect of 500 unleashed horsepower was once again dramatic. This time, the boat lurched ahead but there was hardly anywhere to go.

The cruel-looking man had just come to his feet once again, bringing the pistol to aim when the speedboat crashed into the rocky shore, sending him down for a third time. This time, however, due to the abrupt halt, the cruel-looking man tumbled overboard, all feet and arms in a Wide World of Sports agony-of-defeat ski jumper pose.

Roman had been somewhat protected, wedged between the seats on the deck. Now, however, Konstantinou was on top of him. The terrorist rained down vicious blows from his one arm, cursing Roman with every strike. Roman tried to move his head with each shot, doing what he could to mitigate Konstantinou's surprising power.

Then, a series of blasts could be heard followed by a deafening gunshot from the bow. Simultaneously, Konstantinou's head snapped aft and he crumpled onto Roman.

Just before Roman lost consciousness, he saw a rather large man in a deep blue wetsuit. The man wore a military style weapons belt and brandished a dripping shotgun. He asked Roman something but it was too late.

Roman was in la-la land.

* * *

When Roman awoke, his eyes burned and the bright sunshine did nothing to help his disorientation. As he squinted, he realized he was lying on something firm and flat. Within seconds he realized he was still on the boat. Eva was just above him, sitting on the bench seat, talking on a cellphone. It was a phone Roman hadn't yet seen. She hung up and knelt over him.

"I've got to leave, Roman," she said urgently. "Just tell the truth about everything, okay?"

"What? What are you talking about?"

"I had divers in that deep water where you first stood. But when the curly-haired man said they had your family, I had to tell my divers to wait. We had partial audio on you the entire time. I just want to confirm, though, is your family safe?"

"What?" Roman asked, confused.

"Your family—are they safe?" she asked urgently.

"Yeah, they're okay. What the hell are you talking about? Divers?"

"Yes, they were there the entire time. I had a solid plan but we didn't know about your family. That threw everyone for a loop."

"Who didn't know? What are you talking about, Eva?"

"I'm sorry, Roman. I'm not a nurse." Just then, a large man in a dark wetsuit appeared, whispering something to her. She looked at Roman again. "The divers work with me. They were here to help you."

Unable to come to grips with all this, Roman rubbed his eyes as he formulated his next questions. "How were you talking to divers if they were underwater? And why didn't we see bubbles?"

"They could hear through special headphones and they were wearing rebreathers. I've got to go, Roman. I can't wait any longer. Just tell them everything. Okay? Don't hide anything, even about me. The locals are on the way."

She kissed her finger and touched it to Roman's lips.

As Roman rested there, he watched as Eva disappeared forward. He heard her jump from the boat. Moments later, he heard another motor rumbling. Roman sat up, dizzy but realizing his hands were no longer cuffed. Rubbing his wrists, he stood, watching as a dark gray boat roared away. Eva stood aft, waving to Roman. With her were six people, all wearing dark clothing or wetsuits. They headed straight out to sea.

Roman stumbled forward, amazed at what he saw. To his left, at the point, a number of sunbathers gaped back at him. Several were still completely nude, adding a bit of spice to what was already an otherworldly situation.

Far more amazing, however, was the scene in front of the beached boat. On the shore, at the base of the rocky cliff, were Roman's three enemies. The three men were hogtied and tethered together. The two henchmen squirmed and cursed, but Konstantinou was perfectly still, glaring at Roman.

They were alive but going nowhere.

Roman drank in the scene for a long moment. It really was quite beautiful.

Chapter Eighteen

Following a one-hour surgery to clean up and repair his gunshot wound, Roman spoke on the phone with Wendy and the kids. They talked for over an hour, with each of them assuring Roman they were okay and hadn't been mistreated. The Tennessee State Police were discreetly guarding their house and would do so for the foreseeable future. This provided Roman a great deal of comfort. The time spent talking to his children might have been the sweetest moments of his life.

Thank God they were unharmed.

Roman's doctors held all visitors at bay until the next day. Despite the primary physician's best efforts, he couldn't prevent the phone from ringing. It rang time and time again. Roman finally answered it.

"Yeah?"

"Where is it?" Eva asked.

"Where is what?"

"You know what."

"Before I discuss that, who do you work for?"

"I can't say."

"What did you shoot Konstantinou with?"

"We had live rounds and we also had baton rounds. We used baton rounds."

"And it didn't kill them?"

"They're all alive and staring at life in prison. Where's the item?"

"I don't know what you're talking about, Eva, or whatever your name is."

"We opened the coin and it wasn't there. Do you have the chip?"

"I do not."

"Where is it?"

"Thanks for your help. It would've been easier had you told me the truth. Goodbye." He unclipped the cord from the phone and, with a little pharmacological help, slept reasonably well.

On the following morning, as the sun rose outside his window, a sharp-dressed young lady from the Spanish *Ministerio de Justicia* walked into his room and ignored his order to leave. She sat without invitation and spoke in lightly accented English. In a rather pithy manner, she informed Roman that, unless he immediately cooperated with several investigations, she was fully authorized to have him transferred to the Berga Prison, northwest of Barcelona.

"On whose authority?" Roman asked.

The lady removed several crisp sheets of paper from her briefcase. "As you can see, all of the documents are in order. If you don't cooperate, the two officers outside your room will escort you via commercial aircraft, in economy, to Girona Airport. Though your doctors don't recommend traveling, they do believe you will survive. Berga Prison is quite unpleasant, señor."

Roman eyed the papers. "And does the U.S. State Department have anything to say about this? They tried to see me yesterday, several times."

"We're working in conjunction *with* them, señor," she replied.

"So, this is your collective effort to force my hand?"

She smiled, displaying a row of perfect teeth.

Roman tilted the bed upward. "And if I do cooperate?"

"Then you can stay here as you convalesce. It's a rather simple choice. Cooperate and stay. Remain obstinate and leave." Her eyes wandered the room. "I can assure you the prison infirmary is not this clean, or private. And the inmates there will almost certainly want *something* from you."

"*Something*…yeah, I get it." Roman handed her the papers. "Who do I need to speak with first?"

"Your ex-wife has hired an attorney for you. She's here, as are representatives from numerous Spanish agencies, along with the American State Department and the CIA."

"I'll cooperate," Roman said, deflating at the prospect of providing "something" to inmates at Berga Prison.

He met with his attorney first. She was from Mallorca and had been educated in Spain and the United States. She informed Roman that all charges involving the hotel murder had been dropped, for now. Obstruction charges were pending but, assuming Roman cooperated, he should be cleared of any wrongdoing.

His attorney wanted to know all about Eva, his mysterious German friend. Roman didn't hold back. He told her everything he remembered.

"Who is she?" Roman asked.

"I honestly have no idea. I've spoken to the CIA. I have a feeling they know."

Roman stifled a curse.

"In the end, you used the toilet in the wrong place at the wrong time," the attorney said. "Now, if you'll submit to ten thousand questions from about five agencies, you should be able to move past this unpleasantness and resume your life."

Next up was the U.S. State Department. Roman spoke to them for the better part of two hours, followed by the local Mallorcan law enforcement and members of the *Nacional de Policía* from Barcelona. When Roman suggested there was a leak in the ranks of the local law enforcement, the Mallorcan officials frowned and looked away.

"Well?" Roman asked.

"You are correct, señor," one of them said, appearing angry and embarrassed. "The informant has been found and will be prosecuted to the fullest extent of our law."

"Who is it?"

"That, we cannot say."

When the Mallorcans left, Roman's attorney called them a very proud people. "It's hard for any Spaniard to admit fault in one of our brethren." She smiled. "I believe that's all for today."

"When will I see the CIA?"

"They will be here all day tomorrow."

"Fun."

Just as she'd predicted, the following day was all CIA, from sunup to sundown. Agent Blair Martin, a brooding, intelligent type in his mid-50s, was the lead investigator. Roman told the CIA men every little detail—except he never volunteered that he opened the coin.

When they were two hours into his questioning, one agent produced a photo of Eva. It looked like a driver's license photograph.

"Do you know this woman?"

"Of course, I do. That's Eva."

"What did she tell you about herself?"

Roman explained how he'd seen her before the murder, and how he'd stumbled into her after jumping from the hotel window.

"You're sure she didn't find you?" Agent Martin asked.

"Positive."

"You did say you hit your head. Is it possible you're confused?"

"She was on a blanket and didn't even see me coming," Roman replied. "Maybe she's a spy or whatever, but our meeting was happenstance. I'd bet my *life* on it."

Roman was quite proud that he could now say that without it sounding trite.

When they'd gone over the story from every possible angle, the three CIA representatives conferred. Agent Martin shook his head in frustration.

"Everything you've told us makes sense, Mister Littlepage. Everything but one critical detail."

"And what's that?" Roman asked.

"We think you opened that coin."

"Opened it? How does one open a coin?"

"Don't dick with me, kid."

"I didn't open it. And don't call me *kid*."

"We think you did."

Roman frowned. "Why don't you tell me about Eva? Who is she? Who does she work for?"

"We can't discuss that," one of the other agents said.

"And I didn't open that coin," Roman replied.

"You're in way over your head, Littlepage," Agent Martin said, his words dripping disgust.

Roman displayed a bit of anger. "What do you want me to tell you? I don't have that coin or whatever was inside it. Eva and I did what we had to do, and I had no idea she was lying to me all that time." He crossed his arms. "You people sure as hell didn't help me."

"We know you had it. Why else would Konstantinou have shown himself?"

"I told you I *had* the coin. I've never disputed that. It was hidden at the bottom of that middle olive tree at Cala Tuent."

"It's gone now," Martin said.

"And I wonder who has it?" Roman mocked. "I certainly didn't see who took it. Maybe I was too distracted by Konstantinou's assertion that the CIA pays him more each year than anyone else on earth. Or maybe, just maybe, I was too upset that they had my family, *after* the CIA lied and told me my family was safe."

More unfruitful questions followed from both sides. They wouldn't tell Roman anything about Eva's true identity. At the end of the first day, Roman made them an offer.

"You tell me about Eva, and maybe I'll remember more about the coin."

"I'll see what I can do," Agent Martin said. The agents departed, frustrated.

They returned the next day. And the next. They didn't tell him about Eva. Roman held out—he admitted nothing about opening the coin.

They did share one piece of good news about Konstantinou's network. Though they were certainly irritated with Roman, the CIA agents told him that numerous arrests had been made back in the States.

"Did you get the people who killed my friends?"

"Thanks to quite a bit of evidence we found on Konstantinou's yacht, we're positive we did." The news gave Roman a small measure of comfort.

"Is my family in danger?"

"We don't think so, but their protection will remain in place for the time being."

"Am I in danger?"

"No."

"You're sure?"

"Yes."

On the fourth day, Agent Martin came in alone. He shut the door. "I have some information for you about Eva."

"Let's hear it."

"You'll tell me what happened to the coin?"

"I'll tell you what I know," Roman agreed.

"Her name is Evangeline Christina Solbeck. She's twenty-nine years old and a special agent in Germany's BND."

"What's BND?"

"I can't pronounce it, but it's their foreign intelligence service."

"So, she's similar to you?"

"More or less."

"And the divers that rescued me?"

"They're BND, too. And, as you might imagine, the BND is dealing with a shit-storm from the Spanish right now. The BND is claiming that one of their agents was in distress, and they had every right to defend her. You can imagine the Spanish are pissed off that there was no cooperation, et cetera."

"She *was* in distress," Roman added. "What else?"

"That's all I know. Tell me about the coin."

"Eva took it."

"How do you know?"

"She's called here."

"What was in it?"

Roman told him—told him everything. Agent Martin was furious.

"Is that the truth?" he demanded.

"Go to that house and see if there's any evidence left. I'm not lying."

"Where do you get off doing such a thing?"

"It was mine at the time," Roman said. "I did what I felt was right."

After the CIA, there were no more visitors other than Roman's attorney and the sharply dressed young lady from the *Ministerio de Justicia*. She delivered Roman's passport and several official documents in the event he had a difficult time booking a departure flight. When she'd departed, Roman's attorney strongly advised him to keep all matters related to this incident quiet.

"There is a decent chance you will be allowed to discuss it, eventually. For now, Spain, Germany and the United States respectfully request you keep it to yourself. Your wife and children have agreed to do the same."

"Ex-wife."

"Sorry," his attorney replied, smiling as if he might be flirting. He wasn't.

"Also," she said, "as discussed, please do not speak with the families of your friends about their murders being related to what happened here. The United States government is handling that."

"I hope they're telling them the truth," Roman said flatly.

"I'll leave that to you to pursue," the attorney answered. She shook Roman's hand, providing him with her information in the event he needed her before he left Spain.

* * *

On Roman's last night in the hospital, he was visited by a wiry male nurse who rolled in a large cart teeming with medical electronics of some sort. The nurse shut the door and kicked a wedge underneath before turning to Roman.

"Why did you wedge the door?" Roman asked.

"Be quiet and don't make any loud sounds," the nurse said, ripping backing paper from two electrodes and attaching them to Roman's upper and lower chest.

"Hey, what are you doing?" Roman asked, trying to get up. The male nurse grasped Roman's left arm and twisted it. He pinched the median nerve between Roman's thumb and index finger, crippling Roman and making him cry out.

"Be quiet," the nurse said. "This'll only take a minute." He attached two smaller electrodes to Roman's temples. Then he turned on the machine and removed a phone from his pocket. "Here. Talk. If you resist again, it'll hurt worse next time."

Roman accepted the phone and asked who was on the other end of the line.

"You know who this is," Eva said.

"Where are you?"

"Doesn't matter," she answered. "Where are you?"

"Still in Mallorca."

"But where?"

"You know where…the hospital."

"Has anyone told you who I am?"

"Yes."

"Who?"

"The CIA." Roman looked up at his visitor. "Who is this guy pretending to be a nurse?"

"Doesn't matter. Put him back on."

Roman handed the fake nurse the phone. He typed something into the machine he'd wheeled in and spoke to her. He nodded as he confirmed something and handed the phone back to Roman.

"Can you hear me, Roman?" Eva asked.

"Yes."

"I'm sure you realize this, but you're hooked up to a very reliable and high-tech polygraph. We've gotten your baseline of truth, so…I ask you…where exactly is the microchip that was in the coin?"

Roman hesitated. The "nurse" began to move at him again before Roman waved him off. "Eva?"

"Yes?"

"I destroyed the microchip."

"What?"

"I cooked it."

"How? When?"

"That night, after you came to my bed, I got up early and took it to the barbecue grill out back. I put it in the middle of the burner, lit the grill and

158

turned up the gas until it melted."

"Are you lying?"

"No, Eva, I'm not. Ask the machine."

"Why didn't you tell me before?"

"I didn't know you were some spy. Why should I have told you? At that point, I was concerned with your safety."

She laughed without humor. "Put my colleague back on."

Roman handed the phone to the Asian nurse and followed enough of his German to understand that he'd told Eva that Roman was telling the truth. They spoke a bit more before Roman asked for the phone again, and some privacy. Eva must have agreed because the man walked to the door and said he'd be right outside.

"You used me," Roman said, attempting to speak the words without the emotion that flooded through him.

"I can see why you might view it that way," she replied. "But I also think I helped you stay alive."

"What about my family? You jeopardized them."

"Roman, think back. Just like you, I thought your family was safe. When I learned they weren't, I held my people back. I wasn't trying to get anyone hurt."

She had a point. Something else occurred to him. "But if all you wanted was the microchip, then why didn't you just take it?"

"That's not all I wanted. I wanted Konstantinou, too. In the end, I got neither."

"You could have taken him."

"Not after all that happened. We'd hoped for a clean trade and snatch. I had to leave him so you could explain what happened."

"Well, about the chip, I thought I was doing what was right."

They were both silent for a moment.

"Roman?"

"Yeah."

"I just want you to know that everything that happened between us was—"

He hung up the phone and called for the "nurse." When the man came in, Roman held the phone out to him. "Take this phone, take your little machine and please…get the hell out of here."

Eva's colleague departed. Roman left Mallorca two days later.

* * *

Delta Airlines delivered Roman to Nashville in just under 18 hours. His route took him to Madrid, then to Atlanta, then to Nashville. Although he was feeling markedly better when he departed, he was exhausted and weary by the time he got home. But that didn't stop him from visiting Wendy and the kids. He stayed with them until well after 10 p.m., when he could barely keep his eyes open. Though he told them almost everything, he did edit the story slightly, and the coin wasn't the only part he left out. He also refrained from making any wise cracks about Toby. Wendy didn't mention him, neither did Roman.

Wise move, Roman. You're learning.

When he arrived at his condominium, it was almost 11 p.m. He hadn't slept on his flights, so he'd been awake for 24 hours straight. There were two state policemen watching his condo. They gave him their cell numbers and told him to call if anything was amiss.

"Thanks guys," Roman mumbled. "All I plan on seeing for the next ten hours are my eyelids."

Once inside, Roman was asleep inside of ten minutes. He slept deeply and darkly, having a number of strange dreams. He awoke with the sun. After a quick trip to the bathroom, Roman fell back asleep and slumbered until mid-morning.

At 10:22 a.m., Roman was awoken by the smell of coffee and frying bacon. He rested in bed for a moment, making sure his mind was working correctly.

Would those cops have come inside? he thought incredulously.

He staggered from his bedroom to find the answer. There, in his kitchen, was the Goddess. She wore the exact same t-shirt she'd worn the last time she made him breakfast, along with a skimpy pair of pink underwear. She smiled at him and poured him a cup of coffee.

"Holy shit! Eva, what the hell are you doing here?" he asked, opening his arms and spilling the coffee on the counter.

She wadded up a bundle of paper towels. "I'm quitting my job, Roman, whether or not you want me to stay here. And I don't give a shit about microchips, or my career, or the damned seventeenth state. What matters is I'm here, and single, and so are you." Eva cocked her head. "You *are* single, aren't you?"

"Yes."

"Good. That was one thing I didn't verify."

Roman leaned against his kitchen counter, his knees weakened once again by this woman. "Eva..."

"Yes?"

"Remember when I hung up on you?"

"I do."

"What were you about to say?"

"I was simply trying to tell you that, whether or not I used you, my feelings for you were, and are, real." She moved in front of him, draping her arms around his neck and pulling him close. "You're incredibly brave, Roman. You risked your life so that your family would be spared. You were willing to die." She squeezed him. "Think about that for a second. You seized control—not me. *You* saved everyone, Roman."

He dipped his head and she lifted his chin. They kissed.

"Don't you remember that night in the house above Sóller?" she asked.

"I think about it every hour."

"Do you think I would have done that with you if I wasn't crazy about you?"

He counted the items off on his fingers. "Well, you did tell me you're a nurse; you broke into a house; stole a car; enlisted black ops divers; shot at—"

She play-punched him in the stomach.

They kissed again.

"Were you really there on vacation?" he asked.

"Absolutely."

"Did you know who Konstantinou was?"

"Never heard of him."

"How did you find out?"

"As the days wore on, I was talking to Berlin when you were asleep." She winced. "Sorry."

He shrugged. "About the microchip."

"I'm glad you destroyed it, Roman. No one needs that kind of information."

"What was on it?"

"You don't want to know."

He took a step backward and ran his hands back through his hair. "Holy crap, Eva, I can't believe you're here."

She opened her arms and did a dancer's twirl. "I am, and I came here on a one-way ticket."

Roman walked to the front and peered out his blinds. "I'm sure you saw the cops stationed outside. How the hell did you get in here, anyway?"

She rolled her eyes. "Oh, Roman, we have so much to learn about each other."

THE END

Acknowledgments

If you've read my other books, you already know The 17th State isn't my standard fare. I've always loved tales of suspense—be it television, movies or books. I also desired to create a character that was a little less "super hero" and a bit more of a normal guy. Combine these two notions and, if all goes well, you come up with a Hitchcockian tale. Hopefully, that's what I've done. I do hope you enjoyed the read. It was a fun story to write.

I owe a great deal of thanks to my buddy Mitch Compton. He helped me come up with the title and brainstormed many of the plot elements with me. He's a great friend to me, along with a lifelong friend to tattooed Harley riders the world over.

Liz Latanishen, my editor, had strong opinions about many elements of this book. She was a wonderful guide and helped me torture Roman to the maximum extent. Thank you, Liz.

Dina Dryden helped me put the finishing touches on the book. Her keen eye was fantastic as always. Thank you, Dina.

Nat Shane created another dynamite cover. Nat, you're an incredibly talented person. Keep plying your gift.

Many thanks to test readers Jenny Bell and Scott Valentine. You made this book better.

Please interact with me on Facebook, on Twitter or via email. You can always reach me at chuck@chuckdriskell.com. I return all reader email.

Thanks again for reading my books. Your support is what keeps me going. Please review this book where you purchased it. God bless you.

About the Author

Chuck Driskell credits the time he spent as a U.S. Army paratrooper for fueling his love of writing. During the week, he works in advertising. Seven mornings a week, usually very early, he writes. Chuck lives in South Carolina with his tolerant wife and two loving children. *The 17th State* is Chuck's tenth novel.

Made in the USA
Middletown, DE
08 July 2019